ASTORIA'S SECRET

ASTORIA'S SECRET

A. P. Goodman

ISBN 979-8-9872709-4-3 (pb)

Book Cover by Nitish Mathpal

Visit us on the Web!
www.apgoodman.com

First edition 2023

To Z,
Every day you amaze and inspire.
Never stop being you.

The

Summer

Diaries

Diary Entries

1. Delphine

2. Solei

3. Alcmaeonidae

4. Lena

5. Airess

6. Tao

7. Selene

8. Kohl

Delphine

The trials went bad. Actually, everything has gone bad—the trials, hunting for Kohl, curing the Nulls. Even my first visit with Aglaopheme bombed. THIS PLACE IS SO STUPID! It's not going to stop either. Just wait until Airess finds out the secret I've been hiding! Just wait! That'll really be something. I have to keep her from finding out about Kohl and me. I didn't mean for things to happen the way they did but . . . what's a girl to do? His smoky eyes, his soft white skin, he can be pretty charming when he wants to be, and oh, how he wants to be charming lately! He wants us to run away together. He says The Bad One is under control now, that I help keep it under control. I'm not sure if I believe in it though because the Nulls keep coming into Legacy in droves! Selene can barely keep up! He's so assertive these days, so confident. Hard to believe he was the poor neglected kid a few months ago. He and Lena are basically king and queen now. Getting kicked out of Legacy Academy was probably the best thing that ever happened to her. She knows it too. I've tried to get close to her so many times, and she always shrugs me off. I don't think she likes me very much, but she has no reason not to! Without me, she'd have never known about Kohl! I basically saved her; I basically saved them all! Only Airess gets it. That's probably why we got so close during her rehabilitation. She was barely healed when she agreed to champion the trials with me. Another failing within the Basil family household, Kasim, is really out of his element with everything going on these days. He needs Solei to come back, we all do, if we think some magical item can save the Nulls, but they've been gone for so long. I'm starting to wonder if they're actually studying abroad, or if they just left and didn't want to say goodbye. Of course, no one here wants to hear that though. No one here can say anything bad about Legacy's shining star—their sun. They certainly revolve around Solei in such a manner too. They'll learn soon enough I bet! Solei is nothing but a supernova waiting to explode. I thought Airess and Lena of all people would remember that and be rightfully fearful of them but nope. Those two are probably the most delusional out of everyone. I thought Selene would understand too, being so moon centric. Wouldn't the moon dislike the sun? It made a lot of sense to me but nope! I was wrong again! For someone so uncomfortable being in daylight, he supports the sun bearer fully. Solei can do no wrong. Just wait until they explode. Everyone will have to learn the hard way. Kohl gets it though. He always thought it was creepy that they could get inside of people's heads if they wanted to. Plus, he prefers staying in the dark these days. There's hardly ever sunlight when we're together. Only brief glimpses of the moon, which I think we both enjoy more than we want to let on, albeit for completely different reasons, even if our feelings are based on the same person. He asks of Diablo sometimes, never Selene. Kohl says he's happy for him. It feels true, but I know there's more to it. Diablo was all he had before me. They were almost like brothers, but he never understood Kohl's darker side. Kohl thought for sure, it would make all the sense with Diablo being part devil. They were the only white ones. Now we know better. Diablo was never real, and the bond they shared was likely never real either. I can tell Kohl grieves that sometimes. He mourns that the best relationship he ever had probably never really existed in the way he thought it did, which is only ironic because I hear practically the same thing from Airess about Kohl. It's why I can't ever tell her that the person she keeps obsessing over actually feels that way about me. Well, that, and the fact that there's been a top-priority manhunt for him for months now. That would probably end badly too. What a mess! I thought life underwater was complicated, but the land folk here have our drama beat in spades. This world is so weird up here. Most of the time I don't mind it, but man is it hard to adjust to. Going from a fin to legs was not fun, and freshwater is disgusting. I can hear them calling for me outside my dorm. These Nulls are so needy, and each one of them relies on me for all their answers. Can't they see I have no answers? I have absolutely nothing to offer them. I barely have anything to offer myself, except for my secret half-dead vampire boyfriend. Not exactly something that is in high demand. I wish I had a life of things in high demand.

Solei

Oh man, oh man! I asked her. I can't believe I asked her! I know she said she needed a day to decide, but I can't stop checking my phone every time a text comes in. It's only been Lena though, it's always Lena. She rarely goes a day without texting. I think she's panicking about my visit here. That seems to bother her A LOT. I'd never have guessed that. I assumed she and Selene would be all lovey-dovey and off on their own thing once his drama settled down. If they separated from the pack, it's not apparent from where I stand. It feels the opposite even. They're so involved, so, so involved.

I expected—maybe hoped?—for Airess to be the one to miss text me the most. I think I thought we were closer than we were when I left. I know she had her own stuff going on. Maybe I should've stayed behind more for that? It didn't feel like I had any role to play. When she needed it, I risked sacrificing myself to be her sun, and once she got her fill . . . well . . . she moved on . . . on to her next need, on to her next crusade. I've known for a while, I guess, that I'll never be her patient. I'll never be the bird with a broken wing crying for help. It took a while to accept it though. I've made peace with it now, but that was a long painful pill to swallow.

Now that I'm free from all that, I sometimes wonder if Tao will ever have to swallow the same pill. He's been crazy for that bubblegum healer since he first laid eyes on her, I swear. I didn't fall for her until much later. I remember freaking out if it would cause problems with Tao. It never did though. Not with Tao. He's the constant, level-headed and chill no matter what. I feel bad for him. He's everything Airess doesn't want. It's so conflicting to think about. I want him to be happy, and I never want him to have to break enough for her to be interested.

I suppose it's not just that though. Distance is quite an eye-opener, but nothing compares to Mae. Absolutely nothing! She's incredible. Astonishing. Breathtaking. I am speechless and at her mercy every time she walks into view. I've never been like this before. I pride myself on my composure. I've led my team into battle against one of the worst. I never faltered; I've never failed. I'm the strong one, I know I am. And yet, I'm weak in the knees and tongue-tied even after six months in. Mae's one of those girls that is stunningly beautiful and when she speaks, it's hard to comprehend how someone can be blessed with even more intelligence than the beauty she possesses. She rivals the gods. I know she does, especially after studying them so much lately. Apollo's nothing compared to her.

I wasn't surprised when I found out Mae was sure to have ichor in her veins. I can't see how anyone would be surprised by that. Here, in the beaten off paths outside Athens, she is the oracle of this tiny village. A resource, yes, but also an outcast. She's different than they are, and they'll never let her forget it. She's none but a tool for them to use when it suits them best and a scapegoat to blame when they're at their worst. I get that part. I get being used as a tool and then being discarded when they're done. It crushed me, but it barely seems to faze Mae. She doesn't know any better. She doesn't know what it's like to be safe and loved and supported. I'm not always sure I do either, but I know we could learn together if she gave it a shot. If she gave me a shot. I hope, more than anything, she agrees to come home with me, to come to Legacy. I want to teach her all the things, show her how good things can be. I also know I need to go back. I've pushed that off long enough. I need to resume my responsibilities. But . . . Mae. I don't know how any of those things matter without Mae. Fingers crossed! Here goes nothing!

Alcmaeonidae

Oh my gosh! I'm doing this!

Why am I doing this?

I like my town. I like my space. I like my sitting stone.

Now what? Now I travel across the world to attend some stuffy school with a bunch of entitled godly brats? That sounds miserable.

Why am I doing this?

I mean I know the answer—everyone here knows the answer. I feel like an idiot being swept up by my feelings. Nothing good ever comes from feelings. They cloud your judgment and most times, end in ruin. Whole civilizations have been destroyed because of feelings. I know that; I've seen that. Yet, here I am . . . packing my bags, ready to fly for hours, just so I never have to say goodbye.

I don't think anything could be worse than saying goodbye to Solei. If that possibility existed, this would be it, and it's not. At least, not yet.

I hate every part of this: rash decisions, unknown places, schools, and people. The only time someone talks to me here is when they need something. Then we do our simple business transaction, and then they go far, far away again. I like that. I like silence. Well, silence from people. I need music. I couldn't function right without my music.

Why didn't Solei leave when they found me? Why do they keep asking for only one thing—MORE of my company? Who does that?

They've never asked what their future holds, or even particularly cared that I could tell them almost any-thing they wanted to know. Details about their life, their friends (which it seems they have plenty of (omg so many people and so much drama)), or us . . . I could tell them about us. I could tell myself about us too. Maybe they're too scared to ask a question that could give an answer they won't like. I know that's why I'm avoiding it. If Solei and I don't work out, I don't want to know that. I don't want to know it now. I don't want

x

to know it ever.

It's my miasma. Or the miasma handed down to me by my great great great great great great great (I could keep going) grandpappy. Thanks, grandpa! Cursed forever. LOVE IT!

If that stupid thing is real, it's for sure to take Solei away from me. That sweet soul, that beautiful heart. They deserve so much better than what I am. I'm too chicken to tell them though. They'll have to find it out all on their own. And I'm sure they will—at good ole Legacy Academy, when I'm a world away from every-thing I've ever known. Serves me right though. What I'm doing isn't fair to Solei. I sometimes wonder if it's borderline cruel to share their company knowing I'm doomed for ruin. I just love them so much that I can't seem to walk away. I should, but I won't. Despicable feelings! I'm ruined already.

Lena

I'm exhausted. I'm so exhausted it's hard to write, but I know what I'm doing is good for everyone, and I'm happy to finally be considered useful around here. Valuable even! My days are so crazy. I usually wake up to some text message or note telling me of some new fire to put out, and I know that that's a popular metaphorical thing to say, but literally, I've been woken up to put out actual fires in Ward A. These forgotten gods can really be something else sometimes.

I don't find them as malicious as my dad does, though some definitely are, but they are certainly all entitled. He was not wrong about that. It seems like the weaker they are, the worse they behave. Their powers are failing, they're trying so hard to hold onto who they once were, and then next thing you know the ward is facing a catastrophe because some god was trying to prove themselves, using an ability that is as uncontrollable and volatile as they are. It's a mess. A big gigantic mess!

What I wouldn't give for some help. Airess

tries so hard, she really does, but her healing can't cure temper tantrums, and she has her hands full with Delphine—who I don't particularly enjoy being around. It's not that I dislike her; it's just that I don't really like her. I find her a little much for me and I don't like how happy she gets around Selene. I know that isn't a great reason to not want to be around a person, but it's quite valid for her. Maybe if she were more helpful, or useful, or pertinent to my cause, it would be better? Maybe? Actually, probably not.

That said, I know she's crucial to what Selene has going on, and I'm grateful he has help. He's probably the only person busier than I am—with the exception of Principal Chromwell. I wish I could get him here with me. Wouldn't that be incredible?! He would be an amazing assist in Ward A, but he's championing all the Nulls. Selene, Professor Nakshatra, and Delphine get flooded by new arrivals daily. It never ends. Then there are more bodies to house, more mouths to feed, and some serious trauma to try to help them through. I sometimes wonder if I'd ever see him if the Nulls didn't spill in from Ward A. We're so caught up in our own thing. I miss him so much. I know what we're doing is vital, but what I wouldn't give to go back to our beginning sometimes. Things were so hard back then, but somehow I think they were easier. I wouldn't have believed that for a second, last year. My sweet Selene. I hope he knows I still love him more than there are stars in the sky.

I'm really banking on Solei being able to help them. They always have the answer. They've been completely missing in action, but anytime I ask Tao about them, he gets really dodgy so something big must be coming up with Solei. I text them constantly. I hope they come back soon, and if not, I just hope they come back. I miss my friend. I can tell there's a hole in the group since they've gone. I'm trying my best to hold that together too, but I'm no leader, and no one else comes close to Solei. They do what they do better than anyone else I've met in my short time here. They really are a star, inside and out.

Tao tries to keep spirits up with the group too, but he's also abhorrently closed off emotionally, so that goes about as well as you'd expect it to. I can't even tell you how many times I've tried to bring up to him that he told me he loved Airess when everything crashed and burned before the winter solstice. Selene says I should just drop it, but Tao let it slip! He should acknowledge it! I'm his friend! I could help!!

No one cares when I get upset over that. They just want to keep on keeping on, and when we all have time, we solely talk about Kohl. That's like the only subject all of us have in common anymore.

Airess still wants to save Kohl with every drop of her being. I'm hoping if it happens, then I can get some type of control over my life. Plus, that could control the influx of Nulls coming too! How great would that be? Selene would get a break, and maybe we could even fix Delphine and send her back? (Not because I hate her, just because that's her home (and also where she belongs . . .)) I bet Solei could help with that too. There's nothing they can't do.

Sigh. I always seem to find myself counting down the unlimited number of days until Solei gets back. I need them here. Now!

Airess

I am going to scream! I do not have time to babysit this little abomination while I try to cure everyone else! I have no idea how an angel of wisdom decided this was a good idea, but it is not. This is a horrible idea! How am I supposed to do it all? Can you deny a gift from an angel?

I need to figure out something to help Delphine and the Nulls. Or, if nothing else, a way to provide enough food for the influx that comes in daily. Then, I have to help keep the forgotten gods mellow in Ward A, and heal who I can in Ward B. Lena and Selene are doing their best with those patients, but those two look so stressed out every time I see them. They're always chasing after some emergency—dropping off one person, or god, in need to go rescue another, rarely together too. I would've been too happy for that last semester, but now I wonder how lonely their crusades must be. Mine sure are.

I know I technically agreed to be on the hunt

for Kohl. It's not that I'm not, I just miss him. We had our problems, for sure. I can even acknowledge that I might have tried to cure him a bit too aggressively, but I often wonder if I loved him? If I still love him? I've never been in love. I remember watching Lena and Selene when I first woke up around Winter Solstice. They both looked so happy. It was cute. It made me feel warm inside even though the feelings weren't mine to have. I'd like to have those someday though, I think, as long as they don't go out of control.

Who knows, maybe when the next school year starts, I'll meet someone new. There are always new faces at Legacy. Nothing gets stagnant there, that's for sure. Maybe Solei and Tao will be back to their normal routines then too and could help. I made Tao daily balms during his meditation to help keep him balanced, and he recovered quite quickly in my opinion. I was pretty proud of myself for that. No one asked me to intervene, but I convinced enough staff that someone did, so everything went according to plan. Adults are too easy to fool. They hardly know anything.

I hope Tao and Solei get back to their normal lives soon. I miss having my friends around. And honestly, now that Ina has "blessed" me with such a persistent "gift," I could really use the help. Fall just started, and I'm already ready for it to be over.

Well, I suppose I need to be off to make that abomination a tiny place to sleep. Did you know that dumb angel was going to just leave him in the field? Adults really are (well-intentioned) idiots. He'd be immediately eaten by a Beboy twin, if not worse. This thing can barely walk without falling, let alone survive on its own. Ridiculous! This is all so ridiculous!

I feel like I'm the only one around here that truly understands anything. It's so frustrating being the only one that sees the whole picture, and what's my reward? I get another chore added to my already exceedingly long list of duties. This thing better sleep tonight while I make my rounds at both the wards. I do not have time for an around-the-clock nuisance!

Tao

Hello again,

I feel like I've already spent a great deal of time writing in this journal lately, but I've returned. It seems like this is all I have strength for these days. I've been out of my meditative trance for three months and five days now. I should be closer to normal, but I can't seem to find the strength to get out of bed lately.

The meditation went as expected. I saw the visions Principal Chromwell hoped for but couldn't dare talk about them. I told the headmistress a majority of them. School is going to be so different this year. Not that last year was standard in any way, but I don't see how this year goes well. And lately, I see a lot of things.

That's the other half of my troubles, I suppose. Ever since the trance, my visions are basically on steroids. Every time I sleep: vision. If I take a nap: vision. If I find myself spending too much time on a daydream: vision. So. Many. Frickin'. Visions! It's depleting. I never asked for this.

I can only hope that when I get back into the swing of things, my head stabilizes, and I'm able to achieve a more successful handle on what's real. I cannot spend my life lost in my head. That isn't practical. I'm better than that.

Even now, I can only be away from my bed for a few hours at a time. Lena ignores that though and is relentless. Selene tries to ebb her eagerness, but she's always on some type of crusade. I don't even understand what she's trying to prove. My head hurts even thinking about it. She's so much. Add Delphine into that equation, who is essentially a ball of pure energy, and I am not able to function. Delphine's energy isn't even aimed at me, and I can't process it. The only thing that calms her down is talking about Kohl. That is an instant silencer. His name is my only refuge when I try to socialize these days.

Selene gets super serious the instant Kohl is brought up. It triggers Lena every time. She is so desperate for answers she actually listens for once and doesn't continue to incessantly spout off. It probably helps that Delphine basically goes mute in those situations. I've noticed Delphine talking distracts Lena a great deal. It takes so long for those conversations to find their purpose again. During that time, I'm usually focused on sweet Airess. She always looks as if his name brings her to another place entirely. My heart aches for her. I know what it feels like to be lost in a way that no one can save you.

Every now and then, she'll speak and offer up a sentiment. She's very care based, as we all would expect, but her ideas surrounding Kohl are always tender, dreamy, and slightly vague. I understand those feelings. I understand the space she's in, even if my visions are so different than her obvious grief. I get how it feels to be slightly detached from the life you're living because your mind is taking you somewhere else. I live it every day.

Until next time,
Tao

Selene

I'm not sure what I'm supposed to put here. I don't usually write in these types of things. Lena recommended it though, so I'll try it.

I actually don't hate writing in general. I write quite a bit, but I prefer writing to people other than myself. Lately, all I've done are letters. They've also mostly been to Kohl. I write to him a lot these days. Not that I ever expect him to see them, or to be able to give them to him. I think that chance is long gone now. But, I suppose, I have hope that if I put them out into the universe, he'll somehow know all the things I need to say to him.

I need him to know that I never abandoned him, not even at his worst. I mean, sure, I wasn't thrilled with who he was, but I never intended to give up or walk away. I always thought we could work things out. Whatever he wanted, I wanted to help get him there. He's a good person, or at least, he was when I knew him. Maybe he still is. I'd like to believe in that. That's part of being someone's friend, right? Giving them the benefit of the doubt?

Not many people in this world have had to understand loneliness the way he and I did. I'm not sure if it's for better or worse, but if we weren't legacies we wouldn't have made it. Not that entering portals is safe by any means, but at least it gave us a chance. A win in the realm of a god pays out a lot more than a win in the mortal realm.

I miss him. I know I'm not supposed to, but I do. I can't even voice it to Lena. I've tried. It won't come out. He was like my brother, and now he's the enemy. I hate that. I want to save him, not hunt him.

The one time I said that out loud, I sounded so much like Airess that I've never said it again. She was horrible for him. I never liked them together. She always said I was jealous, but I wasn't. I've felt jealousy over Lena, and that was extremely different than anything I ever felt for Kohl.

I feel jealous every day that so many people in Ward A get to spend their entire day with Lena. I wish she was with me in the portals. I wish I was with her de-escalating Ward A. I miss the days when it was her and I against the world. Now, the only people I see daily are Delphine and Professor Nakshatra, which is still better than it used to be, but they're not Lena.

Not that I don't believe in my cause helping the Nulls. I do. They're lost, abandoned, and ostracized by the home they've always known as well as this weird new place they were forced into. I know quite a bit about those feelings. I get it. I'm grateful I can help, and I'm learning so much from Professor Nakshatra. THEY'RE INCREDIBLE.

I just really liked feeling complete before everyone got this busy. Lena has always made me feel like I'm more than what I see. Her family too. Kasim has been very understanding from the start, and Kamilah is simply adorable. She has the kindest soul; I really enjoy spending time with her. I'd never turn down an invite to the Basil household. I'm sure I'll never be so lucky, but they feel like family to me.

My beach is beautiful, but it's no home. It doesn't smell like cooked meals. It doesn't have the white noise of the TV or doors being shut too hard. No one's voice chatters in the background here. No one gets upset if you come home late. There isn't anyone to even notice. All that exists here is me, some rogue horses, and a world of dreams to visit.

xxv

Kohl

Another day, another portal, another entry.

Tonight I'm in some forest.

I'm not sure who this one belongs to. No one impressive, that's for sure.

I hear howling pretty often, and it's pitch black.

I was trying to find Hela's realm again, without being noticed, obviously.

I don't think I made it.

This one is probably Norse though.

Man, being in the shadows of the main gods is cool.

The first time was basically an accident. Now it's accidentally on purpose.

What I wouldn't give to be a god. Even a God of the dead would be plenty.

Delphine would love that.

Sometimes I think I'm pretty close. It feels amazing.

I can't believe I ever tried so hard to get rid of The Bad One.

He's more useful than I ever expected.

I'd never have realized that without Delphine. I'm so grateful she chose me.

xxvi

It's so different from before. Back then, Airess had me on all sorts of herbs and potions.

She even tried her version of an exorcism once. It was awful.

Then there was the time I thought my great idea of finding a portal near the Underworld would make everyone happy.

If I could find the river Lethe and drink from it, I could forget everything. I could be a new me.

Yeah, Airess went bonkers over that.

Only Diablo supported me. He didn't say it, but I knew he did.

He was my brother up until then.

But, then Delphine got caught in the crosshairs, and he brought her back to Legacy Academy.

That did not go over well for anyone.

Plus, he met Lena that day too.

Stupid Lena! She ruined everything.

Even when I was trying to commit suicide, she ruined it.

I jumped heart first into that terrifying sea beast, and what did I get to show for it? Some stupid pendant her dad made to save me from the poison.

Okay, maybe I actually like that necklace since it ensures I stay in control, but still, the Basil family is the worst thing to ever happen to me.

xxvii

Everyone thought I lost my powers because I looked normal. I believed them for a bit. I thought maybe it was all a convenient miracle.

I should've known better. I don't get miracles.

I left Ward B feeling pretty good. Powerful. I knew I was going to retreat back into the Ward A portals.

Even if I encountered a dying god, I would've been fine, but I wanted some padded insurance for my travels.

That's when I knew I lost Diablo though. Heaven forbid I slightly inconvenience his precious Lena.

Makes me want to puke.

So, whatever, I lost the magical items and he took them back in his backpack.

Delphine saved me though. She had left Ward A too.

She had a plan for us. A plan I am still working hard towards every day.

She deserves the world.

She was ecstatic when I portal hopped. The Bad One figured it out.

I can get to a god's realm as long as they have a connection to the realm I'm in.

All you need is to be a bit of a sneak and have some good snooping skills.

It comes naturally to me, but Delphine has really surprised me with how quickly she learned that too!

xxviii

Life is actually amazing lately.

I've stolen food from at least five main gods.

I even went back to the portal of Aglaope, trying to find my way to Olympus for Delphine.

That's where she belongs. She'd give anything to find her way back there.

I really messed up destroying her old realm, but you'd never know it.

I've seen glimpses of Aphrodite, and Delphine puts her to shame.

I can't even imagine what she looked like healthy.

She has no reason to be spending time with someone like me.

I can't get enough of her. I want her here every minute, every second.

I could hide us away and get us what we need forever.

I'd keep her with me in the shadows. She would always be safe.

I've told her so.

She's less sure than I am.

I know I could do this though. I screw up everything, but I wouldn't put this at risk.

She survived me at my worst, now she could have me at my best for the rest of eternity.

All she has to do is say yes.

xxix

xxx

ASTORIA'S SECRET

Table of Contents

1. Golems and Guesses

2. Arrivals and Additions

3. Qualms and Questions

4. Fights and Favor

5. Oversights and Oracles

6. Family and Friends

7. Mysteries and Mayhem

8. Prisoners and Pacts

9. Moles and Mermaids

10. Truths and Timers

11. Secrets and Scheming

12. Witches and Worries

13. Goodwill and Goodbyes

E. Cuddles and Companionship

{1}

Golems and Guesses

"No! Stop it!" Airess yelled breathlessly. "Why won't you listen to me?"

Tao appeared through the nearby row of crops. "Please stop yelling. It's hurting my head." He bent low to the ground and scooped up the wiggly clump.

"I think they're pretty adorable," Lena said, peering over Tao's shoulder, finally having made her way down the correct path.

Sweaty and disheveled, Airess screamed, "He is a bastardous little akuma!"

"Language!" Tao scolded.

"No. This horrible abomination drives me out of my mind until dusk and is back up at dawn. He is the worst thing I've ever encountered, and that is not an easy list to top."

Lena frowned. "Come on now. They can't be that bad." She offered her cupped hands to the bumbling creature. They looked to Airess for approval, and when their master nodded, they climbed over Tao's fingers into Lena's palms. They squirmed around, settling into a relaxed position.

"I hate to disagree with you, Airess, but they seem reasonably harmless to me. Do they act out even when you cuddle them?" Tao asked sincerely.

"Cuddle him? I would never!"

Instantly retracting, Tao corrected himself, "I meant when you hold them."

"I pick him up if it is absolutely necessary. Otherwise, my only goal is to try to keep him out of my way."

"I don't know, Airess; they seem to like it?" Lena scratched the tiny figure's head. They leaned into it and closed their eyes.

"You two are absolutely ridiculous. I can't believe you're both pandering to him so much. Did you not watch him run, over two miles, in the opposite direction from me? Did you not see him completely disobey me as I screamed at him and chased after him? He tore up at least five hundred feet of roots back there! And does anyone know why?" Airess did not wait for someone else to answer her question. "No! Because nothing this golem does makes a lick of sense. For something created specifically for me, he is the least helpful aide in the history of aides!"

"They must be misunderstanding you. Give them some time. It's been, what, two days? If Ina thought this was a good idea, I'd trust her," Tao reassured her.

The badges around Airess' and Lena's necks started to blink. The girls groaned in unison.

"And so it's totally doable to manage whatever this emergency is, while holding the imp, right? That won't hinder you in any way?" asked Airess snarkily.

Lena gave her friend a dirty look. "Tao, give me your hoodie."

"What?"

"Just do it! It's almost a hundred degrees out anyway. It's not like you need it, and take Cutie, here."

"His name is not Cutie," Airess interjected as she watched Tao follow Lena's orders.

"Then come up with a better one." Lena tied the arms of the hoodie securely around Airess' neck and fluffed out the hood in front of Airess' face. "There." Lena softly transported the squirmy golem into the hood.

"You've got to be kidding me. I hate this!" Airess' face was despondent as the creature stood at her words and started to pat her face.

"Why don't you ask them to go to sleep?" Tao suggested.

"It won't work. He never listens to me. Ever!"

Lena proposed, "Try it without yelling at them. Tell them that's how they can be helpful."

"Fine, but when this fails, you get to corral this monstrosity while we deal with whatever we're being called into." Airess waited until Lena rolled her eyes in agreement. "Akuma, go to sleep. I don't want to deal with you anymore." Airess watched as the golem stared with a tilted head at her.

"Do you have manners, or have you lost those along with your mind?" Lena ridiculed her.

Airess sighed in exasperation, "Golem. I would like you to help me by going to sleep. I'm about to be very busy and cannot watch after you while I'm working." And by the end of her sentence, the little clump of clay was curled up, fast asleep in her hood. The anger at her success was almost as evident as Lena's pride in her clear victory.

Lena threw her arms around her friends. "Now, on to the next quandary!"

~*~

The lights of Ward A were brighter than the outside sun. It was hot and sticky inside. Lena wiped the dust from her eyes as she scanned the crowd. The debris came out grainy and hard; each wipe was more painful than the last. It didn't matter, Lena found exactly what she had hoped to. She instantly grinned from ear to ear.

"Selene!" Lena shouted and waved.

He rushed to scoop his girlfriend up into a hug and placed a single kiss on her cheek. "Hey. I've missed you."

"I've missed you too. We just got called in." Lena showed him her blinking badge. "Oh! And I want you to meet someone! They're adorable, you're going to love them!"

Selene's eyes narrowed, but he let her pull him

to Airess.

Lena was practically bouncing. "Selene, meet Cutie!"

He looked at her apprehensively.

Airess' face was not one of compliance or approval.

It made Selene uncomfortable. "Are you sure it's okay?" He posed to the girls.

"Be quick, we're here to do a job. Also, his name isn't Cutie." Airess leaned forward slightly and pulled the backward hood down.

Peering in, Selene could see a small mound made of four rectangles, a square, and a circle. Not understanding what he was seeing at first, he watched it until it moved. The rectangles acted as limbs, the square as a chest, and that circle was its head. Selene had no problem not calling it Cutie; he found it disturbing.

Airess saw his reaction. She pulled away quickly after and recomposed herself. "If you're here, where's Delphine? Did you guys get called in too?"

"She's with the newest set of Nulls. We pulled another batch from some desert realm about twenty minutes ago. The sand got everywhere. It wasn't my favorite trip." Selene brushed his clothes off, seemingly not for the first time, before pulling Lena back into him.

"The desert? Whose realm was it? I can't imagine that being a great place for a siren," Tao chimed in.

"Professor Nakshatra told me, but I wasn't able to listen at the time. I had my hands full, and truthfully, they smelled kind of bad. I just wanted out."

"Their lives are completely dismantled, and you're complaining about their smell?" Airess asked indignantly.

"I have discovered the undead aren't my thing. And yes, they smell bad."

Airess' face cringed at his response.

"The undead?" Lena looked up to read his face.

"There were hordes of mummies. Most of the Nulls are fine. They're weak and thin but seem human. Some though . . . are slightly different."

"But mummies are real people that died, right? They wouldn't even be gods. So, why would they even have a portal? That doesn't make sense." Tao had found a stool to sit on and was holding his head as usual.

"Excellent question Mr. Vovi. I'm glad you're all here." Professor Nakshatra appeared from behind. She stood and studied Tao for a moment. "Let's go into my study and chat. I've requested the presence of a few others as well."

Lena loved going to Professor Nakshatra's. It brought back so many strong memories. This was where they saved Selene, where Lena let her guard down and allowed herself to feel everything she had held back for months. This was her safe haven. The decor was much different now, but it still had the same gentle lotus smell Lena loved so much. The study was bigger than it had been before. It was less dark but remained dimly lit by the stars hanging near the ceiling. Varying forest scenes replaced traditional walls. Large fluffy pillows and the softest of blankets outlined the center rug. The professor started playing her Tibetan singing bowl. It was time to begin their meditation.

Lena made herself comfortable and kept space for Selene to join beside her. Her eyes closed momentarily, taking it all in. Her soul felt quiet here. She could feel the strength of Selene's hand holding hers, the cool breeze carrying its sweet floral scent, the warmth and tameness of the lights around her, and the soothing vibrations being carefully crafted for them by their teacher.

"Thank you for joining me here today, my children." Professor Nakshatra completed their melody. "It seems I am once again in need of your services. Today, while Selene and Delphine continued their valiant efforts retrieving the Nulls from Amenmesse's portal, I had quite the unique experience. I found a small boy hovering in a corner. Assuming he was scared, I knelt down to express kindness and sincerity. His eyes went wide, and I noticed bright red around his ankle. It was quite striking on this now dull child. I summoned my magic to my hands, prepared to heal, and much to my astonishment the boy scattered. Behind him, he left this." The professor walked around the group and presented a covered glass platter. "I discovered a scrap of vibrant red cloth, a hefty clump of seaweed, and two fish. What I find most confusing is that, yes, the fish are certainly dead as expected, but they are not dried out or rotting. I don't even think they've been iced. Please, come inspect these for yourselves."

Airess was the first one to the plate. She lifted the glass cover and picked up the red fabric. Selene was tentatively holding back with Lena, and Tao appeared to be asleep.

"This is—this isn't right. This fabric doesn't belong here." Airess' voice tried to hide her heightened concern. "Egyptians were masters of textiles, but this piece has ash embedded in its hemline. Volcanic ash." Her voice was becoming unnerved.

Lena leaned forward, pulling Selene with her. The seaweed glistened in the faint light. Lena picked up the bundle to sniff. The saltwater scent was unmistakable. The pile dripped as she put it back. "I am neither a plant expert nor a geography expert, but the desert should not have bunches of wet seaweed sitting in its streets."

Selene inspected the displayed items. He paused for a long while. "I think we should ask Delphine about these. They smell like her world."

Lena was taken aback by his words. *How does he know what her world smells like?*

As if she heard her name on his lips, the doors opened to the room. Delphine trailed in on the coattails of Principal Chromwell who stood as captivating as ever in her flowing robes.

"Salutations, my dear colleague and students! I bring another to join you!" Chromwell ushered Delphine towards the others. As expected, Delphine sat right next to Selene. "Professor, if I may, I have wonderful news sure to elate this lot."

"By all means, Theodora."

"Excellent! Let me read directly from their letter!" From one of her cloaks, the principal pulled out a sheet of loose-leaf paper. "Dear Headmistress, I have begun my journey and wanted to keep you up to date on my travels. I am in London now and should arrive in Astoria by midnight tomorrow. I have my old keys, so if able, I'd prefer to keep my old space. I believe that should suit both of us nicely. All my best, Solei." Principal Chromwell folded up the paper and tucked it back in. She beamed proudly to her students, anticipating their great joy.

Though Tao had still not stirred, Airess was bouncing with glee, clapping. Selene seemed pleased as well until he saw what Lena was up to. Lena had taken to searching her phone. Delphine was not hiding her dissatisfaction of the whole event and wandered off to find anything of higher value.

Hurt, Lena muttered, "They haven't sent any-thing to us."

"Don't fret, child! They have informed me, so I would have the honor of telling you all! I know you, in particular, have been eager for Solei's return for quite some time now, Miss Basil. You've mentioned it often, have you not?"

"No, ma'am. I mean yes, ma'am. I have. I very much wanted to have them home."

"Fantastic! I will prep their room with great haste and make sure everything goes smoothly for tomorrow!" Chromwell took a step toward Lena to ensure eye contact. In a sincere tone, the head-mistress murmured, "And I'm sure that when they are ready, they will text you then, but only then. Patience is always the hardest to manage when it involves the ones we love, dear. Chin up." With that, Principal Chromwell showed a proud smile, gave a nod to the professor, and shut the doors behind her as she left.

Lena put her phone away with a huff and focused on an outside tree. Tears wanted to pour out of her, but she willed them not to surface. She was tired of crying over Solei.

"Oh my gosh guys!!! This is so great!!!" Airess had her hands on Tao's shoulders, shaking him with excitement.

Tao jostled awake. "What's going on?"

"Solei is coming home tomorrow!" Airess shrieked with happiness.

"Hey, that's cool! You have to be excited for that one, huh, Basil?" Tao asked groggily.

"Yeah. It'll be nice to have them back," Lena offered with a half-smile.

Tao couldn't understand Lena's reaction. He looked to Selene for answers.

Selene held out his phone. "Solei didn't send anything to us. It all came through Chromwell."

"Ahh, I see," Tao said slowly, acknowledging the situation.

"Enough about that! What's this??" Delphine dove towards the items displayed in the center of the circle. "Looks delicious!" She lifted up the seaweed to her mouth.

"Stop!" Selene grabbed it from her. Lena watched with scrutiny how he reached for Delphine. "Professor Nakshatra found these when we were gathering the Nulls. We think it's a clue to Kohl."

Delphine's face went whiter than it already was.

"Indeed, my young protégé is correct. What we had been discussing is that Miss Hikona believes the red material to have volcanic ash. Others, as well as myself, could not ignore how fresh the seaweed and fish have been kept. Needless to say, these are not your typical finds in the desert of Amenmesse. Wouldn't you agree?"

Words choked in Delphine's throat. "Ye."

Selene addressed his friend, "I thought these smelled like Souda Bay. Do you recognize them?"

She stared into his fiery eyes and breathed. Taking the offerings from his hand, she brought them to her nose. "The smell is similar, but these don't come from my land, Selene. I'm sorry."

Disappointed, he set them back. Tao came for a closer look. "I'm not one to be able to tell one kind of seaweed from the next, but I know that fish. It's a humuhumunukunukuapua'a."

"A what?" Lena and Airess said in unison.

"It's also called a reef triggerfish outside of its native Hawaiian language. It's a very clean fish, white meat. It tastes kind of sweet like crab. The only downside is the size. It's small so not many people go for it."

Selene's tone turned serious. "You said its name was Hawaiian. Is that the only region it's native to?"

"It's the state fish of Hawaii, but I think it can be found anywhere in the Indo-Pacific region. Where did you guys find these?" Tao addressed his question to the professor.

"The realm we were in mimics the location of Ancient Egypt. One of their seas meet with the Indian Ocean, but water was not a prevalent resource where we were located. Even with our additional information, I do not believe these items came from where we were."

"I'd need to have some more time with the cloth, but Hawaii would make sense for the volcanic ash on this garment." Airess traced her finger over the fabric's hemline.

"Doesn't Hawaii have a volcano goddess that wears a red dress? Pele, maybe? Does that sound familiar?" Tao scanned the crowd. They had no answers, but were all listening intently except for Delphine.

"I'll look. Want to come to the library with me?" Selene moved to a kneeling position, prepping to stand.

"It's about time for me to go home. I'll catch up with you later though, text me?"

Selene was shocked at the idea of Tao passing up a trip to his favorite place, especially when someone was asking him to deep dive on a topic and listen to him drone on about it. Selene made sure not to let his surprise show. "Yeah, of course. I'll text you everything I find."

"Great. See you guys tomorrow." Tao went to take back his hoodie from Airess, reconsidered, and headed out.

Suspicious, Lena asked, "What was that all about?"

"What do you mean?" Airess responded genuinely.

"He's being so weird." Lena knew Tao was acting off, but her thoughts kept bringing her back to someone else. "Hey, in that letter, did you guys notice that Solei said we? And how did Chromwell get a letter from them if they had just arrived in London to come here?!"

"P.C. probably transcribed that from a tele-graphic message. Solei used to send messages in Morse code all the time to Legacy." Airess reached out to her friend. "Are you ok?"

Lena pulled away and stood upright. "I'm fine. Isn't everyone fine these days?" She grabbed her gear and left, slamming the door behind her.

Delphine peeked her head out. "Dramaaaaaa!"

She carried on the ending sound for an excruciating amount of time. Taking up Lena's previous spot, she shoulder-bumped Selene. "Am I right?"

"I have to go. Please forgive my abruptness, Professor." Selene was on his feet, ready to chase after Lena. "I'll look into the Goddess Pele and be in touch soon. Take care."

"You children may depart as well. It seems our meeting has come to an end," the professor addressed her remaining students.

The two girls obliged and made their way into the hall.

Delphine had many more opinions she wanted to express. "Wow, have they been like this all day? Geez."

"Lena was fine in the fields. I wish she'd let me hold her hand, so I could read her. I want to help."

"That'll never happen. Help would lessen her ego."

Airess directed a concerned face towards Delphine.

Delphine shrugged. "I said what I said. Speaking of surprises though, what's with the new style?" Delphine flicked the backward hoodie.

"Oh, this is Cu—" Airess cut herself short. "I'm not sure what his name is, but he's a golem. Wanna see?" She got close to Delphine to show her.

"If you don't know his name, how do you know it's a he? Are all golems he's?"

"I suppose I don't actually know. I've never met

a golem before this one. They're incredibly rare, though they certainly annoys me the way some he's I know annoy me."

Delphine laughed, "Probably better not to assume, eh? I remember someone wise telling me that once upon a time."

"Wise AND beautiful!" Airess posed playfully.

"That goes without saying. You are beyond wise and beautiful." Delphine pretended to bow in honor of her friend. "Whatcha gonna do with it though?"

"I wish I had any clue. All I know is that they have orders to 'Help Airess.' That's what Ina told me when she gifted them to me."

"This lump is from Ina?"

Airess nodded.

"I can't speak for you, but if I got a gift from an angel, I'd give it a real good name. Those favors aren't easy to come by, Airess."

"I know. I just hate him," Airess whined. "I mean them. Sorry. I just hate them." Airess clarified, "They never listen, they're always into trouble, and I swear they never sleep even though I know they have to."

"It's like meeeeee!" Delphine twirled in front of her friend. "And you love me, right?"

Airess gave her a taunting glare that only encouraged Delphine more.

"You love me! You know you do!"

"What can I say? I'm a poor judge of character."

"Wonderful! So be a poor judge of character again and figure out how to love this little lump!"

Airess sighed. "Okay. You win. I'll love the lump." She scratched the golem's head with care. They woke up and stared at her. "Hi buddy," Airess said softly. They waved a rectangle at her. "Let's find you a name, okay? Can I call you by a name?" The creature pounded their rectangles onto their center square. Airess shook her head with a laugh. "Okay you, let's go brainstorm together."

"Auntie Delphine is going to help!!"

"No way!"

"What?" Delphine yelled, flabbergasted.

"Absolutely not. 'Auntie' is not happening." Airess dramatically shielded her golem from Delphine's absurdity.

"Come on!!!!"

"Not even once."

"You're no fun, you hear me? Absolutely none." Delphine was intentionally acting bombastic. Airess refused to give in and kept a straight jovial face. Attempting to get a rise out of her, Delphine leaned close to the hood and whispered, "Your mom is the killer of a good time." But when she said the word mom, the golem stood and tapped Airess' chest.

The sweet gesture melted Airess' grumpiness away. She started crying immediately, cradling the golem's hood closer to her own heart.

Delphine looped her arm in Airess' and laid her head on the bubblegum healer's shoulder. Delphine was quiet the rest of the walk. She had fallen into two mindsets. While she was happy for her friend, she was also jealous of the seraph's favor.

{ 2 }

Arrivals and Additions

Lena woke up to the smell of a hot breakfast. She got ready sluggishly before making her way down to the kitchen. Her mother, Kamilah, was dancing to the beat of soft music while tending the sizzling pans.

"Morning, Mom. Smells great, whatcha cookin'?" Lena took her seat on a stool at the counter.

"I'm making cornbread pancakes stuffed with cinnamon apples."

"That sounds . . . new."

"I saw it on a show! You and your father are going to love it!"

"They made that on your show?"

"They made parts of it on the show. It was MY idea to make it an all-in-one experience!" Kamilah emphasized her pride as she cooked.

"Ahh. Gotcha! That makes more sense. Well, I'm in! I'll try anything that smells that good."

"Who wouldn't? I'm about to plate." This was

Lena's mom's new way of saying she had to focus, and she wasn't going to indulge in a conversation anymore.

It always made Lena slightly nervous watching her mom manage multiple areas at once, especially when fire and glass were involved. It wasn't long ago that folding socks had been too big of a challenge for Kamilah. For most of Lena's life, she had always seen her mother as a source of chaos and uncertainty. It wasn't until her family came to Astoria that she began to truly value their relationship. Lena felt sentimental, admiring how far they'd come.

Life was very different now that Lena's mom had synced back up with her old besties. The three of them were quite a trio. Millie was as straightforward and strong-willed as ever, with a heart that never stopped caring. Ina mimicked the likes of a seraph and was a manifestation of angelic perfection. Theodora, a.k.a. P.C., a.k.a. the headmistress of Legacy Academy, was everything those titles implied; she carried authority with her everywhere she went, and the rest of the world seemed to obey her every command.

Ina was Lena's personal favorite. Ever since Ina came along, things had been frictionless in the Basil household. Ina had spent hours with Lena, training her on her language skills and True Sight. These lessons may also have included significant time on helping Lena control her emotions too, but that was not what Lena talked about at the end of the day. Neither Lena nor Kamilah ever turned down an invite from Ina.

Principal Chromwell was loved by Kamilah, but that was about the extent of the feelings towards her within the Basil household. Theodora spent a good deal of time with Kamilah lately, and Lena spent an even greater deal of time trying to avoid P.C. as much as possible. Principal Chromwell's presence was especially vivacious if Lena's father, Kasim, had obligations elsewhere.

Kasim never directly said anything poorly against Ina or Theodora, but the unresolved tension towards each other from their younger years was palpable. The three of them bickered nonstop. This got exceptionally awkward, not only during the girls' nights Lena's mom hosted but also where they all worked too. Lena and Kasim were assigned under P.C. He was a teacher, and Lena helped take care of the dying gods in Ward A. Ina was around daily to help as well; she functioned as Theodora's personal assistant.

"Ha! Done!" Kamilah gloated, "And I didn't even burn any bacon!"

Lena, who had been setting the table for everyone, stopped. "There was bacon?"

A concerned look spread across her mom's face as she inspected the kitchen. "Why would there be bacon, Lena? We don't typically eat that in this household."

"I know, but you said . . ."

"I said I didn't burn any, Lena! Do you see any burnt bacon in my workstation?"

"No . . ."

"Exactly my point! My dish is more condensed, AND I didn't have to burn any food to do it! Now, let's not wait until the food gets cold. I'll call your father." Lena's mom spoke into a band on her wrist, "Breakfast is cooked. Time to eat!"

"Oh, a new gadget? What'd dad make this time?" Lena reached out to see the newest magical item crafted by the famous Kasim Basil. He had been famous most of his adult life for his magical work, but Lena had only known about this for less than a year. She always thought he did woodwork for a living, not so much crafting powerful ornate staffs like the revered staff Principal Chromwell wields.

"Not Dad, Theodora! She gave it to me last night!" Kamilah displayed her shiny new smartwatch to Lena.

Lena pulled her hand back slowly. She had no desire to get near that potential powder keg. She could hear her dad coming down the stairs.

"Morning! How are my girls today? The food smells great, Millie. It's making my stomach growl!" He kissed them each atop their head before sitting down.

"If growls are coming from your stomach, that is not normal and has nothing to do with my food. Your abnormalities manifested on their own."

"Very fair, dear; these are wonderful," Kasim said with a mouth full.

Her dad wasn't wrong. Shockingly, these pancakes were pretty good.

"Lena, you should take some food to Selene. I worry he doesn't have enough to eat in his cave." Kamilah said this almost every morning and certainly every morning she cooked. Lena had a sneaking suspicion that it was a driving factor as to why her mom was cooking so regularly these days. It used to be her dad covering most of the meals earlier, and now Lena couldn't remember the last time he was the one in the kitchen.

"I've asked him plenty of times if he has enough food, but I'm sure he will enjoy these either way." All of that was true. For whatever reason, Selene loved her mother's peculiar cooking. No matter how weird or how bad it turned out, he was always excited to take Kamilah's meals with him. Even when he visited the house, Lena could barely peel him away from the kitchen, which she had tried to, repeatedly.

"Good. I'll pack him extra," Kamilah said authoritatively. Her watch dinged. Her mom started poking at it haphazardly, mumbling to herself.

Lena looked to her dad to see his reaction. He was focused on his pancakes and even more concentrated on not looking over at his wife.

Oh my gosh, he hates it! I knew it. Attempting to dispel building frustrations, Lena showed her mom what she needed to know. She explained the concept of notifications and how they would direct her to the app that was asking for her attention. She also assured her mother that there wasn't anything actually ringing a bell inside her watch, and no, they did not need to disassemble the gift to be sure, although Lena doubted her father would've stopped that investigation in any way. The family finished up breakfast, Kasim offered to clean the dirty dishes, and Lena went back to her bedroom.

Despite having helped her mother, she hadn't checked her own phone yet today. The delay was intentional. Lena wasn't worried about what would be on her phone, but she was incredibly anxious over what might not be on her phone. Solei was a thought that was impossible to escape from. Even thinking about her dad's work brought Lena's thoughts back to her friend. Solei was Kasim's apprentice, just like she was Ina's and Selene was Professor Nakshatra's.

Lena must have sent Solei over a hundred messages since they left. Solei had yet to send a reply that made up a complete sentence. The lack of response frequently made Lena doubt their friendship. They were supposed to be best friends, but Lena wasn't so sure of that anymore. Turmoil nagged at her to open the group chat that included all of the people who loved Solei, had stood by Solei, and were basically family to Solei. It had been over eight months since their departure. That was a long time to stay silent. They missed out on all of second semester and summer break.

Times like this made Lena want to text Selene. She wanted to have him with her in case Solei still hadn't reached out. To get that though, she'd have to text him, and that was the exact screen she was actively trying to evade. She debated walking the food over to his room in Ward A, but she imagined he was probably out saving the world again and much too busy to be sitting on his beach, lonesome and waiting for his girlfriend to appear. A brief flash of him being on the beach with fishy company crossed her mind. The millisecond of that image turned out to be exactly what Lena needed to pull herself together. She found the idea so revolting she texted him at that same moment.

"Homemade breakfast awaits you! Where can I meet you?"

"I'm all over this morning, but pick anywhere in Ward A, and I'll make it work. Can't wait to see you! XOXO."

Lena smiled. He had a way of calming her that no one else had. She needed more of that in her life and more of him too. Lena missed her sweetheart. She was ready to go to Ward A.

~*~

Lena snapped a picture of herself with a blanket and a picnic basket in front of Selene's door. The caption read "Who could turn down a picnic on the beach?"

Lena thought about waiting inside and having their moonlit meal all set up, but she wanted to do it together. It had been so long since they had done much of anything together. She wanted a short escape with only the two of them.

About ten minutes later, she watched Selene

turn the corner. He was practically running towards her. She only had a second to admire his dazzling smile before he swept her up in his arms. She held onto him tightly, wanting to cry. She could feel her chest tighten. Things had been so hard lately, and she hadn't realized how many emotions she'd been holding back to make it through the day. He was her person, and she knew she was safe within his embrace.

His silky smooth voice whispered in her ear, "Shall we go in?" Selene took her items, made an adorably cute dramatization about the smell of the food, and led them inside.

The view was the exact same every time. Lena found comfort in that. The moon was always full and bright. The sand was always soft, and though she knew it was technically white, it shined a glittery bluish gray. His cave glistened, no matter the time of day, and was a beautiful jet black. It housed a cozy orange fire with an everlasting flame. This was their secret space; their hideaway from the rest of the world.

They walked hand-in-hand along the beach, her head frequently resting upon his upper arm. Neither of them had many words to say, but Lena felt this was the best conversation they'd had in weeks. Needing to be closer to him, she stopped and asked to set up their picnic.

The couple lofted half the blanket up into the air and laid it down taut. Knowing her intentions,

Selene laid down with his arm extended towards her. She curled up close to him, tucking into the crook of his neck. This was her favorite spot when she felt overwhelmed. Nestled in like this, she knew she was protected. He put his head atop hers, wrapped his arms tightly around her, and intertwined their legs. All she could see and smell was him. In this space, no one could see her, not even Selene. She could completely fall apart and not have to worry about keeping her composure. He rubbed her back rhythmically, and she finally let her tears rise to the surface.

"Yesterday had to have been rough. I know how important it's been for you to talk to Solei since they left. Hearing their first message from someone else must have felt terrible."

"That implies their message was even to me! Did they know I'd hear what they had written? Did they care?!" Lena was pounding Selene's chest with her fists. "As far as I can tell, they haven't thought of our friendship once. We haven't had a single quality conversation in months! How can they do this to me? We risked our lives together. They've literally been inside my mind when I didn't even know who I was. They've seen and understood me in ways no one will ever be able to. I've risked my life to bring them back when no one else could reach them, and they were a supernova begging to explode." Her tears were coming down so intensely, and her body was shaking so hard, that her words were barely audible. Selene held her all the tighter. The more she fell apart, the more he'd physically support her.

Lena spent a long while letting go of her emotions. When the wave of heartbreak and fear ebbed, her voice was small. "They've been gone, and basically silent, for longer than we were friends here. Did I lose them? Do we even have a friendship left anymore?"

"My sweet love, that's a lot of pain to carry around for nine months. I can't answer those questions for Solei. What I can tell you is that they'll be back tonight. One way or another, you'll get some answers soon, and I'll be here to do what I can no matter what. Solei and I were never close, but I've known of them for a long time. They've never struck me as someone who is faint of heart; however, I can't deny how they've acted this year. I imagine they must have been going through a lot too. It took them a long time to acknowledge that they were related to Lucifer. Maybe that healing process needed more space than any of us expected."

Lena let out a sigh of exasperation. She hated when she was upset and Selene made sense of things. "I feel like they ghosted me."

"I can understand why you feel that way. No matter what their experience has been like in Rome, you absolutely deserve some kind of explanation. There's no denying that."

"I've needed that for almost the entire time they've been gone. I've yet to see the slightest hope of that happening."

"I know, sweetheart. I know." He gave a squeeze. "Hey, you know what?"

"Hmm?" She looked up to see his face.

"I could never ghost you. You're my person. Staying apart from you is one of the hardest things I have to do." He softly kissed her lips.

Lena's heart swooned. She smiled and booped his nose. "You're my person too."

A cough sounded in the background. Lena looked over Selene's shoulder. It was Delphine. Of course it was. The siren waved. Lena's face filled with disgust.

"Hey guys!"

"Delphine?" Selene sounded surprised. "What are you doing here?"

Lena enjoyed that reaction and nodded in agreement.

"Airess sent me for you; she wants to throw a surprise party!"

"Airess sent you to Selene's realm to ask us about a surprise party?" The disbelief in Lena's tone was evident.

"Yeah! Kind of! She didn't exactly say those words, but she did ask me to find you both, and Tao."

"And your first stop was to break into my boyfriend's house?" Lena had become terse. She could hear Selene's heartbeat pick up.

Delphine glared at her. "I didn't break in."

Both girls turned towards Selene.

"Okay." He lifted up Lena's chin to catch her

eyes in his. "Do you want to go or is it too hard?"

Lena swore she could hear Delphine scoff, but she was too focused on Selene to be sure. "I want to see them come home."

"All right. Then we'll go. I'll escort Delphine out?"

"Yes, please," Lena said with enthusiasm.

"On it."

Lena watched him walk Delphine out. It looked like he was keeping more distance than usual. Lena scanned their area and spotted Selene's forgotten food. She picked up the picnic basket and dusted off some sand. Lena walked with the items into his cave and took a long, deep breath before heading out his door.

~*~

"We need more lights over there! Use the twinkly star ones!" Airess directed from atop a tall overgrown yellow rose.

"Can't Solei make lights all on their own? Why do we have to do this?" Delphine struggled to hook the lights over the correct vines.

"They're going to be so shocked when they see what we've done for them! It'll be perfect!"

"Their shocks are what I'm concerned about!" Delphine grumped as she patted her rose to bring her back down.

"The dorm looks beautiful, Airess. They'll love it. I'm sure of it." Tao spoke over Delphine, eyeing her.

"There. I think we're done too. Airess, do these

petals look like they're leading towards the center instead of leading away?" Selene asked earnestly.

"The dirt lines should be fixed as well. They're both effective at keeping the petals in place and are a sight to see!" Lena added, "Also, here is this little gem. They were a great help today." She carefully slid the golem into Airess' cupped hands.

Airess celebrated with delight. "Perfect! Great job to all of you!" She placed the golem into her cross body sling she made for them this morning. They already felt heavier than they did twelve hours ago.

Lena sat against the wall and admired the room. She had spent the majority of her day working hard on Airess' vision. Soft sparkling lights illuminated plump yellow roses lining the ceiling. Petals and dirt lines decorated the floor in a wonderfully symmetrical mandala. In the center of their small space was a proud display of a large cake. The frosted message of "Welcome Home Solei!" was visible even at a distance. Everything was fairly serene and undoubtedly picture perfect.

"Our time is at 11:45 p.m.," Tao announced to the group.

"Okay, that means we have twenty or thirty minutes until they get here. If you want a break, I suggest you take a short one now. Chibi Chan and I will stay here." Airess rubbed the golem's head when she spoke their new name.

Lena looked towards Selene. "What do you think?"

"I'm fine grabbing our leftovers from lunch, yeah? I imagine this feels rather late for you."

Lena shrugged. "A little, I guess. I have leftovers too. Wanna grab them, and then, maybe I'll rest if we have time?"

"Of course. I'll be right back."

Airess made a disgruntled noise from the extra bed. Tao had evidently fallen asleep and unexpectedly fallen into her lap. Chibi Chan was snuggling into the newfound comfort of Tao's fluffy hair.

"I think you've got your hands and your arms full over there," Lena teased.

Airess' face shook in defeat. "Tell me about it!"

It was a peaceful wait. Muffled sounds of eating and snoring faded in and out. Lights of cell phone screens flickered on and off. Everyone who was awake seemed to be checking their phone constantly for the time.

"Where's Delphine?" Airess asked.

Ahh. That's why this has been peaceful. The mermaid's gone, Lena thought.

"I'm not sure. I haven't seen her," Selene answered.

"She'll miss this! It's already midnight! I can't even ask Chibi for help at this hour."

"Are we even sure she wants to be here for this? She was testy all day," Lena posed.

Disappointed, Airess conceded, "I guess . . ."

Selene stood and threw their garbage away. "If you want me to—"

"Shhh!" Airess tapped her pointer finger on her mouth rapidly. When she had his attention, she pointed to her ears.

Sure enough, there was chatter in the hallway a short distance beyond the door. Lena's ears heard a voice that now felt foreign. The handle jiggled.

Airess hopped to her feet, jostling Tao.

Lena's heart was racing. It was finally happening. She squeezed Selene's hand tight and noticed both their hands were slightly sweaty.

The door pushed open.

"SURPRISE!" Airess yelled, jumping with joy.

Solei's face was shocked to say the least. Airess instantly threw her arms around them with a vice grip. Lena couldn't resist hyperfocusing on Solei's body language. They stood as stiff as a board while Airess fawned all over them. Lena's heart was starting to race at the lack of compassion returned by them. She wondered if she was over-thinking everything in such a quick time, but when Selene started to rub her arm, and not just her hand, Lena knew he was offering extra comfort for the same reason. Tao joined the group at the door. Lena thought he was extending his hand to add to the hug, but instead, watched him offer a handshake.

"Hi. I'm Tao."

Lena was instantly confused. She switched her attention from Solei to Tao and noticed what everyone else had seemed to miss too. There was someone behind Solei. This mystery person was in the hallway and seemed to be stepping further and further away from the room. Lena got up to get a better look. They had bags draped over their shoulders, and a large suitcase was still clenched in their hand. *They were traveling. They were traveling here. With Solei!* A bit mind blown, Lena also offered her hand.

"I'm Lena. It's nice to meet you." But when Lena met the stranger's eyes, she knew things weren't okay. This poor visitor was frozen in fear. *Were they shaking?* "Umm, Solei? Can you come here, please?" Lena could feel them rush past her before the request was fully uttered.

"Oh my gosh! Mae! Are you okay? I'm so sorry! I had no idea they would be here! I had no idea they would do all this! Are you okay?" Solei held the face of the scared human. After a while, the girl nodded. "Okay. Okay. Thank goodness! Let's go inside, all right?" The unexpected guest gave another nod. Solei rushed to get their counterpart inside. Lena and Selene carried the extra bags to the room's door, fully knowing they were no longer supposed to cross that threshold. Tao had stepped out of the room too. Solei got their visitor settled and was ushering Airess out. "Thank you for everything, but I think Mae needs to rest now. It's been a long travel home. We're both kind of beat."

"Sure," Airess squeaked out softly.

"Thanks for understanding. I'll see you guys tomorrow. Take care." And Solei closed the door in front of all four of their faces.

Lena couldn't look away from the spot Solei just stood. She heard Tao in the background convincing Airess of doing something, but Lena couldn't move. Selene waited with her, not saying a word, and only offered physical comfort intermittently. Lena stood and stood and stood. Her heart broke more with each passing minute. Eventually, her shaky breath gave her enough strength to speak.

"Welcome back." Lena cried through silent tears.

{ 3 }

Qualms and Questions

"I'm not trying to be difficult, Selene, but what you're saying doesn't add up. If Tūtū Pele is such a prominent Hawaiian goddess, how could Kohl get into her realm? Not to mention, if that goddess created the Hawaiian islands, wouldn't she be pretty protective of who comes in and out of her territory? Kohl wouldn't exactly blend in there. He'd stick out like a sore thumb," Airess opposed.

"If the ash on that fabric is from Tūtū Pele's volcanoes, everything Selene has said holds true," Tao confirmed. "Sorry, Airess."

"Airess isn't wrong though," Lena countered. "Ward A is the only way we know of to get into a god's portal, and the only gods that come into Ward A are the forgotten ones. Tūtū Pele wouldn't have a portal here. Having current believers equals power and powerful gods don't need caregivers."

Selene agreed, "Even Indra, who had very few

supporters, was a complete handful. If a god that's been banned by their own religion can be as powerful as he was, who knows what a revered goddess of creation is capable of? I don't know how he got there and know even less about how he would have survived there. Kohl would have to be as strong as an ancient god to stand a chance against her, and I just don't believe that to be true."

"Kohl could be as powerful as an ancient god?" Delphine muttered in amazement. It was the only thing she had said so far.

"It doesn't seem likely, Delphine. Based on what I saw in Rome, and what I've learned from Mae, he doesn't fit the mold. There are beings out there that truly have unlimited power. They control so much more of the universe than we even realize." Solei tried to make eye contact with Lena, but Lena avoided it.

"Regardless of how unnerving that sounds, you haven't actually seen one of those gods though, right?" Tao inquired.

Solei shook their head no.

"And Mae hasn't either?"

Solei had a longer pause to Tao's question this time. They knew the answer was yes, but now wasn't the time to disclose that little tidbit. Ultimately, Solei shook their head no again.

"That's what I thought. There's no actual proof to go on for claims like those. I think the best way for us to figure out if this Tūtū Pele situation is legitimate or not, is to have an expert study the ash and the cloth. Between those two items, we have to be able to find some type of identifying factor." Tao looked towards Airess. "Do you know someone who can study the ash?"

Airess' mouth held agape. "I don't know." She thought for a long while before turning to Professor Nakshatra. "Do I?"

The professor led with a warm smile. "That's a mighty big task to pass onto a fellow classmate, Mr. Vovi. I think I shall take these items as well as Selene's astute findings on Tūtū Pele to Principal Chromwell. I believe the headmistress may want a say in all this before we bestow any rigorous task upon Miss Hikona here."

Airess looked relieved; Tao looked annoyed.

"I'll head that way now. Take all the time you need in my study, children. I'll be back in a moment."

"I don't see how I can be of any more use here if we're punting to P.C. I'm going home. Call me if our situation changes." Tao packed up and left hurriedly.

Solei tried to say something to him but couldn't catch him in time. They looked concerned for their friend. "Is he okay?"

"He's fine. He's Tao," Airess dismissed Solei's concern. "It's about time to wake my little one up and head to the fields. Anyone want to join us?" Airess patted the melon-sized golem strapped to her chest.

Lena checked her watch. "My shift starts soon. Sorry, Airess."

"I'll go!" Delphine jumped up at the offer.

"We have Null duties, Delphine. We still have to find housing for the newest three that came in this morning," Selene interposed.

"Oh, right! Bummer." Delphine sat back down.

Lena's badge began to blink. "Duty calls. Want to walk out together?" Lena asked Airess.

"Yeah. Of course. What about you, Solei? Are you up for a walk?"

"Umm . . .," Solei picked up their phone and analyzed its contents intently ",. . . I probably shouldn't."

Lena muttered under her breath, "No surprise there," and continued out the door. Airess frowned but followed close behind.

"Everything okay?" Selene gestured to Solei's phone. "Last night was pretty rough. Is she doing better today?"

"A little. Thanks for asking. It's a big change."

"I imagine the majority of us would agree with you if we had a tenth of the knowledge you do." Solei looked as if they were ready to protest, but Selene held up his hands in peace. "I'm not starting a fight. I merely wanted to say that I know your friends would be a stronger support system for you if they had the vaguest idea of how to help you. They want to be in your life, Solei, whatever that looks like, but you gotta let them know where their place is these days."

"Understood." Solei rose and grabbed their things. "Lena's lucky to have you, Selene. We, probably, all are." They patted him on the shoulder.

"I'm just me."

"'Just you' is more than enough. I should probably check in on Mae though. See you."

"See you." He watched them leave then spent a second straightening up the pillows for when the professor returned. "All right. Ready to go, Delphine?" No one answered. Selene wandered around the study looking for her. "Delphine? Hello?"

She was nowhere to be found.

~*~

Delphine's heart was racing. She had never been to this portal before. Only one person could live in a place like this. This was Kohl's domain. She was certain of it. The sky was pitch black; not even a moon hung above her head. The only light present came from glowing figures wandering in the darkness. The air smelled rotten. Delphine was engulfed with death. Goosebumps covered her arms as she tried to get her bearings. She needed a plan, and she needed it now.

A ghostly sound echoed from behind. Delphine turned to face her opponent, but there was no one visible. There was only an increasing sound of something dragging over the earth. Whatever wanted her attention was drawing near. Panicked, Delphine desperately searched for a way out. Her eyes darted to and fro, searching for a natural source of light or any sign of life. There was nothing.

Out of options, Delphine began to run through the cemetery. The eerie sound called out again, making the hairs on the back of her neck stand straight. Delphine needed to find shelter pronto. She had no idea what was hunting her, and she wasn't interested in finding out. Delphine wished she had her dark vision back, from when she was a full siren. She was used to swimming in pitch-black waters; that was easy. Running blind was practically impossible. Branches tore at her clothes then, soon after, tore at her skin too. It seemed the faster she went, the more often she fell. Her knees were already skinned and bloody from tripping on jagged tombstones.

The constant noises from her falls were causing what little plan she had to fail rapidly. Instead of escaping the horrors around her, she was parading the fact that something alive and fresh was struggling within their grasp. It was like Delphine's actions were screaming, "I'm prey, come eat me," and even without looking, she could tell the inhabitants here were ravenous to receive that message. She needed to revise her game plan.

"Think, think, think! Come on, Delphine! What can you do?" She chided herself. Anxiety constricted her chest. She leaned against a nearby tree for rest. It was slimy, but it was going to have to do for now.

Cold tendrils soon began tickling her arms. "Absolutely not! Hard pass." Delphine yanked her body away from the frigid embrace. The invisible source let out a sorrowful moan that echoed through the land. Faint glimmers of light began to congregate around her. Delphine had become surrounded in a moment's time.

Against her better judgment, Delphine made the decision to climb the mucous-like tree she had been resting on. Her footing fumbled on the slippery bark, but she was determined to get away from her newfound crowd. A misty gray outline stood where she had just been. Delphine watched the mist expand around the base of the tree. She stifled her breathing and carefully made her way towards a sturdy bough.

She watched as the mist circled below. Its movement pattern came across as angry and frustrated. Even most of the dimly lit figures that Delphine could now recognize as spirits kept their distance. However, one desperately wanted to climb up the tree. Its face was set in determination. Delphine knew the look in the eyes of that spirit well. It charged toward the tree but collapsed as soon as it hit the mist's border. The mist enveloped the spirit immediately. She couldn't tell if the ghost was asleep or dead.

The mist grew thicker as it claimed its latest victim. Delphine tried to figure out what was going on. The recently claimed spirit was no longer visible. She wondered if the dead could be killed a second time. Life on land was strange. Before she could make any progress in understanding her surroundings, the mist dissipated. The ground became perfectly clear in its absence. The graveyard was quiet once again.

Delphine assessed her surroundings. Given her current vantage point, she was finally able to spot something helpful. There were flames off in the distance. Delphine didn't know enough to gauge how long the run would take to get to them, but she quickly decided that it didn't matter. She tried to channel her inner strength as she climbed down the tree. She hadn't been very far up, but the trunk of the tree was incredibly slick now. It felt like she was descending on ice. Delphine lost her footing on the way down. She fell with a loud thud. Pain shot through her back and legs. Her hatred for Kohl grew by the second. Every throb of pain fueled her rage further.

Delphine remained still and silent until the pain was manageable. The last thing she wanted to do was to draw another crowd by making a scene. As soon as she felt she could, she started running again in the direction of the flame. The torch came into view quicker than she anticipated. There was finally hope!

Delphine instantly regretted diverting her focus. She flew forward, tripping over yet another part of this world. Swearing loudly, she grabbed a rock from the ground and threw it at a gravestone. *Why was this so hard? Why was everything always so ridiculously hard?* A colony of bats screeched and flew overhead. "Don't you dare poop on me! I am not in the mood!" She threatened as she readjusted herself. The smell of the ground here was impressively worse than normal. She kicked the small log that tripped her as she pulled herself together one last time. It bounced back and tapped her foot. Delphine went to kick it again out of sheer defiance, but it was attached to a larger bump protruding from the tree. She inspected the log closer. She gagged. It wasn't a log that tripped her; it was a decayed leg. And the body it was attached to, seemed to be the core of the rancid smell. Delphine had to use both her hands to cover her screams.

Vomit rushed into her throat, but she held that in too. All Delphine wanted was out. She wanted to escape. She wanted to be far far away from this place. Being absolutely anywhere else sounded better than this repulsive world. She wanted to be laughing in the halls with Airess or saving the Nulls with Selene. Even decorating Solei's dorm room was better than this. She never thought she'd pick Lucifer over anything, yet here she was.

A brief memory nagged at her mind. Delphine recalled something Selene said in Amenmesse's portal: "I'll believe it's dead when it tells me it's ready to die. Until then, I don't trust it." *What if the body is still alive? What if it tries to bite me?* She knew she had to check. She was not going to be turned into a zombie today.

Luckily, Delphine deemed that the body wasn't undead; it was rotting. *Rotting like every other stupid thing in this stupid realm from this stupid person.* This was too much. She was past being overwhelmed, but she kept pushing everything down. She was determined to suppress every emotion and every reaction until she was absolutely certain she was safe. This was not a place to show any sign of weakness.

She pushed herself towards the torches again, barely having anything left in her. Her ankles, her knees, her legs, and her back, all throbbed in pain. One of her legs clearly dragged, her body was hunched, and she was sure she'd be moaning nonsense if she permitted herself to speak. Even though she didn't get bit by a zombie, she still resembled one. As she slowly approached the desired source of light, she noticed an outline of a small stone house.

There was an empty space where a door should be. Delphine hobbled through it. Almost all the walls were within reach at all times. The structure was smaller than expected. She could feel the grooves of carvings on the walls. Too weak to walk any longer, she laid on the bench in the center of the compact structure. Looking up at the ceiling, she saw a small glowing butterfly. It was beautiful. It was life. It was the light at the end of the tunnel.

"Finally," she gasped, beyond exhausted. She wanted to sit, to reach up towards it, to feel the warmth of the living again. Using her last ounce of effort, she extended her arm up to the illuminated manifestation as it descended upon her. As she gently traced the outside of the wing, it turned into fingers, clasping her own. The tiny figure of light transformed into a translucent gray boy hovering above her.

"No one's ever made it into my mausoleum before. Welcome, Delphine." Kohl gave a large sly grin and pulled Delphine into an embrace. Before she could attempt protest, an unseen door closed behind them, and everything in that small space, in that small crypt, burst into shadows.

~*~

It was hard to breathe. Delphine was confined by Kohl, and the air around them was sweltering. She wrestled free. Kohl didn't resist, but the heat only intensified as she exposed more of her skin. The air smelled like brimstone. A familiar sensation of puke resurfaced in her throat.

"What is this place? It's horrible. I feel like I'm inside an oven," Delphine whined, slightly disoriented. She squinted at the area around her. Everything looked black as night or bright orange. There was no in-between. Delphine rubbed her forehead in an attempt to soothe her mind. Her skin felt gritty. Delphine panicked. *OMG, are those my scales? Am I flaking?* She inspected her hand immediately. It was covered in black grime. She checked the rest of her body. She was intact but disgustingly dirty, save the parts of her that had recently been touching Kohl.

"Calm down. We're inside Hephaestus' forge. There's no avoiding the soot in here, but it helps give us cover so I wouldn't wipe too much off."

Delphine revolted. "Hephaestus, really? Out of all the places you could take me, you chose here?" Indignation consumed her voice.

"Yeah!" Kohl beamed proudly. "Last time we were together, you were upset that we only encountered minor gods. I did some research on your religion,

45

saw that the forge was sometimes underwater, and figured out a plan to bring you here! Don't you love it? Hephaestus is one of the twelve main Olympians!"

"Kohl. We're not underwater. This heat is basically melting the skin off my bones."

"I did notice that slight inconvenience, but maybe we're just in the wrong part. We can find our way to the ocean together! I bet it's much cooler there."

Delphine was not having it. He could never do anything right. Her dream of being on the arm of an ancient god rapidly deteriorated. She was sick of being some loser's secret girlfriend. "You don't know anything, do you? Hephaestus may have been underwater in some myths, but typically, he's much more partial to volcanoes. You took a sea creature to a volcano, Kohl. Great job!" Delphine rolled her eyes. Kohl went to object, but he was cut off by Delphine's anger. "Not only that but do you even know who his mother is? Hera! His fricking mother is Hera!!"

Kohl pushed to get a word in, "I know that, Delphine. She threw him out of Olympus because he had flaws. It's part of why I picked him. We know what it's like to be cast out for reasons we had no control over."

"Not 'we,' Kohl. You! You're the outcast. My life was quite lovely before my realm got raided by The Bad One, and now I'm the victim making due with what I have left." Delphine knew how deep that ace card sliced him. She smiled when he turned away in pain. He was never going to get stronger if she didn't push him. He needed to be more like The Bad One, less like himself.

"I'm not the same person I was then, Delphine. I'm better now. I know love now. I have you." He reached for her hand with both of his, gripping onto hers for redemption.

She allowed him to touch her but did not return any affection. "You may have changed, but I don't know that it's preferable. You want so badly to be like Hades, but frankly, you're more like Hera. Hera was the one that cast the sirens out of Olympus. She's who stole my ancestors' rightful place among the gods. She challenged the poor sirens to a losing battle against her stupid muses. I have no doubts that the whole thing was rigged before it started. Then, when we lost because no one would ever be allowed to beat the queen, our feathers were plucked, and we were cast into the ocean to die. What you do with the Nulls isn't a far stretch from that. You strip them of their home, their powers, and basically life as they know it, to fuel your darker side. All for what? So you can play like a bumbling fool in the dark? The Nulls may not be sent into Legacy to die, but it's not to live either. You're no better than she is."

"We've discussed this." Kohl's eyes shifted to black. His voice bellowed deep. Whoever was talking now was not the same soul who was addressing her before. "The Bad One needs to consume. I am doing so in the way that you chose. You positioned yourself to be the one who rescues the Nulls, to be in charge of them. You wanted that upper hand over the newcomers of Astoria. I gave you what you wanted."

Ahh, there he is. I knew he'd come to say hi. Delphine was proud of herself for getting Kohl to flip sides so quickly this go-round. She was getting much more efficient at bringing The Bad One to the surface.

"You speak of Hera, and I can see the parallels from one queen to the next. Isn't that your true goal? To be my queen? And haven't I given you everything you asked for, Delphine?"

Delphine's heart raced, and she couldn't suppress the smile on her face. She draped her arms around his neck and leaned into him. "Perhaps. Though like any good queen, my rule is often contested."

"Never by me," he said in a low growl.

"It's true, never by you." Delphine curled a piece of his long hair behind his ear. "They're onto you. We were sloppy when we went to visit that pharaoh. They found some of Pele's cloth. They know you can hop into realms beyond Ward A. I'm sure it's only a matter of time before they come after you. Those silly do-gooders love a heroic journey."

"It was always all a matter of time. I welcome a class reunion. I'll start planning a nice location for the event. Where do you want to go? I can surpass your wildest dreams." The Bad One watched Delphine squirm with pleasure. He knew the best way to pull her in was to demonstrate his power. "I said, where do you want to go, my Queen? Where shall we lead our prey?"

A proud smile spread across her face. "Any-where you are is where I want to be, my King. I trust you to pick the perfect spot."

"Then that is what I shall do. Now, let's get you back before they notice you're gone. We can't have you missing out on anything important."

~*~

Airess was relieved when she found Delphine. Selene had worked up the group into a panic. Turns out, Delphine snuck off for a nap. She was peacefully asleep in a nook at Ward A. Airess texted the group chat and checked the time. It was early afternoon. She had a few solid hours of daylight left to go. Airess could get a good amount of planting and pruning done if she planned it out right. The walk to the field was quick through her shortcuts, one of which just happened to lead to the new area she had been constructing for Chibi Chan. The golem had gotten strong enough to pull big rocks out of the field to help her crops, and it would have been disrespectful if Airess had simply ignored his triumphs. Coinci-dentally, Airess discovered many new rocks these days and brought them to Chibi as gifts. Where else should they go other than to the golem's new home?

Airess made her way down the secret trail, with a few more rocks than what fit in her pockets, to Chibi Chan's place. The existence of this place was less than a day old. So, needless to say, when someone else was there before her, Airess wasn't sure if she should feel jealous or concerned.

"Hello?" Airess' voice came across as gentle and sincere, but her eyes wanted to find Chibi Chan. Thankfully, he was easy to spot. The clay figure was sitting on the ground. Chibi was placing pebbles off to the side, very similar to the design Airess taught them to make for Solei's homecoming.

The human jumped and backed away. They were stammering their words. The wave of fear they projected onto Airess, without any touch at all, was debilitating. Airess held up her hand, but the emotions kept escalating. "Chibi Chan, help please." Airess had to close her eyes to keep from being sick. She heard her golem's footsteps then the intense fear started to ebb. Airess looked up to see a visibly shaken girl around her own age.

"I—I—I—I'm so sorry. I had no idea. I—I—I—" The girl was shaking.

Airess lifted her finger to her mouth. "Shhh." She waited then gestured that she was zipping her own mouth closed. With both hands in the air, signaling a sign of peace, Airess walked over to a large leaf she had made earlier to sit upon. She watched Chibi hugging this girl's leg. Whoever this trespasser was, they clearly meant no harm. Airess pointed to her leaf and then pointed to an open area next to the newcomer. The newcomer nodded. Airess nestled her hand into the soil, and a vine worked its way around the fresh stonework to provide a leaf for the guest.

Once the girl sat down, Chibi made their way over to Airess. They pounded their chest and pointed to the stones. Airess smiled encouragingly. Then they did it again. And again. And again. By the end, Airess was laughing and congratulating the golem more times than she could count. The little stinker was so proud of their work.

The girl was laughing along too. "They're pretty adorable."

"Thank you. It took me a minute to come around to them."

"I can't imagine how. They're so kind."

"I'm coming to realize it was more faults of my own than faults of theirs. That can be a hard path to work through though."

The girl chuckled. "Tell me about it. I'm Mae by the way. You're Airess, right? The hugger?"

Airess' defensiveness flared for a moment, then she recognized her company. Her eyes grew wide. "Oh my gosh, you're Solei's Mae, aren't you?"

"I don't love being referred to as someone else's property, but yes, Solei is the reason I'm here."

"Mae! I'm so sorry! I had no idea you were going to be there last night, and then everyone was so upset, and I didn't know what to do. We hadn't talked to Solei in so long, and Principal Chromwell didn't tell us everything and . . ."

Mae cut her off, "I know you didn't know. I mean I didn't at the time, though I probably should've, but I know now. It's okay."

"Are you sure?"

"As sure as I'll get."

"Okay." There was an awkward silence, and Airess was failing at trying to find plants to fiddle with. "Did you come here then, so you could tell me that?"

"What? No. That was just an unfortunate coincidence."

Airess' jaw dropped.

"I didn't mean it like that. I just—I wanted to find a bit of an escape. Somewhere where there were fewer people, fewer lights, fewer noises. Everything is so busy at Legacy. I'm used to my environment being more natural and quiet. I'd have gone to a mountain if there was a closer one. This semi-forest seemed as good a spot as any. There were hardly any walking paths. I thought I hit the jackpot when your little friend came out and asked me to line up stones with them. I had no idea this was a makeshift house. It's obvious, I guess, in hindsight."

"We just made this yesterday. It's new to us too." Airess stared over at the golem. "I get needing some time away. I love my friends, and people in general, but sometimes, I need to be with my plants before I can go back again."

"I'm surprised. I thought you all were inseparable."

"We used to be, less so now. Lately, we've been branching off into our own things. It's hard to find an overlap."

Mae couldn't help but notice vines and leaflets splitting near Airess' fingers as she spoke. "Was that before or after Solei left? In every story I ever heard, Solei made it sound like you guys were all a package deal."

A wave of hesitation spread across Airess' face. "If I answer truthfully, I would sound like I'm blaming Solei, and I don't wanna do that. I knew going to Rome was important for them, and now, with you here, it seems even more than I realized."

"They talked about you guys all the time. However, I am learning they did not talk to you guys nearly as often."

Airess could feel Mae's unease, even in a conversation Mae seemed to be engaged in. Airess felt bad for the girl; she couldn't understand why Solei would bring Mae here. That part was said and done though. All Airess could do now is try to make the best of a bad situation. "There are only a few hours of sunlight left, I should tend to the rest of my plants before dark. Are you okay by yourself if Chibi Chan and I go to the fields for the rest of the day?"

Mae's mood lifted. "I can stay? Alone?"

Airess dug her hand deeper into the dirt. Tendrils swirled around Mae, turning her oversized leaf into an oversized peapod. "I am sure Chibi would love your company anytime. Stay as long as you like."

A surprising sting of panic shot out from Mae.

"What's wrong? I thought you'd like the quiet."

"Oh. I forgot Solei told me you could do that. I

love the privacy. I was only concerned how many other visitors might show up unexpectedly, but I wasn't going to ask because I thought that would be rude."

"This home is less than a day old. I don't see why anyone needs to know about it, so I won't tell if you won't. Deal?"

"Deal!" Mae pulled out her headphones, her emotions flowing with satisfaction.

Airess reveled in Mae's happiness. Spending time with Mae was an unexpected emotional roller coaster. It reminded the healer of the early days with Lena. Airess liked it.

{ 4 }

Fights and Favor

*D*ing. Another text appeared on her work phone. Lena swiped it open to check.

"I'm getting reports of an argument on the west wing of Ward A. Are you able to break it up, or do you want me to wait to ask the next shift?" asked Ippy, Ward A's receptionist.

Lena checked the time. She was seven minutes shy of clocking out. As much as Lena wanted to punt the request, she knew she shouldn't. Gods could do a lot of damage in a very short amount of time if they wanted to.

"I'm on it. Ping me the location." Lena closed the screen and headed to the west side of the ward. She knew enough to get around, but hardly anything happened on this side of the building. Lena was only a few steps in when she heard the shouting. The argument wasn't hard to find. She followed the sound to its source. The noise came from behind a withered door. A shriveled gray tree with scraggly black roots made up the entryway. It looked like something out of a dark fairy tale. Lena knocked on the door. No answer. She wasn't surprised. They probably couldn't hear her. There were a lot of voices in the room, but it was hard to make out any distinguishing words.

"Hello?" Lena knocked again. "I'm afraid if you don't open up, I'll have to do so myself." She waited a moment. Her warning did not alter the yelling from inside. As Lena was pulling the skeleton key from her work pouch, the door flung open with gusto.

"Dad?!" Lena gasped in surprise.

"Lena? What are you doing here?"

Still in shock, she lifted up her work phone and showed Kasim Ippy's request. "We got noise complaints about an argument. Who's in there?" Kasim tried to block his daughter's view, but she was too quick. Ina, her mom, and Principal Chromwell were standing deeper inside the room, shrouded in a forest. "What are you guys doing? Why is there so much yelling?" Lena peered at her father.

"It's nothing, Magpie. You can go ahead and let Ippy know everything is good in here," Kasim affirmed.

"I'm not good in here," Kamilah said sharply.

"Mom?" Lena questioned.

"Yes, Lena. I'm your mother."

"What's wrong?"

"Your father thinks he has the authority to tell me what I can and cannot do."

He doesn't?

"That's not true, Millie. I'm solely concerned that your friends here are not thinking about their plan all the way through. I simply cannot see how anyone would believe you jumping into a portal is a good idea."

A portal?!

"I'm standing right here, Kasim," P.C. scolded.

"As am I. Are we not all friends here?" Ina's voice cooed.

"I'm your friend." Millie linked her arm in Ina's.

"This isn't about friendship. This is about the safety and well-being of my wife, something this particular group does not have the best track record with. You want to know if we're friends, but neither of you have been able to answer me on how Millie joining you is a good idea."

"She wants to go, Kasim. Isn't that enough?" Chromwell challenged.

Seething, Kasim retorted, "I can list a plethora of things that aren't enough, Theodora, and your ability to protect Millie is on the top of that list."

"Kasim Basil. Hold your tongue!" Ina's energy was glowing around her.

"No. After our last portal, you were catatonic for years, my wife lost her mind specifically because a goddess envied her, and Averi vanished as soon as we got back home. Who knows what their life is like these days. And now you want to repeat it, with no good reason why. I can't risk that." Kasim turned towards Kamilah. "I can't risk losing you again, Millie. I can't see you hurt like that again." Kasim hung his head to hide his tears.

Ouch. Lena knew she shouldn't be here for this, but she couldn't help herself.

"Again? You've never lost me. I'm right here."

Kasim nodded his head, but he didn't speak.

Kamilah glanced over to P.C. with pleading eyes.

"Kasim, there is something we have yet to tell you. I've had a vision. It was of Kamilah standing in front of an old witch. This was a few sleeps ago; I didn't understand the connection until Professor Nakshatra came to see me today. I was alerted of a disturbance among the realms. An individual is hopping between them without going through the proper channels of Ward A. I believe only one goddess can answer how this is being done. Once I realized that the portal we needed to investigate belonged to the deity I saw before Kamilah, I immediately went to Ina. I had to see if she could lend any insight to what this might be. It's not for certain, but we think they can right the wrongs forced onto Kamilah. This is why we want to bring your wife, and our best friend, with us to see . . ." Theodora checked to see if Lena was still listening in. She was "This particular goddess."

Principal Chromwell's revelation left Kasim speechless.

With pained eyes, Ina stood next to Kasim. "I do not take this venture lightly. However, if my friend wants to be healed, and I believe this to be their best chance of recovery, I cannot walk away no matter how intimidating the situation may be."

Kasim locked eyes with his wife. "Is that true, Millie? Do you want to be healed?"

Kamilah squirmed. This situation was becoming too much to bear for her. After a long wait, she replied in a soft voice, "I don't feel sick. But I know something bad happened to me. I know everyone sounds sad when they talk about it, and I want to get rid of that pain for everyone."

Kasim put his hands on Kamilah's shoulders. He spoke with a loud and stern tone. "Do not, Kamilah Basil, for one second, do this to relieve others. You are a good, kind, and wonderful person just as you are. There is nothing, I repeat NOTHING, that you need to change about yourself to make any of us here more comfortable. I love you for exactly who you are without any exceptions." Kasim's forehead was against his wife's. Millie nodded at his words. Returning to his normal demeanor, he added, "And they better, too."

"That means the world to me." Millie wrapped her arms around her husband. "I can't help but wonder, though, if I would feel better if I met with this Goddess they're talking about. It's a struggle to keep my thoughts together, Kasim. Everything is extremely hard all the time." She squeezed him close.

Lena's chest was feeling tight. She watched Ina and P.C., hoping to find reassurance. Now they were the ones avoiding eye contact. *My poor mom.*

"All right then." Kasim pulled away from the embrace and breathed a large sigh, "That settles it."

Principal Chromwell composed herself, ready to leave the room with her head held high despite her defeat.

Ina put her hand on Millie's shoulder and kissed the side of her friend's head. She looked to Kasim with an apologetic acknowledgment.

When both ladies passed behind him, he spoke firmly, "We need a day to prepare. After that, Millie and I will both accompany you on your journey. I assume that is acceptable."

"Yes, of course!" Ina replied with instant joy.

"So it shall be done." Principal Chromwell tapped her staff on the ground and exited the area, her large cape billowing out behind her.

Lena remained frozen, unsure what to do or where to go.

"I'll see you tomorrow, Lena. Have a wondrous evening." With a simple goodnight, Ina was off in her own direction as well.

Kasim and Millie were in a moment all to themselves.

Lena couldn't find her way out of the interaction. "Umm . . . I don't . . . hi. I'm still here."

Kasim transitioned flawlessly. "Hey, Magpie. Sorry you had to get called in on your old man. Thanks for coming to check on us though."

"Yes, sweetie. You did a very good job," Millie complimented Lena with conviction.

Lena tried to shrug it all off. "It's no big deal." She felt anxious. "I know I'm not supposed to eavesdrop, but did I hear right? You two are leaving . . .," Lena gave herself some time to process and complete her thought, ". . . without me?"

"Oh." Kamilah looked stunned. "Kasim, are we leaving Magdalena?"

"Only temporarily." He assured his wife then turned to Lena. "We will be back before you know it, Magpie. I'm hoping it will only be a single day. We'll go in, talk to whomever we need to, then get out."

Lena wasn't convinced. "You really think it'll be that easy, Dad?"

"I need it to be, Lena. There isn't another option for me."

Butterflies were filling Lena's stomach, and they weren't the good kind. "Will we at least be able to say goodbye tomorrow?"

"Of course. I'd have it no other way. For now, though, I need to get your mom home. I'll see you in the morning, first thing, I promise."

"Okay . . . bye . . . have a good night." Lena watched as her parents walked out of the room and off into the distance. She couldn't tell what she was feeling at first. It was a weird situation to be in. She didn't feel forgotten, but she knew she wasn't a focal point in her parent's decision either. It was strange to watch her parents act like something other than parents. The situation left Lena feeling awkward, uncomfortable, and full of anxiety.

Lena was thirty minutes late by the time she made it back to the reception desk. She hung up the skeleton key and plugged in the ward's phone. Ippy had left for the night too. Lena had hoped to encounter a friendly face before heading home but was grateful she didn't have to recount what happened to her dispatcher. Lena had just put on her coat when someone rang the desk's bell. She debated if she could ignore them and sneak out without notice.

"Hello? Is someone back there?"

Crap. I really should have ignored them. "Yeah, one second." Lena practiced her deep breathing then walked to the counter. "How can I help you, Solei?"

"Lena. Hey." Solei's face gave away their extreme discomfort.

Way to tell you wouldn't have come if you knew I was here, without telling me you wouldn't have come if I was here. "I was about to walk out the door. Can I help you with anything, or do you want to wait until someone else is at the desk?"

"Why would you say that?"

Because you didn't text me back in almost a year. Because you couldn't even be bothered to tell me you were coming home. Because you never mentioned you even talked to someone else, let alone about bringing back someone else with you. Because you literally shut a door in my face your first night back. Because—

"Lena!" Solei reproached.

"What? What do you want, Solei? What else

can I possibly offer you?"

Their face was tense. "I can hear you, okay? I can hear everything in your head, and I'm not saying I don't deserve it all, but I figure you should at least know so you don't accidentally think something you want to keep private."

Lena was dumbfounded. *You can hear me?*

Solei made eye contact and nodded.

For how long?

"Months. Ever since we brought Airess back before her rehabilitation."

Before you left, then.

Solei nodded again. "I wasn't sure how long it would last at first, so I didn't want to say anything. But, it never went away."

So, in Rome . . .

"I could hear you. It was fuzzier though. Standing in front of you, especially with you being this angry, you're basically on a megaphone yelling in my brain. In Rome, even at your saddest times, it was more of a painful nag than clear words."

You did not just call me a nag.

Solei's mouth froze agape.

"Cool. Well. That about does it then, yeah? I need to leave now."

"Wait. Don't!"

Why? You don't even care about me.

"That is absolutely not true, Magdalena Basil."

Lena scowled. "That wasn't meant for you. Stay out of my head, Solei." She stormed out of Ward A.

Solei ran close behind. "I'm so sorry, Lena. Please just give me a chance to explain. You don't understand what Rome was like."

"And whose fault is that? I would've loved to have known, but obviously you already knew that." Lena picked up her pace. She had no doubts she could outrun Solei if she wanted to.

"I did. But, please! Lena!" Solei reached for Lena's arm and pulled her back. "Stop! Please! I'm trying to explain things to you!" It was raining outside, and little sparks reacted to the water droplets falling down Solei.

Lena yanked her arm back. "What right do you have to ask ANYTHING of me, Solei? You broke my heart. You know you did. I waited for you every night, right up to the end, because I'm a sucker. I thought having a mental connection meant something. Turns out, we have even more of a link than I thought, and it means less than I could even begin to comprehend." Lena shook her head staring at her friend. "I thought you were my best friend. And I know you and Airess have your thing, and Airess and I had our thing, but I didn't think it mattered. I thought you got me. I sure as hell tried to get you. I was stupid, and I regret it. Now I just want to be done." Lena turned her back towards Solei. It hurt to even look at them.

"At first, I was just so excited to be in Rome. Then, I found Mae, and the excitement was barely containable. I couldn't wait to tell you. Time got the best of me though, and when I finally got around to being ready to text, things were too bad. You were already so hurt. Tao was beyond repair. Airess was off on her own. I couldn't make myself do it. I couldn't be the strong one anymore; I couldn't be the brave one; I couldn't hold you all together. I needed to be where I was. I wanted to be present for myself and then, for Mae. I knew if I reached out even once, I'd rush back home to all of you, and I really didn't want to do that and screw up everything I was building for myself overseas."

"We were all fine."

"Lena. You cannot possibly think that's true. I know you know better."

"Get out of my head, Morningstar!"

"I would if I could. I'd get out of everyone's head if I could. That's why I was in Ward A. P.C. is supposed to be helping me, but she never showed up tonight."

Lena knew why and tried not to bring that to her thoughts.

"That's a scene," Solei said timidly.

Lena sighed in defeat. Tonight was a mess. *You said "everyone," you can hear more people than just me?*

"You, Tao, and Airess."

That's a lot of people.

"You all are a lot."

Rude.

"But, I love you all. I truly do. But, I needed to love myself for a while too. That was the entire point of the trip, and I had to stay true to it."

"And loving yourself found you a girlfriend?"

Solei's sparks jumped at the term. Their face was unmistakably reddened. "Loving myself found me . . . a girlfriend." Solei sat down on the street curb.

Lena sat next to them. "I'm sure they're wonderful."

"They are. I wish you all had met on better terms. That night was way too much at once for her. She felt completely bombarded. I probably should've handled the whole trip back differently."

Probably?!

"All right, all right. I goofed. I admit it. I was trying to juggle too much, and I messed it all up."

"So fix it."

"How? I keep trying to do more and more for Mae, and it's backfiring every single time. Nothing's going right here. I'm scared she's going to ask to leave. She didn't really want to come here to begin with."

"I've only met her for a second, but 'more and more' doesn't seem to be her thing."

"That's true."

"Also, do you really think a gathering after ghosting us and surprising us with a whole new person would be the same as a gathering after having any contact with us at all? I can't speak for Mae, but the rest of us would have acted a lot differently if we had any sliver of information."

"It's not about you guys. I can handle this. I will

figure something out."

"Sure. How's that going for you so far?" Lena's tone dripped with condescension.

"You don't have to broadcast your thoughts so loud, Lena. I know I'm failing."

"Then let us help!"

"How? I don't even know what that would mean."

"You can start by being our friend again, by letting us in, by no longer being an arse—"

"An arse, Lena, really?"

Lena shrugged. *Simply offering various options. You choose the ones which sound the most relevant.*

Solei flicked a tiny lightning bolt at their friend. "Fine. Step one: Stop being an arse. Got it. Anything else?"

"Give me some time. I'll compile a list for you!" Lena beamed with a smile.

"I bet you will, little cub. I probably can't even call you that anymore. You're running the show over there in Ward A. I can't believe how different things are. Even with all your minds constantly interrupting my own thoughts, I had no idea how much had changed in the time I was gone."

"I get it. There was practically no Delphine when you left, and now there's SO. MUCH. DELPHINE. Everywhere! Isn't it great?"

"Bitter, eh?" Solei teased.

"I eat fish sticks now, too."

"I can hear your mind call them gross"

"And what's it saying now?"

"OMG! Lena. No. You cannot eat fish sticks because Delphine is part—"

"SHH! If you say it out loud, it sounds rude."

"Lena! If you say it in your head, it sounds rude too!"

"But only to you and I. Problem solved! See? This connection thing isn't so bad."

"I will be so relieved and insanely bored once it's gone."

"You missed me. Admit it. I have to be so much more interesting in person."

"Yes, little cub. I missed you, more than you know."

Thank you.

Solei wrapped their friend up in a big hug. "I'm sorry."

~*~

"Dad, it's 2 a.m. We're tired. Solei needs to go home. Can we wrap this up, please?"

"There's only a little more left to do. You got the corn for the magic pouch, I finished bottling the Greek fire, and Solei is finishing the multi-faceted animal whistle. Did you have any luck finding a golden apple, Magpie?"

"No, I don't really think that's a thing, Dad. At least, not in our realm, and I'm not about to hop around portals for a piece of fruit."

"I would never let that happen, Magdalena."

Lena shot Solei a sideways glance.

"Sir, are you absolutely sure all this is necessary? I don't want to doubt you. You're much more knowledgeable about magical items than I am, but it feels a tad overkill, don't you think?"

"Solei, there is no limit to protecting Millie. Nothing will ever be too much if it's for my family." Kasim's tone was solemn.

"Heard, sir."

"I'm walking my innocent wife into a death trap because her friends convinced her this was a good idea. If I could take an armory of items with me, I would. There is no question in my mind about that. I don't have that time though. I have less than twenty-four hours to analyze potential weaknesses and then create tailored magical items to protect my wife against a deity I'm vaguely aware of."

"Are we sure whoever this is is going to be that bad? P.C. seems immensely confident about them being able to help Mom. What makes them such an adversary?"

"She's dangerous, Lena. I have no doubts about that." Kasim's irritation grew with every tick of the clock.

"The goddess or P.C.?" Lena attempted to make a joke to lighten her dad's mood.

"I let Theodora's lack of preparation hurt Millie once. That is one too many times in my book. Under no circumstances will that ever happen again." His voice shook as he stood his ground.

Solei placed their hand on his shoulder. "Then let's ensure that. I know the items you gathered, but what's the overall plan? Maybe I can help. I did pick up a few tricks in Rome."

Lena's ears perked up. *Does Solei have new powers?*

Solei responded with a wink.

Ugh! I forgot you can do that!

Solei stifled their laugh as Kasim began to explain.

"After my research, all I can tell is that this has to be one of the most powerful ancient deities in existence. Not every god can undo another god's curse. If the deity chooses to help us, I have no doubts Theodora is choosing someone that can, in fact, repair the thievery Millie endured. However, if they choose not to help us, and rather anything else, I sincerely believe we will be in seriously grave danger."

"She has to have a weakness, Mr. Basil. Everyone has a weakness."

And yours is named Mae, Lena thought in a sing-song melody. She watched Solei's face tighten in an attempt to control their appearance in front of their mentor. *It's kind of fun trolling you, not going to lie.*

A familiar pang struck Lena's forehead. *You are really enjoying this, aren't you?*

Lena let out a small laugh.

Kasim was still trying to come up with an answer he felt confident in. "I haven't found a single myth shedding any insight. From what I can tell, our best chance is going to be to escape if things go the way they did before. Theodora's witch will be as intelligent as they are powerful. They're definitely no Ward A god."

"Wait. If their portal isn't in Ward A, how are you all going to go through with this?" Lena asked, confused.

"That's a great question, Magpie. I had the same one. Theodora assured me we will be able to access their location through Ward A, and intentionally avoided giving any other details."

"Wow. I'm sorry, Mr. Basil. I wanted to help, but I don't think I have anything to offer here."

"You've been a great help, Solei. Don't downplay your presence. You too, Magdalena. I fear my emotions are getting the best of me on this one. I should have known better, but I had no idea coming back to Astoria was going to be so challenging for me. I can handle hard or scary situations in stride when they target me, but life feels a lot different when the same scenarios revolve around my family instead. I wish there was a way to guarantee a getaway. I wish there was some surefire trap I could spring . . ."

"I don't completely know how this might help, but can we go outside for a second? I want to show something to you two."

Intrigued, Kasim and his daughter joined Solei out in the yard.

"This won't work great on the ground. It works much better when it can flow through a conductor below it, but if you want a trap, this will get you there."

Solei closed their eyes. They shook the tension from their body. They gracefully transitioned to a forward stance, both their hands cupping their left hip. As sparks began to swirl under their hands, they opened their eyes with complete determination. Their hands lifted and threw the sparks across their body as they let out a loud bellow.

A yellow-gold cascade spread out into the night and floated onto the wet grass. The water droplets only magnified the beauty of the woven glimmering net. Layers of humming electrical currents wove tighter and tighter before them. The trap was longer than their arm span.

"Look familiar, little cub?"

Lena had never seen anything like this.

"In theory, it should look like the net Airess wove for us in Indra's portal. That's what I focus on when I direct my energy. I worked on this every time I missed home while I was overseas. Feelings like that give a hefty amount of energy to burn off."

"It's beautiful, Solei. Truly." Lena held her own bracelet at the thought. The magic band had shielded them repeatedly while dealing with Indra. She never took it off.

"I agree! This is magnificent, Solei! How long will this last?" Kasim had his face to the ground, inspecting Solei's work.

"I've never left one alone long enough to see."

"Fascinating. Would you mind leaving this one? I'd love to study it in the time I have left."

"I'd be happy to." Solei stumbled as they spoke.

Lena rushed to their side to keep them steady. "I think that's enough for tonight. Wouldn't you agree, Dad?" Her intonation was more declarative than a question.

"Yes, of course. My apologies. I may have gotten carried away. Thank you both for all your help. Solei, how about I drive you to the dorms? I'd hate for you to walk back in your current shape."

Solei agreed and Lena helped them get situated in the car. After closing their door, she walked over to her dad to give a hug and a kiss on the cheek goodnight.

"Goodnight, Dad. Love you."

"Goodnight, Magpie. I love you too. Thanks again. I'll be back soon."

"Sure thing. See you soon." Lena watched as the car pulled away. *Love you.* Lena wasn't sure her friend heard as the distance between them grew from the car traveling off. She was prepared to use this as her excuse when no response came, but a familiar ache to her forehead indicated that may not be needed.

Solei had wasted no time in responding. *Love you too, little cub.*

{ 5 }

Oversights and Oracles

"**D**on't get over excited, Lena." Even through text, Tao's tone was unmistakable.

OHMYGOSHICAN'TWAITTOTELLSELENE!!

"I wouldn't have even asked you if I thought I could do this alone. I've just—I've never done something like this before."

IT'S FINALLY HAPPENING! THIS IS AMAZING!

"So we're in agreement, right? You're going to get the fresh Japanese cherry blossom from wherever you decide is best, hand them off to me, and then text Airess to meet you at the meditative gardens where I'll be waiting."

"Yes!! Absolutely!! I am so excited!!"

"No. This isn't a big deal. I'm about to do a normal teenage thing that is standard and commonplace. This is completely mundane."

AHH!! Solei can you hear me?! Tao is going to ask Airess out in like two hours!! I am buzzing!! "Right.

Yup. Totally natural. You've got this!"

"All right then. I'll see you in an hour. I'm trusting you, Lena. Don't make this into a whole thing."

"See you in an hour!! I can't wait!!" Lena squeed with exhilaration, and without a second's hesitation, she texted Selene. "You're never going to believe this!! Tao is asking out Airess in the meditative gardens today!! Can you come? You have to be there!!"

She held the phone, awaiting his response. He wasn't coming online. Her emotions were starting to ebb. She justified the delay to herself. *I'm sure he's in class and can't get to his phone. It's no big deal. I need to get the fresh cherry blossoms anyway.* Pulling herself away from the phone, she made her way to her dad's workshop.

Her goal was to find an item that would help her teleport from one area to the next. She didn't think finding a large rolled-up piece of carpet would be this challenging, but the space was a mess. Amulets were strewn all over his desk. Chunks of unfinished wood littered the floor. *I was just in here last night; it couldn't have been that bad then, right?* Lena was pretty sure she'd have noticed, but it was late and she had been exhausted. Lena's ankle got caught in a piece of thick, scratchy fabric. She almost fell but caught herself halfway down. She worked to stretch out the matted cloth, hoping it was what she wanted, but it wasn't anything remarkable. She took a deep breath. The workshop smelled like smoked hickory. It smelled like her dad. She admired the picture hung on the far wall as she tried to come up with other ways to find the flowers she needed. A circular frame held a picture of a glittering bright blue sea and a white sandy beach, just like the one they visited over winter break. Lena smiled at the memories she shared with Selene there. *That trip may be the only good side effect from Delphine's arrival.* Lena picked up the mounting, and the picture inside changed. Not drastically. It was still an image of the beach, but as the frame turned, the perspective shifted as well. The image seemed 3D. She recognized some of the buildings that came into view. A car drove past. *This isn't a picture, this is a live scene! Score!* Lena took the object out of the frame. A squishy wobbly disc fumbled around in her hands. She debated using the traveling disc here in the workshop, but a flash of Selene and her silent phone crossed her mind. *It would be kind of nice to have our own date too.* Now, hoping to try to catch him in Ward A, Lena carefully rolled up the magic item and put it in her bag.

Pain shot across her forehead. *Please don't do this, Lena.*

Ow. *Solei? Why not?*

I don't think this is a good idea.

Oh?! Do you know something I don't know?!

No, Lena. I just—I know Airess.

I mean, we all KNOW Airess and I'll be the first to agree that she isn't Astoria's most stable choice, but I don't think she would intentionally crush

Tao. Even if she says no, I think she'll do it nicely. Don't you? There was a long pause. Lena felt like an idiot standing in the middle of her yard, looking at the sky, waiting for her friend to communicate telepathically. *Solei, I said, don't you?* She waited again to no avail. *Is this thing on? I don't know how any of this works.*

It works. My abilities aren't the problem here.

Ouch. I'm missing something. Can we talk about this? Preferably with actual words in front of each other? I'll come over to you. Where are you?

I'm with Airess, so I guess I'll be seeing you and Tao soon.

That's not great.

No, no it is not.

Lena's stomach was starting to fill with anxiety. Doubts about the setup were running through her mind. She didn't know if they were hers or Solei's. She promised to help Tao though, so that's what she was going to do. She was just going to stick to the plan and hope for the best ... after she had found Selene.

~*~

"AND THEN, after EVERYTHING, I texted you, and you didn't respond so I had to come here instead and find you!!" Lena was talking a million words per minute.

Selene laughed as Lena acted out the morning's events. She always got so animated when she was excited. "That's a ton to take in all at once, huh?"

"Right?! And I had to do it ALONE! Where's the fun in that?!" Lena made a pouty face. "What do you think, though? Why did Solei get so worked up? They're crazy, right? Tao asking Airess out is going to be FANTASTIC and completely overdue!"

He was hesitant to share his thoughts; he knew they weren't going to go over well. "I mean, I don't quite know what Solei was getting at, but I don't think they're wrong. This probably isn't the best time for Tao to be doing something like this, and Airess is a loose cannon under pressure."

"Under pressure? What pressure? It's just a date." Lena's annoyance was sharp.

"I don't want to upset you, but with P.C. and everyone else leaving tonight, there's just too much going on. Professor Nakshatra is a mess trying to prep for taking over the school. My phone is blowing up with new requests and responsibilities, most of which involve me reaching out to Tao, so I know his plate is getting rather full too. It also wouldn't surprise me if Nurse Galen is stepping up to help in either ward. If she is, that would mean extra duties falling on Airess as well. It doesn't make sense for Tao to wait for so long to say something, but now, when the weight of the school is coming down on our shoulders, he's determined this is the best time to make a move? Something's up. He's been weird since he came out of his trance in the spring, and this only magnifies previous red flags. Plus, if Solei says that they can hear yours, Tao's, and Airess' thoughts and then say this is not a good idea, I'm inclined to believe them. I can't imagine a more solid source than that."

"So, you're going to believe someone who abandoned us all over your girlfriend?"

"What? I did not say that!"

"You don't say much these days, do you? At least not to me. I'm off to get the flowers and go be a good friend to Tao. Alone. Enjoy whatever it is that you have planned this afternoon; I'm sure it's vitally important towards something that doesn't involve us."

"Lena, stop! Please."

"I'll see you in the gardens in an hour." Lena's eyes focused intensely on Selene.

His face was filled with despair. "I'm really sorry—"

"Of course; I shouldn't be surprised," Lena groaned. "My mom is cooking a goodbye dinner before the big trip tonight. Will you at least come to say bye and send her and my dad off?"

"Lena, I really want to—"

"Mhmm. Right. I know how that sentence ends. Fine. See you when I see you then, Selene." Lena pushed past him, fury radiating from her body. Under her breath she snarled, "And be sure to tell Delphine hi for me."

"You don't even like her."

"She'll get it even if you don't. Bye, Selene." Lena's heart ached as she took the next turn down the hallway, but her wrath kept her from looking back.

~*~

Tao clipped the stems off half the flowers Lena gave to him. She was confused but kept her thoughts to herself. Surprisingly, she hadn't said much at all. Lena took the shears from him after the last batch and cleaned up the stems. She had him poised next to a stone bench. A bubbling pond with croaking frogs lay behind him. Dazzling rays of sunlight were scattered around. The scent of the cherry blossoms filled the room.

When everything looked picture perfect, she whispered, "You've got this. I'm proud of you." Lena offered a big smile and went to stand in the back corner, semi-concealed by overgrown leaves.

He watched as Lena tried to enshroud herself in a small tree. For a moment, Tao had flashes of their first day together, back at what he believed to be the Old Hag's house. At the time, he couldn't believe she ran straight into that hellscape. Her decision was illogical and unfathomable. Now, it'd be expected. He could even see a way they'd be assigned by Principal Chromwell herself to go in. Life was completely different back then. Things were simpler, calmer. These days he had so much stress he was barely functional, and it was about to get worse.

He shifted his weight from side to side. His palms were sweating. The flowers he was gripping too tightly were turning sticky. He had never done anything like this before, nor did he ever really plan on it. He recognized it was now or never though. Between the visions he had about P.C.'s upcoming journey and the frequency and intensity of the visions as a whole lately, Tao wasn't sure how much longer he could hold up to the world around him. His long meditation may have ended, but the feeling of the trance never did. It had been months since then, and he still didn't feel like he could get two feet into reality. For whatever reason, part of him never let go of the other side despite his best efforts. He hated it. His visions were so strong now. They were instant and consuming. There was no controlling them or being able to push them off. He had to be ready at any given second for them to take over. The only silver lining to these vivid intrusions was that they gave him the confidence he needed. He knew that no matter what answer Airess gave within the next five minutes, it almost certainly wouldn't matter.

If the visions were right, which they had been since the trance, things were going to fall apart as early as tomorrow morning. That meant if his proclamation went well, he and Airess could enjoy one night together. He firmly believed she deserved, at least, one good night. Goddess willing, his ideal goal was to break through the pain Airess has felt for so long about Kohl. He would try to give her peace and safety for as long as he could.

But if the proclamation went poorly, well, a few tough hours would be better than a lost opportunity. Ultimately, he knew he'd do anything to try to make Airess happy, and this was his best shot before their world turned upside down . . . again.

"Lena? I'm here. What's up? What did you need to meet me for?" Airess had finally arrived. It was time for action.

"Hey." Tao peered out around the corner of the path. "Can we sit for a second?"

"Oh! Hey, Tao. Uhh, no offense, but no, not really. Lena asked me to meet her here and—"

"Lena asked you to meet her here for me." He waited for Airess to recognize the intimate setting.

"Oh."

"Here, these are for you. I asked Lena to pick fresh Sakura, and then I cut half short and kept half extra-long. I wanted them to reflect the relationship between Sukunabikona and Ōkuninushi for you. I wanted to give you a little piece of home. I remember you saying that Japanese cherry blossoms were your favorite part of your rehabilitation trip this past winter."

Airess held her hands up in protest. "That's very sweet of you, Tao. Thank you, but I should probably—"

"Please don't. Please stay. Just for a little bit longer?"

Airess found it hard to resist Tao's pleading eyes. She had never seen him so vulnerable before. "Okay. Only for a minute." She sat down on the cold stone bench beside him.

He shook his head in earnest agreement. "I'll be quick. Airess, I've put a lot of thought into this. I—" A loud dragging sound was coming from the entrance. A very large Chibi was slowly making their way down the main path, dragging someone with them on their back foot.

"Chibi!" Airess shot straight up. "Mae? Mae, what are you doing?" Airess ran to help the girl up, but upon Airess' arrival, Chibi stopped walking and lifted the small human off his foot into a standing position. Airess helped dust her off.

"I tried to stop Chibi, but they're too strong now! They refused to be separated from you." Mae was in tears. "I was trying so hard to prevent this."

"You're fine, Mae. This is nothing. Tao just wanted to talk." Airess tried to console Mae, but no one believed the words being said, not even Airess herself.

"I don't know that I would say this is nothing, but I'm glad you're okay." Tao supervised from afar.

Chibi walked up to him and started pounding their chest rhythmically.

"Chibi! Stop that right now. You know who Tao is, and you know I wasn't in any danger." Airess attempted to scold the no longer tiny golem, but it came off more tender than intimidating.

Chibi crossed their arms and stomped in response.

"Are they trying to threaten me?" Tao's tone carried a hint of condescension.

Mae glowered at Tao. "He's a golem. Golems aren't violent unless they're directed to protect. You should know that. Isn't that your thing? Knowing everything? You leave him be. Don't be a bully."

"A bully? Seriously? Who are you to even be involved in any of this? You've been here, what? Like a week? I was trying to have an important conversation with my friend, and you rudely interrupted."

Mae snapped, "I am more than happy to not be involved in your failed attempts and unrequited love, but I didn't particularly have a choice today."

Solei jumped into the conversation before Tao could respond. "All right. We should probably head out."

"Solei?" Tao asked, confused.

"Tao, Solei might be right, want to head out together?" It was Lena chiming in now.

"How many people are in here?" Tao was becoming increasingly distraught.

"Tao, they were with me when I came. I didn't know. I didn't know I was walking into this." Airess tried to be sympathetic. "Chibi, go with Mae and I'll meet you at home, later."

The golem tried to protest, but they couldn't refuse a direct order.

Solei nodded to Airess and ushered an irritated Mae and a crabby golem down the path.

Lena stood there awkwardly, waiting for a cue to either grab Tao or disappear into the foliage again.

"Did you still want to talk?" Airess offered sweetly.

"Was Mae right?"

"About what?"

"About this being a failed attempt and unrequited love?"

"Oh, Tao. Even an oracle wouldn't think you're in love with me. Mae lashed out because she was upset. She's still adjusting to life here. You remember how it was." Airess made a slight gesture towards Lena.

"I see. That explains a lot then." Tao was getting more and more defensive by the moment.

Lena couldn't bear to watch. "Tao—"

"I think you've done enough, don't you?" He spoke to Lena directly.

"Tao." Airess came to Lena's defense.

"I've also done enough for the day. Goodbye, Airess. Sorry for making a fool out of both of us." He threw his carefully crafted bouquet onto the ground.

Lena reached out to him as he passed.

He evaded her reach, sneering at her as he left. "Never again, Basil; never again."

Lena's mouth froze agape. She stared at Airess. She wanted to cry.

Airess rushed to embrace her friend.

"I didn't do anything wrong, Airess." Lena's words were muffled and weak.

"I believe you."

"I tried so hard to make sure this was all perfect! I didn't do anything wrong!"

"I know. Give it time. We'll all be okay." Airess rubbed her friend's back and waited for Lena to come up for air. "Want to go see Selene? I can walk you there on my way home?"

Lena pulled away grumpy but tried to act appreciative of the comfort. "He's with your best friend."

The healer stayed silent, careful not to react. She hadn't heard from Delphine all day. Lena could be right, but there was no way Airess was going to fuel that fire.

Lena felt the outrage in her previous tone. She recognized she was angry at Delphine and Selene, and maybe yelling at her friend that was caring for her was not the kindest of decisions. Remorseful, she apologized, "I'm sorry. You didn't deserve that."

"Oh, I think a lot of us are dealing with things we don't deserve right now. Come on, let's go to my place. I'll grow a mushroom that contours you perfectly; it'll be like a cozy hug." Airess nudged her friend with a smile.

"That sounds lovely. It's been a while since I've snuggled an oversized mushroom." Arm in arm, Lena walked with Airess back to her and Chibi's home.

~*~

I should have listened to you. You tried to warn me.

Don't be so hard on yourself, Lena. You were doing what you thought was best. You were being a good friend.

A lot of good that did me. He blamed me for everything and left in a huff.

He's been going through more than he can

handle lately.

And I'd know that if he ever opened up about anything.

Solei answered sympathetically with their eyes, fully knowing the same had been said about them recently.

Airess and Mae were engrossed with Chibi in the center of the home; they had been making designs with various rocks, stones, and four-leaf clovers for quite some time now. The sun was setting outside.

The three of them seem pretty close.

Mae spends almost all her free time with Chibi. She likes to find clovers for them since they can't pick them up themselves. She seems to find Airess tolerable in low doses too.

Lena had to suppress a laugh.

Solei did not disguise their grin. *I thought you'd enjoy that.*

She really isn't that bad anymore. She was considerably kind to me after Tao blew up. She didn't have to be.

Airess has many incredibly phenomenal qualities. It's a shame a few others go in the opposite direction.

Lena waited for Solei to elaborate. She had almost given up when that familiar ping sprung into her forehead.

Tao isn't the only one who has been enchanted by the bubblegum healer. I'd actually be willing to bet that it's more of an outlier to not fall under her spell than be one of the fallen. Airess is compelling; it's a part of her nature. It's impossible not to notice her, and she'll melt your heart the second she wants to. I don't think she means to be like that in a cruel way; it's just how she's made. She's borderline irresistible. That type of lure causes casualties. Solei focused on a nearby window, intentionally avoiding eye contact with anyone in the room.

Wow. I had no idea.

That doesn't surprise me. It was very clear you were not affected by her beauty and charm.

I don't know. She crushed me when she villainized me last year. I didn't have romantic feelings for her, but I did think she was supposed to be one of my best friends when she flipped on me.

She can certainly be ruthless when she deems it necessary.

Why stick around her then?

It's not her fault. She's no siren, right? I know you're exceedingly well-versed with the likes of those.

In some ways it's fitting they're best friends, I guess.

I can see it. Hopefully, the actual siren has less of a lure than our healer friend.

I wish for that multiple times a day. What about you, though? Did you ever break free, or are you still stuck?

Nah. Mae saved me in more ways than one in Rome. They're the real deal, Lena. They're the one thing I know that's right in the world.

Must be nice. I felt that way once.

And now?

And now I max out on omega 3's daily.

Solei covered their face to hide their amusement, but it piqued the attention of the group.

"What's so funny?" Mae asked, cheekily.

"Lena. She's a goof even when she's quiet."

"Ha! Lena? Quiet? That is something worth laughing at." Airess teased playfully then offered out her hands to her hushed friend. "Jokes aside, though, how are you holding up?"

Lena held her friend's hands for reassurance. "Could be worse. Lost in my thoughts, I guess."

"I can understand that. Are you getting hungry at all? I am. Anyone want to go to the cafeteria for dinner?"

"I think we're going to eat at home tonight," Solei answered, admiring Mae.

Mae beamed at their response.

"My parents are leaving soon. I want to say my goodbyes."

"Aww! Of course!" Airess sounded like she wanted to say more but stopped herself.

"Thanks for having me, Airess. You too, Chibi." Lena patted the golem's head. Chibi stood and gave Lena a big hug, leaving her clothes stained with reddish clay smears. "Nice seeing you all as well. I hope you guys have a wonderful evening together."

"Take care, Lena. Good luck." Solei gave a half

hug.

"Thanks." Lena made her way into the outside twilight. The walk was easy and uneventful, a normal part of her daily routine. The house was dark when she arrived. She walked in, locked the door behind her, and made her way into the kitchen. There was a note on the counter.

"Dinner is in the fridge. I hate to miss our last night together, Magpie, but we didn't have much choice. I'm so sorry. I'll make it up to you when we're back. One day max.

Love you more than there are trees in the forest,

Dad"

Resigned, Lena heated up the food and ate at the table. She was alone and lonely. She analyzed her day for the millionth time. Something about the afternoon with Tao wasn't sitting right.

Solei! Sorry to bug you so soon, but do you know where Tao lives?

Lena waited a while, but there was no response. She debated texting Airess but decided that might be in poor taste. Selene came to her mind. Lena resisted the thought.

Her phone buzzed, almost as if he knew he was on her mind. "I'm so sorry, but I can't make it tonight. Give your mom a hug for me! XOXO"

Annoyed, she responded right away. "It's fine. Hey, do you know where Tao lives? Today didn't go so great, and I want to check in on him."

"No, sorry. Are you sure you want to leave your parents on their last night though?"

Lena rolled her eyes. He, of all people, was in no position to question her presence. "They're gone already."

"I thought that wasn't supposed to happen until later?"

"Yup. Well, I'm going to go figure out this whole Tao thing. Take care." Lena closed the phone and didn't wait for a reply. Her shoes were back on in no time. She needed a long run to burn off the bad vibes of the day, and she was determined to get it.

The search turned out easier than expected. With Professor Nakshatra in charge, P.C.'s chambers were left unattended. Lena knew the student files must be located somewhere within there. She started searching drawer by drawer until she found exactly what she wanted. She typed the address into an app on her phone and was off again to her next destination.

On her way, she wondered if it was weird that she had no idea where Tao lived. *Shouldn't friends invite you over? Shouldn't you think of them when you passed their street?* She felt like everyone knew where she lived. They all knew her parents too. Lena didn't know the families of any of her friends. For a school focused on one's heritage and lineage, there was barely any family involvement.

Tao lived on the other side of town. The houses were smaller in this area and most were not kept in the best shape. Lena almost felt like they were darker as well, but quickly decided that had to be her imagination. A few of the street lights were broken, and many were turned off regardless. The area felt slightly eerie. This wasn't the type of place Lena expected Tao to live in at all. Lena started counting the house numbers, but the yellow taxi was unmistakable. She picked up her pace, trying to figure out what she was going to say when she rang the doorbell.

Tao's house was one of the bigger ones on the street, but that wasn't saying much. Their door was decorated with a bright red and gold sign and characters from a language Lena assessed to be Chinese. The door opened before Lena could knock.

"Hello. You must be Lena. My husband told me you'd be stopping by." A thin woman answered the door in a beautiful long dress. She had perfect posture and came across as extremely proper. She looked like an older, female version of Tao. Their resemblance was striking. "You may come in. Tao is in his room and is unlikely to come out, but I'll show you which door to sit by."

"Umm. Okay. Thank you." Lena walked in, more uncomfortable than she expected to be. She stayed silent as the noise of the house engulfed her. Small children ran around the main room. Tao's family was big. Lena never would've guessed.

Mrs. Vovi knocked on the door in front of her. "Tao, Lena is here. You should come out of your room to greet your guest."

Lena did her best to not be awkward while she waited next to his mom.

Looking downcast, the thin woman turned towards Lena. "I will bring you a sitting pillow and a cup of tea. My apologies for my son's lack of manners." With a nod, Tao's mom made her exit.

Lena sat on the floor and gave another small knock on the door. "Hey. It's me. Your mom seems nice. She said your dad knew I was coming. Makes sense with your abilities, huh?" Lena could hear some shuffling inches from the door, but Tao remained mute. "I know it's kind of late. I hope I didn't ruin your dinner. Your house smells amazing. I'm sure whatever it was, it was delicious." Lena could tell she was starting to ramble and didn't quite care. "I spent some time with Airess and everyone after everything. Solei had some interesting observations to make. You should reach out to them sometime. I think you would relate to the thoughts they had. It could be comforting, you know?"

Tao's mom delivered the tea and pillow to Lena. Lena thanked the hospitable woman and adjusted. The tea was warm and soothing. "Your mom brought over some tea. There's a cup for you too, if you want it. I'm sure you're used to it by now, but it's good. I've always liked green tea." As the quietness continued, Lena found herself liking it more and more. It was therapeutic to be able to talk out loud to someone without interruption.

"I'm sure they're not your favorite beings right now, but I don't think Mae, or Chibi, meant any harm. Mae was actually quite devoted to trying to protect your moment with Airess even though they knew the ending. And Chibi, well, Chibi is Chibi. They're real attached to Airess. Which makes sense, I guess, right? I mean Ina made Airess their master so they kind of have to follow her at all costs. I don't think they have much of a choice in all that. Though, Airess definitely speculates that they have some additional moods and feelings that are all of their own. She's really come around to them. Remember how much she hated them? She would've squashed that little lump into a clay ball if she thought she could've avoided punishment for it. Now, she's completely adopted the role of caretaker. Which, of course, she has. That's so Airess. Everyone's forever caretaker." Lena paused for a moment, as she thought she heard something. She couldn't tell if it was a laugh or a sniffle, but it sounded like Tao was rather close to the door.

Lena wiggled a few of her fingertips under the door. "I'm here."

To her surprise, he put his fingers on top of hers.

She waited for him to say something, but when that seemed improbable, she continued on. "I went home for dinner, after my time at Airess', who by the way has made the cutest and coziest little hut for herself and Chibi, and I guess my parents and everyone else have already left to do whatever it is they're trying to do. We were supposed to share a final meal together tonight. I thought it was kind of a big deal. One last hurrah before the big trip. They made food which was nice. My dad did, I guess. But, it wasn't quite what I was going for. Selene was supposed to join too, but I'm sure it doesn't take your visions to see how that's been going lately. He's all about his purpose now, and that purpose seems to involve Delphine and the Nulls more than me." Lena gave herself a moment to reflect. The sting of Selene with an overzealous Delphine never dulled. "Sometimes I wish Kohl would've eaten her."

Tao's laugh wasn't concealed this time.

"That's what he does though, for real, right? I mean, I don't want her dead. That's not nice, but . . . like . . . ya know . . . maybe if she had gotten chomped here or there, she'd be less of a nuisance."

"Lena, you should not wish for one of our friends to have been eaten by a vampire. You're better than that."

"I don't wish for any of my friends to be eaten by a vampire. I wish for someone I one hundred percent have no interest in being friends with to be slightly nom-ed on by a vampire. That's different!"

Tao pulled his hand away and Lena knew it was to rub his forehead. He always did that when he thought she was being too much. "That is not okay." He tried to come across as stern, but his laugh was too prominent.

"Soooooo . . . do you want to talk now? Or else,

I can keep going. I've become quite the fish connoisseur lately. I am happy to go into great detail about all of that."

"I'm going to assume that's due to an increased interest in identifying various aquatic species since the professor discovered the reef triggerfish in the middle of the desert and not an increased interest in eating fish because you hate a siren."

"You're welcome to believe in whatever you feel is best for you. I won't stop you."

"Lena, I don't even know what to say to you sometimes." He exhaled loudly. "But, thank you for being here. I regret how I acted earlier. I know I wasn't the nicest I could have been to you when I left."

"That did suck, but what you were going through probably sucked worse. Gods know that I've taken my frustration out on you before. Turnabout is fair play I guess."

"I like to think I'm above acts of retaliation."

"We're all very aware of your high opinions of yourself, Tao Vovi. What we're not aware of are your emotions. You hide your feelings deeper than any of us can reach."

"I could not have been more transparent about my feelings today, and that went worse than even I anticipated. Why were so many people there?"

"Airess was traveling with a group; that's not out of the norm for her."

"I suppose not. I can't imagine constant company like that."

"I don't know, sitting on the floor and talking through a wooden door screams your love of people to me." She could hear him groan at her mockery. She was happy things were getting closer to normal.

"Your point's been made." Tao opened the door. "Don't come in though. My parents will have my head if I have a girl in my room."

"Deal." She handed him his cup of green tea. "Your mom may have given the impression that you stay in there rather frequently as of late."

Tao was downcast in his reply. "Almost always. I leave to go to school, but I'm only making it a few hours there each day. It's too hard to function around people. There's so much noise and chaos."

"You used to love Legacy Academy."

"My needs have changed now . . . my views . . . everything."

"Your needs? I've never heard of you needing anything ever."

"Well, now you have. Congratulations." His sarcasm was dry.

"Come on. Talk to me. You clearly need it, and honestly, it would be good for me too. Help yourself, or pity me. I'm not really in a position to care at the moment. But let me in," Lena pleaded. She wasn't sure how he would react. In an attempt to keep the mood from getting too heavy, she added, "Figuratively speaking, of course."

Tao stared at her. A million things swarmed his mind. "I don't particularly want to."

"I know, but I don't particularly care."

"I'm aware of that too." Tao let the silence linger.

Lena didn't budge.

"All right. You win. But first, you should probably meet my family."

{ 6 }

Family and Friends

Tao brought Lena to the couch in the living room. His father sat in his own reclining chair off to the side. His eyes were closed, and he was still as a statue. He barely looked awake, but Lena could tell he wasn't asleep. There was a way about him that let her know he was listening in. Tao's mother bustled around from one spot to the next. She ushered the other children into the center of the room. There were three of them, all around the same age. They couldn't have been more than five years old.

"Lena, this is my father, Biêt, and my mother, Hùfú."

"It's nice to meet you, Lena. We've heard so much about you."

Lena glanced over at Tao. She was sure not everything they were told had portrayed her in the best light.

Tao played aloof. "I bet you didn't know, but

my dad is actually the mayor of Astoria. He's held that title since before I was born."

"Oh wow." Lena couldn't imagine anyone being in charge in this town other than P.C.

"I thought you'd be surprised. And my mom . . ."

Lena couldn't be sure, but she swore there was a glance exchanged between Tao and his parents.

"My mom keeps us kids here safe and cared for." Tao nodded at his parents as their faces indicated approval.

A little one from the floor handed Lena a piece of paper filled with scribbles.

Mrs. Vovi laughed. "That's Yùnqì. He must like you."

Lena addressed the wobbly toddler. "Thank you for such a great gift. It's lovely." Lena pressed the piece of paper close to her chest.

Out of the corner of her eye, Lena was certain there was that glance between Tao and his parents again. She was dying to know what that frequent look meant. It was easy to see how Tao grew up to be the way he was. The whole family was as enigmatic as they were gracious. There was a whole conversation going on in this house that Lena was not part of.

Tao's mother broke Lena's thoughts. Mrs. Vovi placed a large plate of various foods in front of the teenagers. "It's been long since we've had a guest in this house outside of the family. Tao is not always the proudest of our household." She was talking to Lena but looking at Tao. He avoided her stare. Mrs. Vovi turned towards Lena. "I'm grateful you came tonight. It's a nice change of pace for all of us."

"Yes, Lena. Thank you." Tao's father's voice was quiet but firm. He spoke with a succinct intonation and closed eyes.

"I appreciate you having me," Lena said, quickly swallowing a mouthful of food.

"I hear your parents are embarking on quite the journey in the near future," Hùfú commented.

Tao's body tensed.

"Yeah, I guess they left before I got home today. I didn't know you all knew each other."

"We actually have yet to meet. I typically stay close to home. I've been watching over this house, and my family's children within it, for over two decades now. Biêt's role within the town lends to a similar path, so I enjoy being by his side. He does a fantastic job overseeing the safety of us all." She gave her husband a sweet smile.

"My dad and Principal Chromwell work together very closely." Tao's words heavily implied that Astoria and Legacy Academy were not autonomous of each other.

"I had no idea." Lena never even thought about the town much.

"Not many people do." Tao's tone remained heavy with implications.

"I see." Lena got the hint; there were eyes everywhere.

"It's for the best." Mrs. Vovi cut off their conversation. "Without such strong camaraderie and support between the school and the town, you never would have had the opportunity to meditate this summer."

"And that's supposed to be a good thing?"

"It was a great thing! You were able to help your people at such a young age! You honored yourself, your family, and your school. What is better than that?"

"Living, mother. Living is better than that. Not being overrun by visions. Not feeling torn between two realms." Tao's words carried an edge to them. "I want to know what's real. I want to not be so lost in my head that I'm scared I won't be able to find a way back out. I want him to help me!" Tao pointed at his father.

"Tao, that is not an appropriate conversation to have in front of company. You need to apologize to your friend here, and then it's probably time for Ms. Basil to head home." Mrs. Vovi spoke as if Lena was not within arm's reach of her.

"You're never going to understand if you never listen," Tao implored, waiting for his mother to respond. She remained as composed as ever. Frustrated, he huffed over to the door. "Come on, Lena. Let's go."

Lena nodded, grabbed one last snack, thanked his parents, and chased Tao out of the door. She found him in the driver's seat of his car and climbed into the passenger seat.

"That was intense, huh?" Lena said, stuffing her face with her final snack.

"They don't listen! No, I take that back. She doesn't listen and he doesn't talk! How am I supposed to get better if neither one of my parents acknowledges anything is wrong? How am I supposed to go back to living a normal life?"

This was the first time Lena had ever seen Tao truly angry. "Tao, I'm not the best source of advice on how to have a normal life, but I completely understand what it's like feeling like one of your parents is hard to reach."

"You're the only one out of all of us who got to live without any of this stuff. You just found out about Legacy and Astoria last year. Don't you miss your old life?"

"Honestly?"

"Always."

"Not even once, not really."

"I find that highly doubtful."

"I won't deny that all this is harder, scarier too, but I'm alive. To use your words, I'm living. Before knowing all this, it was fine, but it never felt satisfying. No one would have understood my mom, so I never got close enough to anyone to give them the chance. I fought with her nonstop. I didn't go out, and I never had anyone over. Plain and simple, I didn't fit in, which I'm sure is incredibly hard for you to believe." Lena bumped her friend's arm with her elbow until he cracked a smile.

"I hope you're not ashamed of your mom anymore. She's utterly fantastic. And we all think so, just so you know."

"Thank you. I'd never have figured it out without Astoria." Lena let that sentiment linger on their drive home. When they reached her house, she added, "Your mom might be great too, you know? Maybe you two just need to get to know each other better. That's what I had to do."

"Maybe. I didn't think that was a problem we had until recently."

"Now that's a topic I can give advice on!"

"Spending multiple seasons in meditation?"

"Having one singular event that flips every-thing you ever knew upside down."

"That's fair."

"Right? I thought so too."

Tao leaned his seat back and closed his eyes.

"You going to be okay?" Lena asked, concern-ed.

"Who knows? I certainly don't, and if my father does, no one else would know."

"I might've guessed he had a similar gift as you."

"Because, once again, P.C. needs to be overly involved?"

"Ouch. Salty much? I was going to say because his name means knowledge."

"That too." Tao thought for a moment. "Wait,

how did you know that?"

"It's kind of what I do."

"Hmm."

"Your whole family is like that but you. Your mom's name means talisman and your brother's name means lucky."

"He's not my brother."

"He's not?"

"My mom watches over the kids within our extended family. The triplets are actually my cousins. My aunt and uncle live with us too, but they weren't home yet."

"That's a lot of people in one house."

"It's eight. It's always been eight; I anticipate it will always be eight."

"Is that why you don't invite people over?"

"No. I mean, my house is typically chaotic, but more than anything, I used to love my freedom. The library was my happy place. It was quiet, and I could be alone. No one had any expectations of me. I haven't been able to enjoy that for months though. I don't feel like I've been able to enjoy anything for months."

"Is that why you asked out Airess, to try to enjoy something?"

"No . . .," Tao's face looked pained as he addressed Lena.

"Then it was because . . ."

"You know I hate talking about my visions, Lena."

"I also now know that your visions are an overwhelming burden for you lately. So, again, let me help. I'm here, and I have nowhere else I need to go. My parents are gone who knows where, my boyfriend is missing in action, probably with a mermaid deep within some random portal I'll never learn anything about, and it's not like our other friends are dying to hear from me. They've got their own lives now, too. Airess has Chibi; Solei has Mae. I have no one right now. I'm readily available to help you with your problems. Plus, then I can avoid confronting my own." She let out a playful grin.

"You make a compelling argument. I assume you know Delphine isn't a mermaid?"

Lena stared at him blankly. She was un-amused.

"It's a common misconception! It was worth verifying," Tao protested.

"Was it? I don't feel there's ever a situation where it's worth bringing her name up." Lena shrugged.

"There's probably plenty to unpack there, but I concede to your original request. I'm not yearning to go back home and that's the only place that requests my presence currently, too."

"You don't have duties at the school with P.C. gone? Selene may have mentioned something like that when he was telling me how busy he was going to be with his own newly found obligations."

"Ahh, yeah. I'm supposed to perform routine

meditations to keep an eye on things around the school. As you might have surmised though, I'm not very inclined to do those."

"Wow, Tao Vovi a rebel, who knew?"

"Not my family, that's for sure."

"Want to come in for some tea? I might be able to make a bad version of sahlab if you want? That's my preferred drink when receiving bad news. My dad's kind of a pro at it." Sadness creeped into her voice.

"I'm pretty smart. Maybe I could help? Is there a recipe?"

"No, but there's the internet."

"Ahh, research then! That's basically my love language. Let's give it a go."

Off they went, straight towards the kitchen.

~*~

"I still don't get it. Everyone thought Ina was the Old Hag, and clearly, she is anything but that."

"I know it doesn't make any sense. Visions never do, but I'm telling you, come tomorrow morning, the Old Hag is living back in their house."

"But it's Ina's house, and she isn't an old hag!"

"Yes, we've covered that already. I don't know what else to say, Lena."

"Do you have any other information? Is it actually Ina, only grotesque, and maybe another name they're going by? Or is it someone else taking over Ina's place, someone we could look up?"

"Listen, if I could give you the picture in my

head, I would. All I know is come tomorrow, the Old Hag's house is going to look worse than it ever did, and it'll be occupied by something worse than we ever thought of. That's it. That's all I know."

"All right. I understand." Lena racked her brain for what to do next. "I guess, then we plan for the worst."

"And how do you envision us doing that?"

"I don't know yet, but maybe our friends could help?"

"Aren't they off with oracles and mermaids? Isn't that how we ended up here to begin with?"

"Yeah . . .," Lena paused. "But now we have sahlab?"

"That's true, and it's rather delicious if I do say so myself."

"It is way tastier than I expected that to be. I'll give you that."

"So, sahlab and a group text?" Tao suggested.

"Sahlab and a visit to Ward A. Airess has a shift later tonight, and hopefully, we can catch Selene on his way home. Solei will be a harder challenge, but I have a plan for that."

"All right then. Let's find some thermos' and pack up."

The two were out the door in less than fifteen minutes.

Solei! Solei! Solei!

What's up, little cub?

Bad news! Can you meet Tao and me in Ward

A tonight?

Does it have to be tonight? I'm exhausted.

... yeah ... kind of. Tao strongly believes we're going to have an unwelcome visitor in Astoria tomorrow. We want to prep for it.

No promises, but I'll see what I can do.

All right. Thank you. Hope to see you soon.

The pair lucked out, and Airess was at the reception desk when they arrived at Ward A. Understandably so, Tao asked if he could go look for Selene while Lena looped Airess into the plan.

"Meet you and Selene at Professor Nakshatra's?"

"Too risky with them being one of the only adults left here. How about the library back at Legacy? The school should be empty at this hour."

"Sure. See you there."

Tao tried to slink off to the side, but Airess had eyes on him since his arrival.

Lena waved to her friend and walked over. "Hey."

"Hey. I didn't expect to see you two together, let alone here. I thought you went to spend the night saying goodbye to your parents?"

"That was the plan, but they were already gone by the time I got home, so I wanted to check in with Tao. I think something's off with the trip, and Tao does too. Have you heard anything from anyone yet?"

"Nothing much, but it makes sense. From what I heard, Nurse Galen has been in Ward A all day but not for our normal duties. Ward B has had almost no staffing, and I'm not sure who was covering the nurse's office at Legacy today. I got called in early by an intern. At least, I'm assuming they're an intern. I didn't recognize their name at all. I came in as soon as I put Chibi down."

"Weird. Have you tried to message Nurse Galen?"

"No, I was looking through the paperwork here to see if I could find anything out myself. No one's filled anything out all day though."

"Who was scheduled before you?"

"Ippy . . .," Airess said with an uncertain tone.

"Oh." Lena was practically speechless.

"My sentiment exactly."

"Well, that kind of brings me to my next question. I know things with Tao are beyond awkward right now, but we're meeting in the library later tonight to try to talk about one of his visions. He thinks come tomorrow morning, we're all going to be in a lot of trouble. We want to try to get ahead of it if we can."

"He wants me there so badly he ran off at the sight of me?"

"He's going to try to find Selene to bring him to the library too."

"And your first choice was to come see me instead of going to find your boyfriend?"

"I adore you but obviously not. We're all going through things right now and are doing the best we can."

Airess nodded her head. "I can agree to that. Who else is invited?"

"Solei."

"And Mae?"

Lena grimaced.

"I suppose it's not worth asking about Delphine then?"

"I personally wouldn't," Lena emphasized.

"I'll go, but it's a mistake not to invite Mae. She's an oracle. If we're really in danger, she could help."

"I don't think that fact was missed by Tao."

"Ugh. He's so frustrating sometimes!"

"I understand. Grab my badge too if you want. Maybe I can help sort things here afterward."

"Won't you need sleep?"

"Depends on how bad things go at the library."

"Based on today, you should probably have this then." Airess tossed Lena her Ward A badge, grabbed the work phone, the skeleton key, and walked with her friend to the library.

"How bad do you think whatever this is is?" Airess inquired.

"Bad enough for Tao to tell us about one of his visions." Lena held open a heavy door for both of them.

"I've known Tao since the first day I came here, and he's never come close to talking about his powers. Kohl talked more about his skills than Tao ever did."

"Which is why, when he says we need to meet to talk about this, I push for all of us to meet to talk about this. Because whatever 'this' is, it's clearly important."

"It almost makes me nervous."

"Being close to me isn't going to help with that. We'll figure it out though. Whatever it is."

"I hope so."

Knowing what her friend needed, Lena reached out for Airess' hand for support. The two made their way into the library, set up a table for five, and held hands while they waited for the others to arrive.

Surprisingly, Solei and Mae were the next to arrive. At first, Lena was excited to chat and catch them up on everything, but the mood they brought with them was clear. They were nonplussed to be in the library right now. Lena tried a few times to say Solei's name telepathically, but it only seemed to make them ignore her more.

Thirty minutes later, Tao and Selene finally made it through the doors. Tao gave Lena an instant look as he walked in but quickly dropped it as he pulled over an additional chair and addressed the others. Selene sat next to Lena, giving her a kiss on the cheek as he reached out to hold her other hand.

"Thanks for coming on such short notice every-one. I see we have some extra guests too, so the more the merrier I suppose." Tao began.

Daggers were shot from Solei's and Mae's eyes at him.

That must have been the trigger to their poor mood, Lena thought.

"I, unfortunately, don't know much. I never do, but I think it's important to share the little I do know in this one specific case. When we wake up tomorrow, Astoria will be under attack."

The room erupted in chatter. It was hard to understand one person over the next.

Solei stood with their palms outstretched, calming the chaos. "We're going to need more than that, Tao. What do you mean that Astoria is going to be under attack?" Their tone was calm when they spoke, but their stare was intense.

Lena wondered if they were reading his mind without him even knowing it. Tao would freak out if he found out that was happening.

"I know, but what I have is limited. All I know is that it's related to the Old Hag. I've seen flashes of their face; it's hideous. The flashes don't last long enough for me to make much past their gro-tesqueness. I also see wreaths made of wheat and wildflowers. Sometimes there is corn too, but that is hit or miss. More than anything though, I feel fear, chilled to the bone, cold sweat-inducing fear. These visions have left me shaking and screaming."

"I know I'm new here, and wasn't particularly invited to this shindig, but doesn't Legacy Academy have its own protection? It's a magical school; I can't imagine that nuance is ignored when it comes to outside visitors," Mae contested.

"To the best of my knowledge, yes, Legacy does have some basic protection. However, we're not talking about the school. I'm talking about the town."

"Your dad's the mayor, right? And has similar gifts? If nothing else, they've seen you come out of these visions in a bad way. Can't he do anything?" Solei didn't understand why this wasn't his dad's problem.

Tao gave an uncertain look to Solei and Lena. He wasn't aware Solei knew about his dad. "My dad doesn't believe in getting involved." For the first time in his presentation, Tao's delivery came off sheepish.

"You've told him Astoria is getting attacked, and he doesn't want to get involved?" Mae's tone was accusatory.

"I feel the same way you do but no. I've had as much conversation as he would permit, but he doesn't believe that is his role."

Frustrated, Selene added, "I can't imagine it's a coincidence that someone is coming to invade the town while P.C. is gone?"

"I feel that's likely the case as well, but have nothing to confirm that," Tao affirmed.

"Have you told Professor Nakshatra?" Selene pressed.

Tao dismissed the idea. "I don't think she will be much help outside of the school."

"She's good enough to run the school while

P.C. is gone," Selene responded defensively.

"Of course. Her magic is incredibly valuable and permissible within school grounds."

"The way you say that makes it sound like you think her magic is not permitted in the town." Lena attempted to clarify.

"That is unfortunately correct. Unless it is proposed by P.C. and my father approves it, magic is not allowed anywhere outside of Legacy Academy. Technically, it shouldn't even be allowed in Ward A, but you try telling that to a bunch of entitled dying gods."

"Tao, that doesn't make any sense. I play with electricity all the time outside of Legacy. Lena's dad literally has a workshop filled with magical items. No one has ever said anything."

"That's true. I've even seen Kasim use some of them in Lena's house," Selene added.

Lena didn't want to say anything that would make her dad look bad, but they weren't wrong. Even Lena had used his items frequently, and she was hardly ever inside Legacy Academy these days.

"I don't know what to tell you, Solei. Those are the rules. I can't speak on what my father knows about or chooses to have P.C. enforce."

"He doesn't even enforce his own rule? That's weird, isn't it?" Mae was being skeptical once again.

"It's hard to say who makes the rules between himself and P.C., but as I've said, my father doesn't believe in getting involved."

"What's the point of having rules if he's not going to do anything about them? Plus, if he's not going to do anything about them, why would Professor Nakshatra stand down against this thing coming to Astoria? You're talking in circles." Mae was getting more and more upset.

Selene answered reluctantly, "Professor Nakshatra isn't likely to oppose P.C. I can't see her going against a direct order. She's incredibly diligent and loyal."

"I also highly doubt P.C. would put someone in charge that is likely to disobey them. She is not unkind, but control is something she's very attached to," Tao added in a snarky manner.

Airess spoke for the first time. "So, what do we do then? The mayor doesn't care, P.C. is gone, and Professor Nakshatra isn't likely to get involved."

"Great question, Airess. I want to scope out the town tomorrow morning, investigate, and then get this monstrous beast out of here as quickly as possible."

"I get that Tao, I'm sure we all want that, but how?" The healer's voice was desperate.

"I'm not sure. We won't know until tomorrow morning."

"Wait, the whole point of this meeting was to tell us something bad is coming and we have to wait until it's already here to do anything?" The frustration from Mae was unrelenting.

Solei attempted to comfort her. "I can think of

one way around that . . ."

"No. You are not dragging me out of my safe space, into this stuffy building, to listen to your friends argue and adhere to stupid rules that don't make sense, just so you can then ask me to use my powers which you know I avoid."

"That wasn't my plan, Mae. However, it seems like now is as good of a time as any, doesn't it? You could help the team so much!"

"Why would I want to do that? These aren't my friends. This isn't my town or my home. There's a literal Academy filled with adults way more adept to handle this situation than I am. Why do I need to get involved?"

"Because it's the right thing to do. Isn't that important to you?"

"Other than this group, who says this is the right thing to do? I think this is much closer to the wrong thing to do. This isn't my responsibility. I have no ties here."

Solei was visibly hurt by Mae's comment. "I think I misunderstood, then. I thought you had a rather strong tie here."

"Don't do that. Don't turn me not wanting to help your friends engage in a battle they don't need to be in into an attack on us."

"I can't stand by and watch my town, and my home, get destroyed. This is my fight. You say you won't help them, but what you're also saying is you won't help me."

"Knowing more about what's coming will not solve your problem the way you think it will. It doesn't work that way. It NEVER works that way."

"How would you know? You won't even try."

"Enough. I'm not doing this. I want to go home. I didn't want to be here to begin with."

"That's exceedingly clear. Here's the key, Mae. Go home, whatever that means to you."

Mae stared in disbelief. Solei glared defiantly in the opposite direction. This exchange had become more awkward than Tao's stunt earlier.

"I'm happy to go, but you need to know that this is a mistake. This whole thing is a mistake." She whispered something into Solei's ear and then walked out the door.

Tears began forming in Solei's eyes the moment the door closed. They tried to wipe them off discreetly. Without speaking, Solei got up and walked out the door as well.

Lena looked to Tao for guidance. He was focused on Airess who, not surprisingly, was not focused on him.

Selene continued to evaluate the plan. "Tao, how do you expect us to get all this intel on the intruder when we have to run the school?"

Lena could feel the weight of Selene's "we" not being inclusive to her or Airess.

"These visions hold me hostage whether I'm at the school or not. I'm tired of feeling scared. I'm tired of being a prisoner of my mind. I want to do something. I'm ready to take action, and this is my chance. It's my priority."

"How can you say that when you're supposed to help with the safety of the school?"

"If Astoria goes down, there won't be a school to take care of." Tao was firm in his response.

Selene shook his head in disapproval.

Another disagreement was brewing amongst the group. Lena wondered who would storm off this time. It was making her stomach hurt. She hated all this tension. She stood up to try to break the room's energy. She planned to go look at some books to link the clues they had together. Once her hands were free of Airess and Selene, her head was crippled with panicked thoughts.

Lena! LENA! Why aren't you answering me?! Mae isn't here. I went to go chase after her, and she isn't here. What if the Olg Hag came early? What if something happened to Mae? We have to find her, Lena! Lena? Lena! Please answer me. You have to help me!

Selene rose to her rescue and steady her. "You all right? You're not looking too good."

"I need to lie down, I think."

"There's a place to lie down in one of the reading nooks. I'll show you." Tao led the way to a soft warm leather chaise lounge chair.

Once she lay down, she responded to Solei's onslaught of messages. *Please calm down. I know you're scared, but it's hard to handle so much coming at me at once.*

I'm sorry. I just have no idea where she could be! She hates leaving our room. I don't know why she isn't here! I'll never forgive myself if something happened to her.

Doesn't she like being with Chibi Chan too?

She does, but not at this hour.

Go look there. I'll wrap up here and try to meet you there afterwards.

Okay. Thanks, Lena. Please don't tell the others. Mae is having a hard time being around the whole group.

I can tell. I don't think she's particularly fond of me, but I'm happy to help.

I don't think she's particularly fond of me either at the moment.

We'll find her. Go check by Chibi, and I'll be there soon.

Thank you.

Of course.

Selene was waving his hand in front of Lena's face. "Hello?"

"Oh! Hey . . ."

"What was that? You spaced out for a minute. I almost called Airess over."

"My head's just being funny. I'm okay though. What a night, huh?"

"Yeah, I feel bad for Solei and Mae, but I don't think Mae's exactly wrong."

"What?"

"I mean there has to be someone better off to handle this than us, right?"

"Tao doesn't seem to think so."

"But Tao doesn't know everything."

"I kind of thought that was his thing."

"Maybe Mae knows more."

"She didn't even use her powers."

"So? Maybe being an outsider looking in gives her a better view."

"Because you were an outsider and you had a better view?"

Selene was taken aback. "That's harsh."

"Is it? Or is it what you're actually trying to say?"

"Everyone's worked up from the fight earlier. We can have this conversation later. Do you need water or anything?"

"You know, I'm not sure which is less probable at this point: that you're going to have free time later or that you plan to stay here with me now."

"I have no idea where any of this is coming from, Lena."

"You have no idea that you're never around? That seems fitting."

"I missed one dinner, Lena."

"One dinner this week. How many times the week before? The month before?"

"I'm around as often as I can be. You know I have responsibilities."

"I do too, but I still try to make time for us."

"We just had breakfast on the beach, I listened to the Tao thing earlier today, I'm here now, and I never miss anything that Professor Nakshatra gathers us all for. There's only so much I can do, Lena."

"Well, I'm glad you never miss anything Professor Nakshatra asks you to do. Clearly, that's most important." The bitterness was dripping from Lena's every word.

"She's my mentor Lena! I'm supposed to do what she asks of me!"

"And what about Delphine? I'm sure spending all those extra hours with her is an added bonus?"

"I do my very best not to say anything, but I don't get what your problem is with her. She's always nice and funny and doesn't do things like this."

Lena could feel her entire face getting hot with anger. "Things like this?"

"I mean, she doesn't ambush people. What you see is what you get with her. She's simple. There's not a ton of layers to uncover with her."

"I'm sure you would know. You spend more time with her than anyone else, even more than your mentor."

"I don't understand what you're mad about. Are you mad that I go to the things I'm supposed to go to with Professor Nakshatra or are you mad about the time I spend with Delphine?"

"I don't know. Neither. Both." It wasn't true. Lena knew she was mad about the time he was with Delphine.

"I can't help either of those things, Lena. That's a part of the duty I agreed to take on here, just like you agreed to take on duties within Ward A."

"My duties don't make me look like I'm cheating on my boyfriend." Lena spat out.

"You think I'm cheating on you?"

"Sometimes, yeah, I do."

"I would never do that, and with all the things you know about me, that shouldn't come into question for you."

"You say that like it means something, but if you asked me if you'd miss a family dinner at my house the day before my parents were leaving for a portal, I'd have said you'd never do that either."

"I had no choice. I had to help with things around Legacy."

"Were you with her?"

"What?"

"Were you with Delphine instead of being with me and my family?"

"Didn't that dinner fall through anyway?"

"Answer me, Selene. Were you with her?"

"Yes, Lena. I was with her. We were helping with the Nulls."

"That's all I need to know then."

"I can't believe you're acting like this."

"I'm sure you'll have someone to complain about it to later. I have to go though."

"You were just complaining that we never get time together, and you're going to leave in the middle of us being alone?"

"If this is what it looks like being together, I don't want this either."

"What do you want then, Lena?"

"I want how things were before you spent every day with Delphine."

"I can't give you the past."

"I get that, but I don't know if I want this future."

Selene sighed in frustration. "I don't know what to do."

"Welcome to my world. I really do have to go though. I'll text you tomorrow. Are you going to meet up with Tao in the morning to look into whatever this being is?"

"Lena, I—"

"You have other things you need to do. Got it. Okay. I'll see you when I see you then."

He reached out for her. "It doesn't need to be like this."

She pulled a way from his touch. "Then change it."

~*~

Delphine had been waiting outside the library for hours, brooding. *How dare they not include me! Give them time. They'll see how valuable I am sooner or later.* An angry Lena caught Delphine's eye. *Ms. Hoity-Toity looks livid. This is great! What if they got into a fight and broke up? This could be my chance!* Delphine wanted more than anything to ditch icky

Kohl and upgrade to Selene. Keeping The Bad One on the side would ensure a solid safety net, too. It was a flawless plan. She peered into the doorway. Selene was still in there with the others. He was doing that thing he did where his arm was propping him up against a wall; he always did that when he was overwhelmed. *Perfect!* She was more than ready to enter the room and offer herself up as his emotional support.

{ 7 }

Mysteries and Mayhem

Mae wasn't with Chibi either, and Solei wasn't taking it well. They had taken off before Lena made it back. It felt weird for Lena to be walking around Airess' second home without her. A large lifeless Chibi occupied a majority of the space. He had gotten bigger since the last time Lena had seen him. Lena nestled into a large mushroom in the corner of the room. Solei was combing through the fields while she waited behind. The thermos of sahlab jabbed her side from her backpack. She pulled out the drink and poured herself a cup. It was nice to feel its warm hug. It was past midnight, and Lena was feeling the toll of the day weighing upon her. She wanted an emotional rest. She figured it couldn't hurt to close her eyes for just a few minutes.

Lena's sleep quickly transported her into a sea of feathers. Soft, brilliant, white plumes glided all around her body. It felt divine.

"There you are again, child. It has been some time."

"Hello? Who's there?"

"You lie upon my feathers but cannot recognize my presence?"

"Sorry, feather identification is not my strong suit. Would you mind showing me your face?"

"My face is too powerful for a mortal like you to comprehend. I am descended from the messenger of God."

"Which god do you serve?"

"The one and only! The all-true and righteous one! I'm assigned to watch over you and your family periodically. I do not prefer your realm to my own, but I am aware of it. In fact, the last time we met was in your realm. I believe you had just avoided being hit by one of Lucifer's kin."

"Ahh. You're who I met in the rings."

"Indeed. Your wits are functioning this time around. I'm glad to see that. There was concern previously."

"You remain as charming as ever. Jibril, right?"

"That is the name my line uses, yes, but there are many names that humans associate with my lineage."

"I didn't know gods could visit humans in their dreams."

"Gods typically cannot. Though, there are a certain few who are more privy to special treatment than others."

"Is that why you're here now?"

"You are not one of those few, and I am no god. I am a messenger. I said this. Please keep up, child."

Lena had to suppress a groan. She was swiftly remembering how exasperating this angel was. "If you're a messenger, then I assume you have a message to share?"

"Ah! Now we're getting places! I do undeniably have a message to share. It is quite urgent and of most importance."

"Would you like to share it then?" Lena's patience was wearing as thin as the angel's tolerance.

"Is that what you prefer to know? You would like the message before you even know the sender?"

"Aren't you the sender?"

"No, child. I am the messenger. I've said this thrice."

"Fine. Yes, I would like to know the sender. Is it your God?"

"I fear not; though he asked me to relay this to you, it is not from the one true God. It is, however, from one of his kin. You tend to refer to her as your mother."

"My mother? Why would she send me a message?"

"A prayer, actually. As I said, some mortals are allowed special treatment. Her prayer was received by the highest of lords, and now I pass it onto you. May you feel blessed by his gracious gift."

Millie's voice began to echo all around, "To the God Almighty, I fear I have lost what I've always held most dear. I have separated from my family and am on my own journey now. My husband is shackled to a chicken. My sweet daughter knows not of either of our circumstances. She will expect us home, and no one will come. Please, lord, please do not let her be alone. I've made countless mistakes in my life, but none as large as this one. I already question my journey's worth, but if Magdalena feels, even for a moment, that she is unloved by us, I've succeeded in the biggest failure of all. There is no repentance for an act like that. Please. I do not deserve your favor. My mind is unable to hold long enough to consistently be devoted or faithful. However, I simply cannot exist in a world where I've deserted my child. I've already put them through so much. I could not survive abandoning them too . . ."

There may have been more, but Millie's sobs left any other words incomprehensible. The message concluded in the middle of her heaving sobs. The white feathers dissipated until only the mushroom Lena had laid earlier on was visible. Her eyes were red and wet. Her chest felt tight. Mixed emotions consumed Lena. She felt horrible for whatever her mom was going through, and she was scared for whatever was happening to her dad, but there was also this element of clarity to her mom's words that felt . . . off. While Lena knew without a doubt those words came straight from her mother's heart, they also felt foreign. They were so normal, intelligent even. They didn't feel like they came from a lady who haphazardly bundled socks together and forgot about it a few hours later.

Solei burst into the hut. "Are you okay? What happened? Did you find out something about Mae?"

"Solei, I'm sorry, but no."

"I heard you crying. It sounded intense."

"It was just a bad dream," Lena lied poorly.

"Last time you had a dream, they all turned out to be real."

Memories of her sweet rendezvous with Selene made her blush. "Those were the days, huh?"

"Reality isn't better than a few fleeting moments in an unstable world?"

"Not lately, it isn't."

"What happened in the dream?"

"I received a visit from a messenger of God."

"Oh? Which one?"

"Don't ask that. I did. It didn't go well."

Solei let out a small laugh but encouraged Lena to continue.

"I guess my mom sent out a prayer, and it was granted. They delivered her message to me."

"Which is good?" Solei was hopeful, but their tone indicated they knew otherwise.

"She wanted me to know that she and my dad aren't coming back, but she loves me, and she didn't want me to be alone."

"That is not the greatest news I've heard all

day."

"Better than nothing, I guess? But, yeah, not exactly what I wanted to hear."

Solei wrapped their friend up in a tight hug. "We'll get them back, little cub. I don't know how, but we will."

"We'll get Mae back too. I don't care who shows up tomorrow."

"All of us forever."

Lena squeezed harder. "All of us forever."

~*~

Mae watched the embrace between Solei and Lena. It felt a tad like spying since she could see them, but they could not see her. She was still beyond furious with Solei, but a part of her heart hurt for her partner. They had no idea what they were getting into. Mae had tried to protect them all but failed miserably as usual. It was par for the course at this point. Mae could defeat an army of enemies but had never been able to keep a friend. Solei was the exception. At least they were, so far.

"Back again so soon? And so far away from your body? I'm surprised at you, Mae. You ought to know better than that."

"I'm well aware of the health consequences. Some things are more important than my longevity, Apollo."

"Someone's spicy tonight. You're lucky I'm as proficient in medicine as I am in prophecies. You're eavesdropping too, I see. Another new trait! Color me impressed. I love a good spy session."

Mae stood in front of him and blocked his view. "They aren't yours to look at."

"Oh Mae! I can get used to this side of you! Jealous and in love. Those traits sometimes make the best art. Where has this been all your life?" Apollo was jittery with excitement. Though, to be fair, he was an easily excitable god.

"Enough. I need to know more."

"Why? I told you all I know, dearheart. You know how this game is played. This isn't our first go-round." Apollo booped her nose.

Mae growled in response. "I know what you told me earlier. It wasn't enough. They didn't want to listen to me. I can't stop them."

"We both knew that was going to be the outcome, deary. It's their destiny. You can't fight that. I could help you write a song about it or a poem? Your generation really undervalues poems. It could be just the inspiration they need before they charge off into battle!"

"Logic should be able to combat any of your nonsense."

"For being an oracle, you're rather skeptical." He judged her. "Come on, Mae. Loosen up! We've started crusades and ended generational-long feuds. We have a good time together. We should enjoy it and bask in my beauty and all I have to offer you!"

"Do we have a good time together? Or do you have a good time while I filter out what's relevant and what's tripe? My body dies more and more every time I summon you, and you float around poking and prodding me like a child's toy."

"I have always loved each and every one of my oracles. You are no exception, Mae. Although, if you really wanted to make me happy, you'd wear my laurels. I don't get why you're so against them."

"They're tacky, and I'm not doing it."

"They're gorgeous and handcrafted by a god! You're so insolent sometimes. It can be very un-pleasant for those trying to help you."

"Then give me what I want, and you can be done with me."

"I gave you everything already. I always do."

"I need more. I need to save them."

"I suppose there might be a way for me to dig a little deeper. If . . ."

"If what?"

"If you let me look into the future of you and your cutie pie in there. I can't resist such a Greek tragedy."

"You and I are both Roman, not Greek, and absolutely not. They're off limits."

"Potato, potato. As long as people love me, that's all that matters. But exactly which one of those humans is off limits? I need you to be slightly more specific. I'd hate to help and make an oopsie." Apollo gave a sly grin.

"You don't need to know."

"Come on! You don't talk to me for months,

Mae. MONTHS! And then you show up twice in one day all demanding? How is that fair to me? Shouldn't I get something in return?"

"You're. A. God. You don't need anything else."

"But it's so boringgggg. I need more, too! Give me gossip! Give me love and struggle and strife! I live for this kind of stuff."

"You're alive because you're one of the world's favorite gods. Don't exaggerate."

"Nothing is more thrilling than a doomed love story, Mae. Even Zeus can't turn his head away from those, and trust me, he is plenty good at turning his head if you know what I mean."

"Why does my relationship have to be a doomed love story? It could have a happy ending."

"HA! Good one, Mae! That's exactly the type of comedy I'm looking for!"

Mae's face was stern and serious.

"You weren't joking. Really? Maybe love does make humans dumb after all. You know how being an oracle ends."

"I can change that."

"You can't change destiny, Mae. We've covered this."

"I can if I don't use you ever again."

Apollo scoffed, "I'm offended. How could you deny me? I'm irresistible."

Mae rolled her eyes. "It's not as hard as you think."

"Says the person who called upon me twice in

one day."

"Clearly for nothing."

"What more do you want? I already told you an ogress is coming tomorrow who wants to kill you all, and there's no one in the town that's going to stop her. I don't see what else you want from me. As far as prophecies go, this one is pretty cut and dry." Apollo was starting to get testy.

Mae knew if she pushed him much further, he would start to act out. He was surprisingly tolerant as far as gods go, but his entitlement only let her push so far before a temper tantrum started. "It does seem rather straightforward."

"See? I'm good to you! You should be more grateful."

Mae gritted her teeth. "I'll consider your feedback."

"Nothing else? You're sure you don't want me to look into the future of either of those lovely humans behind you? I'm more than willing."

"Positive."

"I'll find out which one you call yours whether you tell me or not, Mae. I am a god after all."

"You remind me of that frequently."

"It's because you often seem to forget." He booped her nose again. "Ta-ta for now, dearheart." He disappeared right before her eyes, transporting her body to where they met in his wake. It was a cruel and disorienting little trick of his. He left her stumbling and bilious, directly outside the hut's window.

"MAE!" Both Solei and Lena screamed in unison as they watched the oracle collapse unconscious.

~*~

Lena's head was killing her as she turned off her alarm. It was nine a.m. Tao was due over any minute. She hoped he was dragging as much as she was. She checked her phone with high hopes of a delay. *Ugh.* He was already on his way, but he was at least bringing donuts so that was a plus. Nothing from Solei, Airess, or Selene. Not that Lena expected much from them, but she wasn't sure if the investigation of the Old Hag was going to be a duo mission or not.

Solei had their hands full with an unconscious Mae, and with the short staffing at the wards, Airess was overseeing all of Mae's care. She probably would've insisted upon that anyway, but there wasn't much choice in the matter during the middle of the night last night.

The doorbell rang. Lena quickly threw herself together and went downstairs. Solei was sitting on the couch with an iced coffee.

"Make yourself comfortable, I guess?" Lena joked.

"Thanks! I already have," Solei smirked. "I could tell you were busy, and I didn't want to rush you. There's a coffee on the counter for you and Tao. Should be your favorite flavors."

Lena glared at her friend suspiciously.

They shrugged in return. "May as well use my perks while I've got them."

"Fair enough. How's Mae doing?" Lena sat beside her friend.

"In and out, but that's honestly better than I expected, so I'll take it."

"How are you?"

"Groggy but working on it. You?"

"Same. I didn't get much sleep last night."

"Me neither."

"And Tao makes three. He just parked out front."

"If he catches you in his head, he's going to flip out."

"I'm not in his head, not yet. Merely aware of his presence."

"And the coffees?"

Solei winked. "Magic!" They wiggled their fingers in the air as sparks danced around them.

Lena groaned and went to open the door. She beat Tao by a few seconds.

"Hey . . ." He was surprised.

"Hey. Heard the car door shut. Come on in. Solei's here and has coffee."

"Great. I have donuts. It is just us three today?"

Solei interrupted, "I fear so, my dear comrade. Airess is taking care of Mae in Ward B, and Selene is otherwise occupied."

"Ward B? Is she okay?"

"She will be. She has Airess."

"Hard to ask for a higher quality caregiver than her." Tao tried to mask his hurt from the day before.

"I know what you mean." Solei patted their friend on the shoulder.

Lena wanted to lighten the mood. She was too tired for another day of drama. "So! Shall we commence the planning? Where do we start?"

"Have you not seen?" Tao asked in disbelief.

"What do you mean?" Lena asked.

"You must not have seen outside yet today. It's almost impossible to miss, little cub."

"What is?"

"Ina's property. It's three times the size it normally is," Tao informed.

Lena was in disbelief. "No way! That'd be ridiculous."

"It smells worse than ever too," Tao added.

"Being subtle is evidently not one of the Old Hag's magical skills," Solei said as they slurped their iced coffee.

"Why come in so ostentatiously? Clearly magic is at play if they've brought such a big display." Lena wanted to know the angle.

"Unmistakably so," Tao concurred.

"Why break the rules so intentionally?" Lena continued.

Tao was at a loss. "I don't know. I guess that's what we need to find out."

"Indubitably," Solei playfully agreed.

The walk over to the Old Hag's house was spent mostly talking about Airess' previous work and how it compared to the monstrosity that lay before the town now. Lena had a hard time believing the house was going to live up to its hype. Solei and Tao started complaining about the smell once they were on the correct street. Lena quickly joined her friends as the group hunched over, gagging, before pulling their shirts over their noses.

"It smells like rotting flesh!" Lena shouted.

"I don't know what it smells like, but it's wretched!" Solei responded.

"There could be a corpse flower? That's a plant that would smell like rotting flesh," Tao suggested.

Only a few steps deeper into the stench and Lena could see for herself that there was no corpse flower. A fence of pointed spikes started to line the yard. Each spike was adorned with a human skull, some of which still had pieces of their previous owners attached to it.

That was it. That did Lena in. She instantly started throwing up in the street. Solei jumped out of the way.

"Do you want a clothespin or something to plug your nose, Lena? Would that help?" Tao offered.

Lena gave him an incredulous look, pointing to the halfway decomposed skulls. "How is a clothespin going to help with that?!"

"The rows of thistle? Is that what's bothering

you?" Solei questioned.

"What are you talking about, 'thistle'? There is an entire fence with severed skulls on top of it, and you want to talk about the plants?!"

Solei and Tao gave each other a confused look.

Lena caught their glance. "You don't see it, do you?"

"Tell us what else you see, Lena," Tao implored.

Truly not wanting to look back, she forced herself to anyway. "I see the source of that god-forsaken smell. Past that are tons of trees. Maybe pine trees? They're so dense it's like they form a wall blocking me from seeing anything behind them. Above all that, there are some birds. They look black and kind of big, but not otherworldly."

"We see the black birds too, little cub."

Tao closed his eyes to listen. "They sound like geese. Their presence is a little out of place but nothing menacing."

Deflated, Lena acknowledged, "I don't think we're going to get any more information from this side of that fence."

"I think that's probably right. Are you going to be okay? Do you need to turn back?" Tao asked, concerned. His offer was sincere.

"No, and also, no." Lena knew things were not going to get better once they entered that forest. "Let's go before I change my mind."

Resigned, the two friends followed behind

Lena. The scene appeared nothing like Lena described. They had been traveling for quite some time before they even saw their first pine tree.

"Wait. Stop!" Lena crouched down, and her friends mimicked her movement. "What do you guys see over there?"

"A pine tree?" Solei answered.

"It's rather large, but once again, still within the realm of reason," Tao deduced.

"I see an eye."

Worried, Solei commented, "Attached to a body like it should be, or no?"

"No, no. Not a real eye. I think it's a house? But the window is so clearly an eye. It even blinks with its shutters. It's staring directly at us."

"To be clear, you're seeing a house, and it has one window, and that window is functioning as an eye?" Tao clarified.

"No. I'm seeing part of a house, and that sliver of the house has a window that's functioning as an eye."

"Understood. And where is the house located within the forest?" Tao continued.

"It's not."

"What do you mean?" Solei was struggling to follow.

"It's not within the forest, I mean not really. It's even with the forest's canopy. It's probably thirty feet off the ground? I don't know, but it's nowhere near ground level. We should get closer."

"Lena, we should study this more before you approach it."

"I want to see what's holding it up. Stay back."

"I highly advise—" He watched Lena ignore his advice and advance in on the tree.

As soon as Lena started to move, the house rotated 180 degrees, turning its back to her. After another one of Lena's steps, it ran. Lena turned, dumbfounded, towards Solei and Tao.

Solei was the first to speak. "Umm, Lena. I don't see the pine tree anymore."

"Me neither. What happened?"

Lena thought about how to describe what happened in a way that made sense. "The house turned its back on me, and then it ran away . . . the house ran away . . ."

"Tao, how can a house run away?"

"I . . . I don't know."

"Do we head back then?" Lena suggested.

"I don't think we have a choice. I have no idea what we're up against. I feel like I always know what we're up against." Tao was irresolute.

"Hopefully, we can figure it out quickly then. Time to head back to Legacy, friends." Solei took the lead as they guided the group back to safety.

"To Legacy," Lena said supportively.

~*~

Tao had started to feel funny on the group's walk back; he was certain he was going to fall into a vision before he got to Legacy's main doors. He took a minute to rest while Lena held him upright.

"I'll get Airess," Solei asserted.

Barely coherent, Tao pleaded in protest.

Lena nodded in agreement from behind him, and Solei sprinted into the school.

"I b k ynow." Tao couldn't even open his eyes as he spoke.

"Maybe talking isn't the best choice at the moment. Staying conscious is enough. Solei will be back soon." *I hope.*

"Appns al he tim."

"Shh. I've got you. This time you don't have to do it alone." Lena could feel Tao sink into her more. *Solei, are you close? He's not in a good place. We'll lose him soon.*

"Here." Solei was running at top speed. "Airess had this ready to go. She didn't even have to make it."

"Bless that beautiful bubblegum healer." Lena grabbed the green vial from Solei. "Okay friend, say ahh."

Tao swallowed the liquid with ease. The fog within his brain started to subside. He felt peaceful. "Wht is hiss?"

No one on these steps was going to be able to answer that. "Something from Airess," Lena dismissed.

"Is good." Tao's eyes remained closed, but at least he was smiling now.

"How's Mae?" Lena asked.

"No longer in Ward B, so that's good."

"Wow. She's out already? Back to your dorm?"

"No. Airess and I didn't talk much, but when I glanced over to Mae's bed, Airess said, 'Chibi.'"

"That makes sense too. They'll take good care of her."

"They're probably her preferred company at the moment anyway."

"You want to go check on her?"

"I know I'm needed here. I'll stay."

"Please, don't. We're fine. He'll be back to normal soon."

"M gud now."

Both friends ignored Tao's mumbling.

Promise to let me know if things get worse?

I promise, but I trust Airess. We'll be good. Go check on your sweetheart. That's where I'd want to be if I were in your shoes.

Thank you for understanding, Lena.

Longing to be by someone I love is not a hard stretch for me.

I'll be in touch soon.

I hope not. Go talk things out with her. Figure out how to make it better.

Will do. I'll make it work.

Lena opened her phone as she waited for Tao to become cognizant again. There were no notifications to scroll through. She debated texting Selene and letting him know everything that happened this morning. She wondered how much he would care about it all. She opened the app to check when he was last on. He was currently online. She wasn't sure what she expected, but she didn't expect that. If he was free, why hadn't he messaged her? Who was he messaging instead? Her mind rapidly filled in possible answers. She knew what she wanted to do. She also knew there was no outcome from her next action that would make her feel better. She decided to do it anyway. Against her better judgment, Lena opened up a chat with Delphine. She had to be careful not to hit anything by accident. She waited for the information to populate. As expected, Delphine was online too. Lena closed her phone.

She looked down at Tao. He was making a noise that sounded an awful lot like snoring. She sat on the steps for a long while waiting for him to wake up. She watched students come and go without a second thought as to why she was sitting on the stairs with a boy on her side that wasn't her boyfriend.

A loud screech sounded behind the school. Lena heard a few screams, but no one came running out of the building.

Solei didn't miss a beat. *Did you hear that?*

Yeah, it sounded like it was behind me. Could you tell where it came from?

It was pretty close. My guess is in the fields.

Want me to go check it out?

Are you still with Tao?

I can figure that out.

Okay. Keep me posted.

Will do.

Lena jostled Tao. "Hey bud, we're going to need to walk a little. Can you do that?"

"Mk. Where we goin?"

Lena knew Chromwell's office wasn't too far off from the entryway if she took the shortcuts. "To the headmistress's chambers."

"She not there no more."

"I know; that's why we're going to put you there."

"Okie dokie smokie." And he lifted up his arm pointing in the general direction of where they were headed.

Walking with Tao was slow but not impossible. She laid him down on one of the sofas in the expansive room. He insisted he didn't need to lie down, but Lena thought it was the safer choice than sitting him up. Once she was sure he was safe, she went off to investigate the fields.

By her account, she estimated it was mid-afternoon, but the sky in the fields was closer to dusk. Lena listened for clues around her but couldn't pick up anything. She scoured the rows of crops Airess had planted. She knew this area like the back of her hand. She had been here countless times over the past few months. When she got to the edge of the last row, close to the muddy pit where the livestock tended to dwell, she could hear familiar laughter. She knew instantly it was the Beboy twins. She hadn't seen them in almost a year, but they left a lasting impression. They were hooting and' hollering after something. At one point, Lena wasn't sure if they were yelling out of anger or joy.

Wanting to enhance her hearing, Lena cautiously approached the source of the noise. The livestock fields were not the same as Airess' crops. There wasn't much other than mud and manure for coverage or concealment. Unfortunately, Lena imagined that was intentional. This ground was prime for catching something that got away from you. Lena wished she had her mother's cloak instead of her own shield.

They weren't hard to miss. Two large disgusting ghouls stood at the top of a small hill. A single tree was their only shelter. They spoke in a language that was hard to understand. Not because the language was complex, but because their articulation was atrocious. Lena concentrated on their chant.

"One little mouse, two wild dogs, three hungry bellies to get their fill of."

That doesn't even make sense.

A cackle erupted from the tree. It sounded very similar to the screech Lena heard earlier. "Boys, I think we have another guest. It would be rude not to invite them to the house." The tree pointed directly at Lena.

That's not a tree, that's a gigantic ogre.

The twins laughed maniacally and stalked toward Lena. A small shape rose from the mud.

"NO! LENA! RUN!" *OMG! That's Airess!* She was in serious trouble, and it looked like Lena was now, too.

Lena knew she should run away as fast as humanly possible. She should get Solei and Mae and Chibi. She could come back later and save Airess. That's what Airess would want. Two of them being on the ground in the mud wasn't going to solve anything. Lena did what she knew she had to do. *HELP! EMERGENCY! AIRESS! BEBOY TWINS! GIANT OGRE! GET CHIBI!* Lena yelled this on repeat in her head to Solei. Then, she braced herself for sprinting in the muddy field, anticipating the way the ground would move below her. She channeled every instinct she learned on the training field all those months ago, and she charged straight towards both twins with no intention of stopping.

{ 8 }

Prisoners and Pacts

"You're going in the wrong direction, Lena!" Airess barked from the ground. "Turn around!"

Lena's eyes were locked on the Beboy twin closest to her. There was no turning back now. She was set to crash into the oversized brute head-on. Her shoulder was dropped, her arm braced, her head tucked. Three. Two. One. Lena thrust her wrist towards the ground, creating a barrier around her. Just as she'd hoped, the first twin slid over the top of her. The second one tried to stop, but his momentum was too strong. He was set to fall on top of her shield. It couldn't have been more perfect. She readied a punch and blasted him straight in the face with her iridescent dome. He didn't go far, but Lena could tell he felt the hit. She dropped her protection and rushed over to her friend.

"Airess!"

"Lena!"

"What's going on?"

"You need to go! I need to do this!"

"Stop that. I can get us out of here!" Lena could hear the grunts of the twins preparing for their next round.

The towering ogre that Lena previously thought was a tree leaned forward. They were of female nature and undeniably resembled the rumors of the Old Hag. Her features were horrid and cut deeply into her green skin. She was covered in wrinkles, warts, and moss. She smelled of death; dust escaped her mouth when she spoke. Her nose was long, pointed, and crooked. Lena had to tilt away from the face's protruding features to keep them from touching her while the ogress addressed them. "Why such haste, my pretties? There's always room for more at dinner." The hag smiled, exposing her sharp jagged iron teeth.

Lena had no doubts about what the intended meal was supposed to be. She whispered into Airess' ear, "When I say go, we run."

Airess didn't whisper back. "You run. I need to handle this. I know who she is and what she wants."

"Why didn't you tell us that yesterday?!"

"There's no time, you need to go now."

A colossal withered hand with sharp nails and stained red tips reached out for the two girls on the ground. Lena instinctively enacted her shield again. The ogress crowed with delight. "All the easier to grasp you with, dearies." She scooped them up in one hand and started carrying them back towards the center of Astoria.

"No!" Lena threw herself against the shield, but it didn't budge. They were firmly secured by the grasp of the ogress. "I could drop my shield, and we could lunge to the side. What do you think?"

"I think you should've listened and left."

"We're past that now so how about something else? Perhaps a plan that focuses on us getting out of here?!"

"It's no use, Lena. This is the plan."

"The plan is to be captured?! That's an awful plan, Airess! I'm quite confident she wants to eat us!"

"Of course she does. She's Baba Yaga."

"You're on a first-name basis with her?! I missed the moment you two became best friends. Where was this information yesterday, Airess?"

"I didn't know it yesterday. If I did, I'd obviously have said something. I knew it today though. As soon as those brutes came over and started teasing me that their grandma wanted to meet me, it all clicked."

"Their grandma?" Baba did mean grandma in most Slavic languages, but Lena knew the Beboy twins were from another culture entirely. "I don't see how they connect."

"I don't think they were being literal. I imagine they thought they were being clever with their setup, but what they said reminded me of something Kohl warned me about a long time ago. It was probably a few years ago now, but there was this one time I was working late in the fields experimenting on a new crop, and he came over to take a peek at my new creation. I had hoped it was the start of a solution for Kohl, ironically. He caught onto my intention too quickly, though, and we started to fight. The argument wasn't too surprising; those occurred fairly often between us. But the twins heard us yelling and started making their way over from the livestock farm. They thrive on other people's strife and weaknesses. When they approached us, they backed us up against the tree line and were talking about how they hadn't eaten a good meal since their grandmother came and how they were starving. Kohl said they could take him if they left me, but they used that opportunity to separate us. The one pinned me up against a tree. I tried to use my powers, but I was too in my head and wasn't able to get anything to grow. The twins made a slew of crude and inappropriate comments once they pinned me down. I'd never felt so threatened. Eventually, Kohl couldn't take it anymore. He used his powers, which, as you well know, he never did willingly. It was incredible. He is something else entirely when he goes all in. The twins scattered to the winds immediately. I went from bracing myself for certain abuse to marveling at Kohl in the blink of an eye. He gets rather extreme when he's worked up. From then on, anytime he'd lose out to his powers, it always made me feel like he could protect me from anything. I liked feeling invincible with him by my side." Airess held those memories close for a moment.

"Anyway, that first night, we didn't know what the twins were, at least I didn't. We knew even less about who their grandma was, but Kohl said the story reminded him of someone from his culture called Baba Yaga. He told me Baba Yaga was an evil witch whose primary objective was to feast on little children. I, of course, couldn't help but react over how despicable that was. I suppose I got a little self-righteous because, during a later fight, he brought it up again. He said that it was funny how I hated the twins for being their natural selves, but I admired the person who single-handedly invites child killers onto school grounds. I told myself he was overstating things and lashing out for dramatic effect, but it stuck with me. I know almost all of Kohl's coping mechanisms, most of them not being ideal, but lying isn't one of his go-tos. He's always felt his truth is worse than any lie someone could make up about him." Airess was solemn in her delivery. "When the twins came up to me today saying their grandma was in town and they wanted me to meet her, I knew exactly who they were referring to. I don't know what the end result will be, but I knew I stood the best chance to handle this out of everyone else in the group."

"Why you? Why couldn't it be all of us?"

"Because what if things go bad? You guys shouldn't have to deal with that."

"Umm … hello?! Things always go bad, Airess. Today isn't the day to go solo. It's all of us or none of us. I promised Solei no one would be left behind, and I meant it. We need to get out of here."

"We can't jump. It's too far down, and even if I grew something to break our fall, she would notice. She would probably notice the second the shield drops."

Lena peered over the edge of the warty hand. Airess was right that it would be quite a fall.

"We're here, my pretties." The ogress raised her palm to her face. "Til this time, only the pink girl has agreed to dinner. Do you also accept, little girl?"

"Why would I do that?"

"Because them's the rules. Baba can only have friends over if you accept the invitation."

"Rules set by whom?"

"Not for you to know. Do you accept my dinner invitation or not? I'm not known for my patience."

Lena whispered to Airess, "You're going no matter what?"

The healer nodded.

"Fine," Lena called out to the Old Hag. "I accept on one condition."

"I didn't know you were in a position to make deals, little one."

"Airess is tiny. You won't feel full on her alone. I'm not much bigger. Let me bring over more like us."

The witch's smile sprouted on her face again. Her teeth varied from needle-like pins to serrated blades the size of a stone pillar.

~*~

Solei was rummaging through Kasim's shed as

hastily as they could. What do you grab when you have no idea what you're up against? They had tried to convince Mae and Chibi to join them. Neither of them budged. Airess needed help, Lena too. Solei couldn't stand by and wait. They needed to act in the moment. The panic in Lena's thoughts left them feeling scared and desperate. Being alone in the workshop wasn't helping. This was all on them, and they had no idea how they were going to handle this all by themselves. They threw the five best weapons into their bag and thought of one more that could potentially be the most useful of all: Tao.

Tao, it's Solei, please answer. Solei's hands were shaking while they waited. *Tao, I'm begging. I know this isn't the most ideal way to show you this connection I have with you, but I don't know what else to do. Lena and Airess are in trouble. I need you, we all do. Please respond.*

Solei pictured Tao as he was the last time they saw him—raw, vulnerable, and happy. That's how they felt when they were in Rome with Mae. Their heart hurt at the thought of giving that up, both for themselves and for Tao.

I'll come find you. Where are you? With the silence fueling their anxiety, they dug even deeper into the connection. They closed their eyes to see through Tao's. He was still in Ward B. Nurses were surrounding him, concerned. Alarm, that maybe he was in just as much danger as the girls, set in. Solei had to push; Solei had to hear what was going on.

"I can tell you're upset, but yelling at me isn't going to fix anything. You need more rest, sir."

"I DON'T NEED REST! I NEED TO HELP MY FRIENDS! WHERE ARE THEY? WHERE IS SOLEI!"

Oh crap. Tao! Speak to me through your thoughts! I'm not there!

Solei watched as his eyes shifted positions.

He had lain back down in bed.

"Sir, are you okay? You're turning pale."

He looked to the nursing assistant, and Solei could tell he wasn't saying a word.

Tell them you're fine or you're going to scare them even more than you already have.

Nothing.

Tao. Tell them you're fine then respond to me in your thoughts. I can hear you best that way.

He kept staring at the fidgeting assistant. When the aide picked up their phone to call for help, he apologized and informed them that he didn't know what came over him, but he would be all right now. He was relieved when she left immediately after. *That information would have been useful a few minutes ago, Solei. Any time, actually, before sending your hysteria of our friends being in dire straits, would have been ideal.*

I never expected you to start randomly yelling for me. I've only ever done this with Lena before, and we've never had this problem.

While I love you telling me I'm more irrational than Lena Basil, maybe instead, you just get me out of this situation, and tell me where I'm supposed to be.

You need to convince the staff you're healthy enough to leave. I'm at Lena's house now then—

Screams filled Tao's and Solei's ears.

Tao ran to the window to survey the scene. A giant hideous ogress stomped by. That had to be the Old Hag. The floor beneath him shook harder and harder as she neared. The hag's strides were long and rapid. She was too tall to make out her full appearance. Her shoes were black and pointed. Her legs were withered and green with moss-like patches. Tao tried to get a more advantageous view of the ogress as she left. He was able to make out that her clothes were dark green and tattered, some strands looked similar to tree branches the way the fabric hung on her, and that the hand closest to Tao was cupped as if she was holding something. From certain angles, he could see a blue glow escaping through the hag's gnarly fingers.

I know that light. That's Lena's shield!

The Old Hag has them then. We have to follow her.

I'm by Kasim's shed. I'll track the hag head-on. I can guide you to where I'm at.

Sounds like a plan. They're distracted here. I'll get my stuff and go.

Solei kept the connection partially going in their mind but redirected most of their attention to give Tao space. He needed it. Telepathy was clearly not going to be a strength of his. Solei had tracked the hag to the edge of Ina's house when Tao started to call for them.

Solei! Are you here? Can you hear me? Sollllllllleiiiiiiiiiiii—

Yes, yes. I'm right here. What do you need?

I need you to establish a connection again.

What do you mean?

There's something here you need to see, and you have about fifteen seconds before it's out of my sight.

Irritated, Solei paused their pursuit and focused their energy so they could see through Tao's eyes again. It was Chibi, a tremendously large Chibi. They were running behind Ward B flailing their arms in the air. It had something around its head too, but the image was difficult to discern. From a distance, Solei thought it might be a strange hat.

It's a python.

What?

The thing you think is a hat. It's not a hat. It's a python.

Chibi did not find a python in the fields. Those types of snakes don't live around here. It's too cold. They like warmer weather and trees.

I don't think all of that is true unless it is a green tree python. Most pythons actually prefer hollows or abandoned mammal burrows. But, yes, the point about their climate is accurate. Astoria is not known for its subtropical weather.

Annoyed, Solei responded, *I don't see why*

correcting me is relevant, but either way, it makes no sense for Chibi to have a python.

I have a few ideas. I'm going to follow Chibi's tracks. I think they'll lead me to where we want to go. Do you want to go ahead or wait for us?

I'll go ahead; I'm already at Ina's. Keep me posted?

Yeah, I'll try. You too?

On it. Over and out.

Solei switched from the frequency of Tao's thoughts to Lena's. The transition made them feel a little dizzy but nothing they couldn't handle. Lena's mind actually felt like a bit of a reprieve. It was familiar and less frantic than Tao's.

I don't know if you can hear me or not, but Tao and I are on our way. We're coming for you. I'll be there soon, Lena.

~*~

Lena had just made a deal with the devil or perhaps, a goddess even worse.

"This is a horrible plan, Lena."

"Thanks for your vote of confidence, Airess. It means the world." Lena's snark was transparent.

"There are so many reasons why everything about your plan is wrong. First, you cannot convince Professor Nakshtra to let this horrible ogress into the school. Second, why do you think you could even convince Professor Nakshatra to do this in the first place? Everything about this is flawed."

Lena eyed her friend, pointed to the Old Hag,

and then Lena's own ear. She desperately wanted to imply that the ogress could hear her, so she couldn't speak out her actual plans. Airess remained ignorant though. The healer's attention was diligently dedicated to telling Lena all the ways she was going to fail. This had been going on since the ogress agreed to Lena's pitch, and the journey to Baba Yaga's house had begun. Part of Lena's idea was to ensure Airess would be safe in the Old Hag's home herself before leaving.

"There's nothing else I can tell you, Airess. Baba Yaga and I agreed to it. The deal is done."

"Can you at least make sure you tell Delphine while you're there?"

Lena could feel her face contort at the mermaid's name. "Why? She's a Null. She can't do anything."

"You're above that, Lena. Don't be so rude. She may not have all her powers, but she's talented. You'd be able to see that if you got to know her. Selene gets it."

Lena gave her friend a serious "Did you just say that?" glare.

"I'm not implying anything, I swear. Delphine just gets left out so often, and she could be a good addition to the group. She's brave and strong, and if she ever gets her siren powers back, we'll all be a more powerful team because of it. You have to be able to see that."

"I know you two are close, but honestly, I don't

feel like that girl is anything but trouble."

Airess put her hand on Lena's. "I don't like admitting something bad can happen to me, but if it does, Delphine has been there when I've been completely depleted. I trust her to know what to do and to be able to help me if things go poorly. You have Selene. Solei has Mae. I'm picking Delphine."

"Those relationships are not all the same thing. Not by a long shot."

"She supports me more than Kohl ever did."

Lena wasn't sure if she wanted to say the sentence forming in her mouth, but she couldn't ignore the elephant in the room. "You could have Tao, you know. You want someone who is willing to take care of you and show up? Pick someone who's already been doing it. He's been at your beck and call well before I even came to Astoria."

"Tao's different though, I don't want something like that."

"Different how?"

"He's so serious all the time. There's no wiggle room with him."

"I barely understand what that means, but he jokes around the same as the rest of us. He's forever giving Solei grief."

"I don't mean how his personality is. I mean, I guess I kind of do but not like that. You get what I'm saying, right?"

Lena shook her head. "I absolutely do not know."

"I don't want to say it out loud, Lena!"

Lena's face was blank. She was totally lost. What was so wrong with Tao?

"Tao isn't like Kohl," Airess said sheepishly.

That was beyond obvious.

"Tao doesn't have struggles like Kohl. Tao isn't unstable like Kohl. I'm used to relationships where if someone says something to me, I get to choose whether I believe that it's real or get to convince myself it was fake. Either way, I don't have to deal with it unless I want to. Tao isn't going to be like that. Every single word Tao says to me is going to be real, and I'm going to be responsible for how I respond to every real word. That's a lot of pressure, Lena. It's a big ask."

"Is it? I've been upset and angry for months because I can't remember the last time my boyfriend was in the same world as me for an entire twenty-four-hour period, and it crushes me. Every day is an almost unbearable amount of pain. The only thing I want in this world is to be in his arms and know that neither of us wants to be doing anything else or to be with anyone else. I think the idea of never doubting the words or acts of someone you care about sounds extremely awesome. It'd be nice to have that kind of stability with all the weird stuff that goes on around here."

"I don't want another responsibility . . ."

"Is that all he would be to you? You guys have been friends for years."

"Friends are easy. Friends don't hold you accountable."

Lena let out a laugh. "Do you not remember last year? I absolutely held you accountable for the beliefs you had about Selene."

"That's exactly my point. That wasn't our best moment together. We fought for months."

"But we worked it out."

"Because I turned into a plant and lost all my powers."

"You truly expect me to believe that you accepted Diablo as Selene because you lost all your powers? The Airess I knew back then would have figured out a way to blame him for that happening before they ever would've forgiven him over it. Don't try to kid me or yourself. That wasn't the reason, and we both know it."

"I guess, maybe, it also had to do with him risking his life for us."

"Just a little bit though, huh?"

"Yeah," Airess smiled, "just a little bit."

"I can't speak for you, but in my opinion, if you can get over the Diablo issues we had, you can surely figure things out with Tao. If you don't have feelings for him, then it is what it is, but don't fall into the 'I only like bad boys' trope. You deserve more than fulfilling a stereotype."

"I love saving a damsel in distress, isn't that what you told me?"

"Past Airess wasn't the only one who had

some growing to do. I'd like to think that we're both more evolved now than we were last year and that we have been lucky enough to grow in the same direction."

"I'm glad I have you, Lena."

"I'm glad I have you too. I'm going to fix all this for us. Just trust me, and we'll be okay."

"I'm trusting you with my life, just like last time. I don't seem to get much of a choice around you."

"Hopefully things won't get to that point this time. I have a plan."

Airess nodded, acknowledging Lena's words, and began to stare off into the distance. Lena knew her friend hated feeling helpless and wondered if that was stealing her thoughts, or if it was Tao or Kohl rendering her speechless.

Lena tried to make herself comfy and searched what she could on Baba Yaga on her phone. She knew it was futile, and her signal was spotty, but she needed to do something. The internet rarely knew what a god or deity was actually like. Her head ached from time to time, and she knew she needed a clear mind going into the next stage of the plan. Once they arrived at the Old Hag's hut, it was agreed that Airess would be imprisoned there and Lena would have two hours to convince Professor Nakshatra to let the ogress come into Legacy Academy and invite the students over for dinner. During that time, Airess would be completely safe, albeit trapped. However, if

Lena did not get the appropriate consent within those hours, then Airess would be eaten. Lena was certain she wasn't going to let that happen.

She thought about texting Selene. She had actually been thinking about it since the second she got scooped up into the hag's hand. What would she say though? Every text she thought of sounded pathetic or needy. Even if Lena was currently both of those things, she wasn't going to write it down as proof. She thought about texting Tao too, but he was rather out of it the last time she saw him. He had himself to worry about. She wished Solei would respond to the mental cry for help Lena had sent earlier. Solei always seemed to know what to do.

The trees grew denser around them. They had to be getting close to the ogress' home. Luckily, no morbid smell had overcome Lena this time. The large branches of the pine trees felt like fingers reaching out to touch the girls. The branches looked normal and innocent enough, but the duo avoided them instinctually anyway. As expected, the house that stared at Lena when she had been in the forest earlier was their destination. It did, in fact, have two windows for eyes and shutters to close them when necessary. The door was large and almost familiar. It was withered like the hag herself and had black roots stretching out into the panels of the house. The mouthlike doorway opened, and Baba Yaga pushed the teens inside her dwelling. The hut heaved as if it were breathing. For a moment, Lena and Airess were alone.

Things on the inside were closer to normal than Lena anticipated. The house was clean and tidy. There was a large cauldron in the middle of the room, notably large enough to fit a few adults, let alone small children. The visual was off-putting, to say the least, but the rest of the cabin felt rather ordinary. The walls looked like your standard cabin. The windows had old-timey embroidered curtains, and the cabinets were composed of basic wood. Herbs were tied in bundles, their jars standing on the countertop next to a mortar and pestle. There was a small twin-sized bed with cleaning supplies in one corner and a wood-burning stove in another. While Lena analyzed their surroundings, a normal-sized Baba Yaga walked through the entryway of her house.

The Old Hag's features were even pointier and sharper in her smaller form. She was fierce looking and terrifying. Lena could feel the fear rising within her. She couldn't imagine how Airess was feeling right now knowing she'd be, at best, trapped with this monster for two hours alone.

"Which one of you plans to affirm the pact with Baba Yaga?"

Lena stepped forward. "I made the pact."

Baba Yaga closed in on Lena and sniffed her. Her nose was the size of a hand. It took up a third of the hag's face. "Your bones are not my favorite, but Babas has taken in your kin before. If I can accept the tougher meat in your lineage for dinner, I will accept yours as well."

"What do you mean you accepted my kin for dinner? Who have you met in my family?"

"Is that the information you seek? Baba Yaga thought you wanted freedom. Which one is it, my pretty? There are different prices for different favors."

"I want both."

The ogress snarled at Lena. Iron teeth jutted from the hag's mouth. "Too greedy! Don't waste Babas' time! I shall eat you both and save myself the trouble!"

Airess stepped in, with her poise, and slightly condescending, demeanor. "Forgive her, grandmother. She struggles sometimes. We, of course, would be grateful for all the help you can give us, but more importantly, what can we give you?"

Lena's face was incredulous, and Airess' face very much told her to shut up.

"Baba Yaga does like gifts and has three hungry stomachs to feed after so much travel."

"Three is, indeed, a lot of stomachs to feed . . ." Airess' tone was shaky.

Lena cut in. "I will solve that for you. I will feed all three of your bellies if you allow me to go to Legacy Academy to talk to the one in charge."

"How will you feed Babas? The only way students can come here is by their own free will. Babas can only invite guests over, never compel guests to come."

"Then I will get them to come here willingly."

"You propose now that you will go to the school and get the one in charge to allow you to bring students here? Enough to feed three of Baba Yaga's bellies?"

Lena answered without acknowledging Airess, "Yes."

"What does this cost Babas?"

"If I bring enough students to this house, you let my companion go."

"One life for many others sounds like a good deal to Baba Yaga. Your friend is very important to you, yes?"

"My friends and my family are what I cherish most."

The Old Hag studied Lena. "There is truth there." There was another long pause. "Babas has decided. You will be free to go to your school, talk to the one who is in charge, and gather other guests for dinner. If you bring enough of the others back to end my hunger, then your friend can find freedom too. If not, I will come to collect you myself and finish you both."

"One hour?! That's not fair! Before you said I had two!"

"That was then, this is now. Do you accept or reject this new pact?"

Lena didn't feel like she had a choice in the matter. She needed to leave. She needed to go get help. "I accept," she spoke confidently and sternly.

"You have a good heart like your mother, but

there are still strains of deceit like your father. You'd have been luckier to only have her genes."

"Don't talk poorly about my father. We made our deal, and you were clear that my family stayed out of our pact."

"Ah, yes! You listen like your mother too! What you say is true. Baba Yaga did say that. I accept this. I like that in you. If you do well on our first pact, maybe Babas will bend the rules and allow a second."

"You'd tell me about my family after all?"

"That all depends on you and your actions, my pretty. Now go. There's no time to waste. Your hour starts now." And with that, the Old Hag shoved Lena out the door, slamming it shut behind her.

Lena fell onto a bed of pine needles. The fall was softened, but the needles were sharp and sticky. She gazed up into the house. It blinked its shutters back down at her, turned its back, and with one swift movement, the house used one of its strong chicken legs it stood upon to forcefully kick a stunned Lena wholly off of Ina's property.

Lena screamed as she flew straight into Chibi, knocking them both into a thin tree. It collapsed behind them. A few of Chibi's clay blocks flew off to the sides. "OMG! "Chibi! Are you all right?!" Lena checked over their body for any extra damage.

They shook their head no.

"Stay right here; let me get your other parts. I'll be right back!" Lena sprinted off to find the one leg block she knew of. When she came back, Solei was there.

"Little cub!" they yelled. "I saw you fly over my head!"

"Solei!" Lena sat the block down by Chibi and embraced her friend in a tight hug. Tears instantly started falling. "Solei, things are so bad—"

"You can say that again. This arm almost knocked my head clear off!" It was Tao. He was coming up from a side path and knelt next to the golem. He attempted to assemble their two missing pieces.

"Tao? You're okay?"

"I almost got impaled by Chibi's arm but other than that, yeah. Why?"

"The last time I saw you, you weren't doing so great." The sadness in Lena's voice was building.

"Nothing I haven't dealt with before. Your situation, on the other hand, doesn't seem to fit that mold for any of us. I saw the Old Hag walk past Ward B. She was disgusting."

"She's so much more than that, too. I guess her name is Baba Yaga, and she's horrible! She has Airess, and did something with my parents, and now I'm stuck trying to find more kids for her to eat! You have to help me! We can't let her do this!" Lena was hysterical.

"Okay, okay." Solei tightened the hug. "Is Airess safe currently?"

Lena nodded her head buried deep in Solei's chest.

"Are the Beboy twins still a threat?"

Lena shook her head no and mumbled something that was barely audible. The noise vaguely sounded like "Fields."

"Then let's head to Legacy. It sounds like you have to go there anyway, but perhaps we can find something along the way to help us, too."

Lena let out another barely audible mumble. This one sounded like "Delphine."

"Lena, I can't hear you. That sounded like 'Delphine,' and I know that couldn't have been your answer to Solei," Tao remarked.

Lena pulled away, assuring Solei that she'd be fine, "It is, unfortunately. Airess asked me to find Delphine. So that's what I'm going to do."

Solei and Tao were baffled. That was the last thing they expected to hear from Lena.

"Are you sure?" Solei clarified.

"I'll find Delphine; you guys talk to Professor Nakshatra. I know people were against it yesterday, but we have no choice. We need her. If we can get Nurse Galen too, all the better. Ideally, they can help with Chibi." Lena gestured to the standing, yet stumbling, golem.

No one had room to disagree.

"We stay together for now though, and you tell us everything on the way," Solei asserted.

"Also, any chance you saw a python when you crashed into Chibi?" Tao asked nonchalantly.

{ 9 }

Moles and Mermaids

Lena wasn't sure where to find Delphine. Her mind kept telling her Selene's room, but she was convincing herself that those were only toxic thoughts and not actually insightful information. She checked the fountain she had first met Delphine in, a few of the classrooms she knew Delphine had classes in, and the common areas of the academy, all to no avail. Lena's last ditch effort, before reaching out to Selene and asking where the mermaid was, was to check Ward A's logs. Lena was fairly certain Delphine was assigned a room there. It took using a password that didn't belong to her, but Lena was able to figure it out. She also made a mental note to thank Airess later for having her memorize Nurse Galen's login information during her first week.

No one seemed to be on duty at the desk which left Lena's stomach feeling uneasy. There was always someone scheduled here. She grabbed the skeleton key from beside the door with ease. Despite the desk's eerie emptiness, Lena was still concerned about returning the key before anyone noticed it was missing. That bothered her more than breaking into the mermaid's personal space. After she had the key in her hand, she headed straight towards Delphine's room, eager to be done and return back.

Ward A was split into different sections. They tended to be organized in a logical fashion, except when they weren't, and the ward did whatever it wanted to do because that's how anything related to gods and deities seemed to go. Delphine's room was one hallway over from the Aglaope portal Lena and Airess had gone through the year before. Lena didn't like going past that portal; it had been a bad experience overall. That realm did hold plenty of first memories though. It was Lena's first portal, Lena's first encounter with a supreme being, Lena's first time feeling Selene's arms around her. Lost in thought, Lena missed the wet siren escaping out of the same door Lena was reminiscing over. Per the usual, they crashed head-first.

"Ow! Earth to Basil! Didn't you see me?"

"Ouch! No. Why would I see you coming through a portal?" Lena rubbed her head and scanned the area to make sure she was where she thought she was. "What are you doing here?"

"In Ward A? I live and work here, Lena."

"Obviously, I know that. I meant in this realm in particular."

"That's a great question! That's my home! Want to come see?" Delphine began opening the door.

"What are you doing, fish brain! You'll let the monster out!" Lena used Delphine's hand to close the door. "That's not where you live! That's Aglaope's lair!"

Delphine wasn't able to hide her surprise. She didn't expect Lena to know that. "Silly me! Must have gotten that wrong again! Whatcha doing around here anyway? It's not often you visit the Greek Seas of Ward A."

Skeptically, Lena replied, "I was going to your room, actually. Airess wanted me to come find you for her."

"You were coming to my dorm with that skeleton key? All in the name of Airess? I know a Hera-like scheme when I hear one, Lena."

"Airess is in trouble, and she asked me to come find you to help her. It's as simple as that. It's no secret that this isn't my first choice."

"And why is that? I'm an absolute joy. I never understood why you don't like me. I even helped you the first time I saw you in Ward B!"

"You did. I appreciated that. Thank you."

"Not going to answer why you don't like me, huh?"

"Do you want to answer why you were in Aglaope's portal?"

"I already did; that's my home, Lena."

"Again, that's not the realm you're assigned to."

"I don't care what the paperwork says. Aglaopheme is one of the original sirens. It wouldn't surprise me if she was even there when Hera had her stupid muses pluck out our feathers and cast us into the water off of Mount Olympus. If she would just wake up, she could be the key to everything!"

"'To everything?' What is 'everything?'"

"You wouldn't even know. You think you know so much, Lena Basil, and you don't know anything!"

"As much as I've enjoyed this conversation, I'd like to get back to my main point. Airess needs your help. Do you need to change, or anything, before I fill you in on what's going on?" Lena waved her hand to the puddles of water pooling around Delphine's dripping outfit.

"I don't need to change at all," the siren said indignantly.

"Fine. Shall we go then?"

"You can tell me what you need to here."

"No. I can't. You need to come with me, so we can go to Airess. I explained that."

"I'm not going to Airess, but you can tell me what's going on."

"Why would I give you any important information if you're not even going to help?"

"There you go! Gatekeeping information as always! You never include me even when Airess directly asks you to!"

"I'm the one trying to get you to go to her! You're the one being exceedingly difficult!"

"I have more important things to do than go be someone's sidekick, especially by the hands of you!"

"No one's asking you to be a sidekick. I don't know what you have going on in that warped mermaid head of yours, but Airess wants you there because she cares about you. She might be the only one that cares about you. And you're not going to go because of your ego?"

Delphine's voice came out as a silky purr as she grinned, "Oh trust me, Lena. I guarantee you Airess isn't the only one who cares about me. Which reminds me . . .," her voice went back to her annoyingly chipper self as she held her phone up to Lena, ". . . I've got to go! I'm needed somewhere else! Thanks for the talk! See you soon!" There were five missed calls from Selene on Delphine's phone, and she physically rammed them into Lena's face.

Lena wanted to punch Delphine in the worst way. Taking the higher ground, she yelled, "Wait!" pulling the mermaid's attention back to her. Lena's hand caught Delphine's necklace in the process, and it snapped off into Lena's grasp.

"Did you just pull my necklace off of me? You're such a creep! Give it back right now!"

Lena stared at the charm in her hand. "Why do you need this?"

"Umm because it's mine, and it was on my body, that's why! How entitled are you?"

"My dad made this." Facts were linking together in Lena's mind. "This is what he gave Kohl when Kohl was poisoned by the serpent in Aglaope's portal. It takes out all the toxins trapped in Kohl's body and helps purify him. Why would he take this off? Did you find this in the siren's realm?"

Delphine's lips were pursed, and her stare was targeting Lena. If looks could kill, they would have. The siren was turning beet red.

"Why do you have this, Delphine?"

"You know what? I don't need it. I don't need any of this! You're the worst being I've ever met, Lena Basil, and trust me that's saying a lot. You're going to regret every minute you ever mistreated me! You wait and see!" Delphine spun on her heels and stomped the whole way down the hall.

Lena was stunned. She slid to the floor. She didn't expect to enjoy finding Delphine for Airess, but this was still more than she was prepared for. She wanted to text Selene but couldn't bring herself to do it. Delphine meant to hurt her with his missed phone calls, and it worked. That attack hit a bullseye on Lena's heart. Part of her, though, wanted to go to Delphine's room more now than ever with the skeleton key. *Why did she have Kohl's necklace? Why did she bring it into Aglaope's portal? What did that other name she called Aglaope mean?* There were so many questions, and Lena wanted answers. She just hoped it would take much less than an hour to get them.

With a big deep breath, she forced herself to send Selene the infamous "We need to talk" message and communicated a long detailed monologue to Solei in her mind about everything that just happened. Without waiting for either to respond, she walked hastily to the mermaid's room, skeleton key already in hand.

The door was easy to find and even easier to open. Lena expected the entrance to be gaudy with elements of Delphine all over it, but it was untouched. So untouched, in fact, that it still looked like a standard door and not even like a full-on portal yet. When Lena entered the space, sand greeted her toes. The space opened up to a bright sunny day overseeing a beautiful white beach with crystal blue waters. The scene was picturesque. Each component was pristine. Hills formed behind Lena with lush greenery decorating the landscape. Older castle-like buildings, seemingly made of stone, sat upon the hilltops. This realm smelled like summer. Every aspect of it was serene. Lena went to sit on the shore to take more in. The serenity here was alluring. She couldn't get enough of it, and she never wanted to leave.

A clunky bottle tapped against Lena's foot on the shoreline. *Awe! A message in a bottle. That's too cute.* Without hesitation, Lena picked it up and opened it.

Delphine,
Do you ever get these?
I've sent countless messages to you,

and you don't respond.
Where do you want to meet tonight?
I can take us anywhere you want.
XO,
Kohl

OMG?! Is that Kohl, like, THE KOHL?! Lena pushed to her knees and vigorously started searching for more. Each bottle she found was in the vicinity of the previous one, always slightly deeper into the water.

Delphine,
Don't be mad at me.
I had no idea you would hate
Hephaestus so much.
I thought you'd like being in an
Olympian's realm, since you're always
talking about how you deserve to be
there.
I'll take you anywhere you want to go;
just meet me at my mausoleum tonight.
Kisses,
Kohl

D,
I'm rushing, so I don't have a lot of time.
I found a way to get from the Greek
portals to Ward A, just like you wanted.
Find me later.

Delphine,

I don't think this plan is a good idea.
I know you keep talking to him about it.
I'm begging you to reconsider.
Can't we start over, just the two of us,
somewhere?
Please?
All my Love,
Kohl
~~P. S. I can't stand to go back~~

The last line was erased so hard there were still rubber fragments in the letter, but the words remained rather evident.

Lena went to find another, but as she breathed, water began to fill her lungs. She started coughing and couldn't find the footing she needed to reach the air. Sounds of laughter and singing filled her ears. The noises calmed her. She knew she couldn't breathe but wanted to swim deeper to hear more. Her chest started to glow. Lena used what little strength she had left to swim deeper into the ocean. It wasn't working. Frustrated, she started kicking and fighting her resistance. She thrashed to and fro until her body couldn't hold up any longer. At peak exhaustion, her eyes started to close. The world faded to black, but the musical accompaniment was exquisite.

~*~

"Lena! Wake up!" He had gotten her out of the water and onto her back. He double-checked to make sure he turned her head to the side, ready to start the Heimlich maneuver. She had fought like an angry badger as he tried to pull her out of the water. Her body was limp and awkward, but he was able to do a rep of five abdominal thrusts before he needed his first break. "Come on, Lena. It doesn't end like this." She smelled like the sea, and he couldn't help but notice how beautiful she was to him even while unconscious. Not a breath of life was left in her, but she still held a smile on her face. He missed her smiles. Those weren't as common as they used to be, and it pulled at his heart. He was rushing the steps, but he needed to get air into her lungs again. He gave another rep of five. "Lena, you have to wake up now. I can't begin to imagine how hard this is for you, but you need to do it. You have to come home." He had given ten thrusts total, and his arms were already hurting. He was losing his composure. Emotions were beginning to steal his own breath away. He had never considered a world that she wasn't in. Whether they stayed close or not, she would always exist. That much was always true. That much needed to stay true. He wasn't going to give up no matter how hard it got. He started another round of five. Much to his relief, Lena started coughing up water after the second push.

~*~

Her chest burned. Everything burned. *Why do I always hurt so much? Where are the delightful songs? Why couldn't I have just stayed in the ocean with the music?* Instead of opening her eyes, she scrunched them closed and pulled away from her rescuer, curling into the fetal position. She didn't want this. *Why is someone touching me? Go away! This burning needs to go away too. Oh no . . .* Lena's body lurched as she began to throw up.

"Believe it or not, that's a good thing." He rubbed her back. "I've got you. You're safe."

Lena squinted one eye open, a scowl staying on her face. "Selene? Why are you here?" She wiped herself clean, getting sand all over, and tried to appear lucid.

"I was with Solei when you told them what you were going to do. We were in the middle of being scolded by Professor Nakshatra. I left as soon as I heard."

"Why would you care so much that I was going into Delphine's room?"

"Do you honestly think I wouldn't care that my girlfriend was walking right into the bay where sirens are trained to lure humans to their deaths?"

"When you say it like that, it sounds like impending doom. I thought it was just going to be a lame bedroom with stupid posters of boys on the walls."

"Delphine doesn't even use this room. She avoids it at all costs."

That matches with Kohl's notes too. "I found letters from Kohl. I think they're planning something. In some of the letters, he sounded real into her."

"I don't think she has anything to do with Kohl, Lena. That was probably just the siren song messing with your head."

"I found them on land, Selene. I'll go find them again and show you!" Lena tried to stand but fell face-first into the sand.

"Hey, let's not move too much. You were unconscious for longer than you should've been. I wouldn't have even found you right away if you didn't have this." Selene pointed to her chest.

"My heart?"

"The insignia glowing on your heart."

Lena stretched out her neck to look. Sure enough, there was some inscription shining a pale red on her skin.

"You were impossible to miss in the water. Both of us got lucky with that. What is it? I haven't seen it before."

Lena shook her head. "I don't know." Her face was getting worried.

"What lured you in so deep by the way? Did their songs get to you?"

"Those letters, mostly. The music was evidently enchanting too, but I kept going deeper so I could read more until I lost my footing. I tried to get back, but I swallowed water instead. It hurt, but the music felt soothing so I kept trying to get closer to that to feel safer. I had hoped it'd heal me."

Selene was torn. "If I ask you to stay here and beg you not to move, will you do it?"

She agreed but wasn't thrilled to have him leave so soon. Thankfully, he was back in a minute's time. He scooted back in to be her physical support and handed her two previously opened letters. Once the couple was settled into place again, he read them.

"See?" Lena said.

"I do." His tone was sad. "That kind of sucks. I'm not going to lie."

"Why?" Lena's jealousy was rising once again.

"Too many people are going to be hurt over this, and I hate that."

"Like you?" Lena pressed with a note of snark in her tone.

"You've got to let that go, Lena. I'm only here for you."

"Then who are you so worried about?"

"First off, Airess."

"Oh . . ." Lena hadn't thought about that. This was going to crush the bubblegum healer. Not only was Airess' best friend ditching her, but Delphine was seeing Airess' lost love behind her back. Lena glanced back at Selene, her mouth still agape.

He gave her a hug and kissed the top of her head. "I think we need to go back to Professor Nakshatra. Fair warning though, she was rather angry at all of us when I left. I'm not sure what we're going to be walking into back at her study."

"Par for the course, I guess," Lena opined, taking one last glimpse of the crystal blue bay before her.

~*~

"Didn't you children learn anything after en-

184

countering Indra? Gods are not to be messed with! They will kill you!" Professor Nakshatra has not stopped her lecture in the time it took for Selene to retrieve Lena. The professor's normal white hue was replaced with a blueish-black outline.

You should've told me you were coming. I'd have told you not to. Solei suggested to Lena as she got herself situated on a pillow with Selene.

It's fine.

You look like you lost a fight with a fish, you all right?

No, but it doesn't matter right now.

"Professor, I am deeply sorry for our over-sights, but unfortunately, I have other information you need to see." Selene handed Kohl's notes to the professor. "When I went to rescue Lena, she was drowning in the siren's waters. These letters are what drew her in."

"I see." The professor set them on the table after her review. "Where is Delphine?"

"Last I saw her, she was stomping away from Aglaope's portal towards the front of Ward A," Lena aided.

"Actually, I know where she is." Sheepishly, Selene added, "She texted me. She said she's waiting on my beach."

Again?! Lena went to ask questions, but Professor Nakshatra cut her off.

"I will go find the girl and bring her back here. Do not, and I repeat, do not leave my study. Not under any circumstance. Do you all understand?" The four scolded teens conceded. "I mean it. Stay here. I'll be back in a breath." There was a faint click as the professor left.

Selene turned to Lena. "Before you even ask, no I didn't give her a way into my realm. I don't even know how to do that."

Lena had more questions like why could Delphine get into his bedroom unannounced and she couldn't but thought to wait on those for now.

Tao chimed in. "Ward A doors are all magical. Unless you're the resident or are a registered user of the skeleton key, you can't get in."

"Those can't be the only ways. She literally crashed right into me as she was coming out of Aglaope's portal. She kept calling it her home."

"The letters mention a few times too that Kohl could take her anywhere and that he had a way to get into Ward A," Solei added.

Tao lacked answers. "I don't know, but I've been with P.C. when she seals all the doors in Ward A, and I'm telling you that's a rigorous process."

"Hey, I know this is off topic, but did you guys make any progress on helping Airess? Or do you know how much longer we have for Airess? My phone died in the water." Lena posed to the group.

"Weird, the clock on my phone is glitched. You guys?" Solei inquired.

Both boys found the same. None of their phones were working properly.

"Can Professor Nakshatra do that?" Lena asked Selene.

"I don't know. She's certainly never covered that in any of our training, but she's never been any other color than white before either. I've never seen her mad before."

"I noticed the color shift too and thought it was strange. What is her chosen culture, Selene?" Tao had his thinking face on.

Selene was puzzled. He shrugged off Tao's question. He had never asked the professor anything about herself before.

"It feels similar to my own. I wonder if she belongs to an Asian culture?" Tao wondered aloud. Then, he pointed to Lena's chest. "I don't think she practices anything like that though, at least not to the best of my knowledge."

"Wait, you know what this glowing red thing is?!" Lena's hand framed the inscription.

"Of course I do. You don't? I thought languages were your specialty? You always brag about it."

"I read and understand languages, Tao. I don't make shiny red tattoos that don't look like traditional words onto people's bodies!"

"I mean, sure, it's not the BEST handwriting, but it clearly says 'seek' if you squint a little."

Lena caught sight of reflection in the professor's gong. "No. It does not. Why would I even have that written on my chest? What language is this in?"

"You put it there, obviously. As far as the language, it's loosely Mandarin. Kind of. Yùnqì is still young. He'll get there eventually."

"Yùnqì wrote this on me?!"

"Who's Yùnqì?" Selene whispered. He was ignored.

"No, he wrote it on a piece of paper, and you put it to your chest, imprinting the image onto you. You absorbed the talisman."

"I had no idea I was doing that! What small child writes talismans and hands them out!"

"I told my mother that you were clueless about your actions. She told me I was being rude."

"And at no point did you think telling this to me was a good idea?!"

"What was I going to say? 'Hey, Lena, maybe don't adhere ancient symbols to your skin without any prior knowledge.' Like you'd have received that message well."

"I'm not receiving this message well!"

"My point exactly. I'm going to go look at the books here and see if I can find anything. It'd be useful if you did that too since you stake so much claim into knowing all the different languages."

"I do not do that; you're taking a few comments way out of context."

Solei cringed, and Lena caught Selene laughing.

"That's so unfair! I do not do that!" Lena shouted at both of them.

Selene kissed Lena's cheek. "What do you want to do next? I don't think we're going anywhere until we're released."

"That's probably for the best," Lena said, assuredly.

"Why's that?" Selene asked.

"Because I have this." She pulled Kohl's former amulet out of her soggy pocket and handed it to Solei. "Delphine had this around her neck, and it's no longer full."

Solei was shocked. How could anyone have emptied this besides Kasim? This creation was slightly before their time as Mr. Basil's protégé, but they had studied his work on this amulet extensively. He had created this item personally. "The spell Kasim planned to use to cleanse this gem involved an Ancient Egyptian ritual. The purification spell was not recognizable to me at all, and I was reading the instructions for it. This amulet is based off of some seriously old and powerful sorcery. It connects to a person's life force and drains all poison out of one's body, so it can carry some seriously nasty toxins inside."

Tao put down his book to insert his opinion. "That type of magic can kill someone if they're not careful."

"Selene, didn't you say you pulled a few Nulls from an Egyptian realm recently? Wasn't there something then, too, about powers only a god could harness?" Lena tried to recall.

"Yeah, if that piece of red fabric was from Tutu Pele herself, whoever took it would've needed to be one of the ancient ones to withstand an attack from her. She's one of the most revered goddesses in the world. There's no limit to the power she can hold. I didn't think there was a chance in Hades that Kohl could be anywhere near that type of magic, but maybe he can. That's kind of scary to think about." Selene's vision was hyperfocused on the necklace. He ached to know what had happened to Kohl since their last meeting.

"If Kohl can stand up against Tutu Pele and drain this crystal, he's much farther gone than any of us have ever anticipated." Tao's tone was matter-of-fact.

"And how does Delphine play into all this?" Lena asked.

Selene, unsurprisingly, was the one to answer, "Delphine really hates not having her powers. I could see how she'd be drawn to someone she thought could solve everything. Maybe even someone who could make her better than before."

"But he'd have to be draining the life out of others to build up his own powers, right? That's how the Nulls exist? Would she be able to just let that happen?" Solei was trying to make sense of it all.

"The Nulls are completely drained of their powers when they're attacked by the darker side of Kohl. If he is a Slavic version of a vampire, I could see how that would all link together. As far as Delphine goes, that's harder to believe. I can't see Delphine standing by while all this happens. Even less so that she goes to him in her free time. Some of this is getting too far-fetched for me." Selene was clearly struggling.

"She could be making sure you all never get too close. It could explain why we've been searching for months," Lena offered.

Solei agreed, "I mean, that makes sense. Delphine could be leading you all in the wrong direction and keeping him clear in another direction. All in hopes that he can help her get her powers back sooner than later."

"I also think Delphine is a mole for Kohl. I'm sorry, Selene," Tao concluded.

Solei tried another route. "I wasn't at the trails you all had for her, but it seems like they were a bust."

"A total bust," Selene confirmed. "We spent days running various tests and exercises trying to spark something divine in her again, but it was all pointless. Kasim even brought a bagful of magical items, and Airess went way overboard on bringing plants that could potentially help, but nothing worked. It was a total waste of time."

Lena stayed quiet. She had thought it was a nice vacation together with her family and Selene. She had no idea he felt that way. He'd never mentioned any frustrations to her.

Selene huffed. "Whatever. It doesn't matter anyway." His tone was defensive and angry. He kicked a pillow across the room.

Everyone's eyes widened at his reaction. They looked at each other, but no one had anything else to offer. They had said what they believed to be true.

Tao went back to studying the books. Lena tried to reach out to Selene, but his broodiness kept her at bay. Solei asked Lena to help them check on Chibi in the corner, but it was just an excuse to pull her away from the tense situation on the floor with Selene.

"Do you think he'll be okay?" Solei asked, concerned.

"Yeah, but he's hiding something. I can tell."

"What do you think it is?"

"Something about her, I'm sure."

"Moles and mermaids, they're kind of the worst, huh?"

Lena's agreement was emphatic. "The absolute worst."

{ 10 }

Truths and Timers

"I HATE STUPID LENA BASIL!"

"I know, my love. I know."

"I hate how she's always so sure of herself, how she always thinks that she's in charge, and how she is always ruining EVERYTHING!"

"All the more reason for us to leave. I can take you anywhere you want to go, Delphine."

"I wanted to be here! I wanted to show Lena that Selene would show up for me before he would show up for her and tell Selene how STUPID his stupid girlfriend is!"

Kohl tried to hide his wince. "Selene doesn't matter. He never did. We should go, though. I don't mind using Ward A as a transfer point, but we shouldn't be hanging out around here. It's too dangerous. We'll get caught if we stay too long."

"I have nothing to get caught for. I belong here." Delphine's tone was as presumptuous as ever.

"I belonged here once too, but you were right. If I had stayed, I could have never been myself. I'd always have to try to be less. With you, I'm so much more. Together, we're such an unstoppable force. Let's go before Legacy ruins more good things for us."

"It's true. They'll never accept you anytime The Bad One comes into play. He holds the secret, though. I know he does. They once said he could be as strong as an ancient god!"

"So. Come. With. Me." Kohl was tugging on her hand.

She pulled away without a thought. "I know this wasn't part of the plan, and I don't want Airess to be in trouble, but if some other drama has their eyes off us and P.C. is already off grounds, there's never going to be a more opportune time to strike than now!"

"We've gone through this, Delphine. I'm happy to get away with you anywhere, anytime, but I'm not in this to hurt people."

"Where was that mantra when you raided my home? You're such a hypocrite. Look at me; you did this to me! You owe me Kohl."

"I love you. I hate that my other side hurt you, but can't you see how much better things have gotten since we've been together? None of this would've happened otherwise."

"The other side of you doesn't have a problem taking what he needs in order to survive."

"Of course he doesn't. He's selfish, vain, and

unkind. Don't you hate that he's created so many Nulls for you to take care of?"

"The Nulls love me, and plus, it gives me all the time with Selene and leaves him with no time for stupid Lena."

"The Nulls are dull and void. They don't feel much of anything. They're barely living."

"How dare you! I'm a Null, and I'm going to be running this whole place as soon as you stop being whiny and help me."

"You aren't a Null, Delphine. You were rescued."

"Yeah because Selene saw enough in me to save me."

"I know we see things very differently when it comes to that day, but either way, you weren't affected the way everyone else has been. The Bad One tried to steal your soul, but he lost and you won. You may have gotten covered in Hades' waters and stuck in this realm, but you're still you. It's beyond anything I could've ever imagined. You're beyond anything I could have ever imagined. So, again, please come with me."

"No. We need to do this now. We need to bring a main god into the Academy, let them wreak havoc, and then I'll come in and save the day. No Lena Basil, just me."

"Isn't it us?" Kohl confirmed, warily.

"I mean, yeah, but no one's going to believe you helped, right? They all think you're the absolute worst, ESPECIALLY when The Bad One comes out to play."

"You keep bringing him up. I don't see why he has to be in this at all. You fixed the necklace, right? I can stay me."

"Oh. Right. About that, Lena stole it from me. Sorry."

"What! Delphine! That is not okay!"

"I said sorry; what more do you want? Blame her. She sucks."

"Delphine! I cannot control the other side of me without that necklace!"

She shrugged. "Like I said, no one's going to believe you helped me when they all think you're the enemy anyway. You'll probably get blamed for letting Zeus in or whatever, but once I get all the credit and get to run the show, it won't matter. I'll come back for you, and you'll be fine."

"Delphine, if I can't control him, he may actually be the reason things go bad. Not in theory, in reality. He's capable of anything, and with all the Nulls he's been devouring lately, he's too powerful to begin with. We need to get that necklace back, and we need to starve him out."

"No way! If he's gone, I stand no chance at getting what I want!"

"Don't you want us? I can take care of us. I've worked so hard at that these past few months, and I'm sure of it. I have no doubt in my mind that I can do this for us."

"And what? I just become some loser's girl going from place to place with absolutely nothing to my name?"

"You'll be mine. I'm already yours."

"Even if my plan fails and The Bad One does go rogue and destroys a whole bunch of stuff, I can still be queen in whatever world he makes this place. My plan or his, I win either way."

"You've talked to him about this?"

"Uh . . . duh!"

"How can you be with me if you're plotting all this with him?"

"It's tragic, really. A side consequence."

"What?"

"Yeah. I have to pretend I like you, so then I can get access to him. I've tried to do the whole one without the other thing, but it's harder to influence his choices that way."

"Influence his choices?"

"I get you to take me where I want to go, bring The Bad One out, watch him do his thing, then run off to Professor Nakshatra and get to be the hero because of my 'expert knowledge.' Both the teacher and Selene think I'm amazing, and I get all the attention I deserve."

Kohl wasn't sure what he was feeling. Part of his emotions were in shock, part were in pain, and another part felt like it all made sense. "You're playing me."

"Only half of you. I genuinely like what your

other half can do for me."

"What about all that stuff in Ward B last year? How you thought I was worth so much more than they were giving me credit for? That I could be great? That together we could rewrite our destinies?"

"I mean, it worked out, didn't it?"

"Not if you were using me! That's miserable!"

"You liked it way more than I did. I don't see why you're complaining so much. I even went through that nasty portal of yours that one time. That was so generous of me."

"That's my home, Delphine."

"It's disgusting, Kohl. Anyways, when is The Bad One coming out? I could really use some good timing here with him."

"No. I'm out. This is over."

"You can't resist me, and we both know it. Even without my siren song, you're completely enthralled with me."

"I wasn't addicted. I thought I was in love."

"Eww. You sound like Airess when she talks about you. It's not the best look, Kohl."

"Why would Airess talk to you about me if you and I were dating?"

"That's a laugh. Obviously, no one could know about this."

"She's your best friend."

"Right, but no way she would be if she knew I was here with you."

"Is any part of you true to your word?"

"I'm always true to my word. I tell her all the time she's my number one girl, and she is. I chose her because she was the most powerful person here until I got you to where you are now. I may not have my powers, but I was sure to position myself with those who did."

"All of this is just a power play?"

"Some of it is just for fun, if that makes it any better?"

"You're nothing like who I thought you were."

Delphine dusted herself off and glanced out of the corner of her eye. Then, she started screaming. "Help! Help! You're not taking me away again! Go away! Go away!" She threw herself to the ground and started crawling away.

He reached out to help her, unsure of what was going on, when he felt a pain shoot from the tips of his fingers to the rest of his body. He was completely immobilized.

"That will be enough, child." Professor Nakshatra stood before him, cradling Delphine in her arms. "I think we are long overdue for a conversation."

"Agreed!" Delphine chimed in. "All of Legacy is going to know what you've done!"

Professor Nakshatra raised her right foot, aiming to stomp on the boy's toes, but before she could make contact, he turned into a shadow. "I demand you show yourself at once!" She commanded.

The shadow swirled lower to the sandy beach, spreading itself out. Once it touched the sea, a bright circular light flashed. It sucked up the entire shadow then collapsed in upon itself.

Amazed, the professor mouthed, "It's true—" Her blue hue shifted back to white.

"You have to go get him! We were so close this time!" Delphine begged.

The mentor studied her pupil. "We should get back to the others waiting for us. I think there are a plethora of topics to discuss."

"Yes! Of course! Anything to help!" As Delphine stepped out of Selene's realm, she couldn't help but blow a kiss to the portal The Bad One had escaped through.

~*~

Lena caught the clicking sound on the door again and knew Professor Nakshatra was on her way in. Anxiety bubbled in Lena's belly. She wondered who would be the first to say something. Sure enough, in walked the professor. Delphine trailed close behind, and once she was inside, the door shut with another click. Lena was surprised to be locked in once again.

"Children, there has been a revelation during my recovery of Ms. Souda here."

Delphine interrupted, "Yes! It was horrible! I—"

Professor Nakshatra was not having it. "I'm able to tell the tale, child. You should sit and rest."

Delphine addressed the teacher, "I was there longer with him though!" She then turned to the group. "I saw Kohl! He was in Selene's room!" She waited for a validating reaction from the group. None came.

"Sit," Professor Nakshatra asserted.

Visibly grumpy, Delphine listened. She sat on the pillow next to Selene then scooted closer towards him. He got up and walked over to Lena, Solei, and Chibi. Delphine scoffed out loud.

"Please gather as close as you're comfortable. I have some important information. It's true that I was finally able to catch eye of the one you call Kohl. Truthfully, I was rather surprised at first. He looked just like one of you. When I arrived, Delphine caught sight of me and started screaming for help. I aided her, as one should, and stunned the boy in front of her. However, when I went in to gain further control of the situation, he turned into a shadow. From there, he crept out to the water, and I was able to see what we have all suspected. I can affirm that Kohl is able to create portals within portals. I am astounded. Part of me did not believe it to be true. This is where I turn to our resident expert. Delphine, it seems you and the boy have grown rather familiar with each other. I would like you to please explain to the group how his talents have come to be."

Delphine looked around, ready to play her part. "So, I was waiting on the beach for Selene since he had called me so many times today. I knew I had right to be worried about him." She looked over and smiled his way, ignoring his current demeanor.

"Stop! That is not the boy I wish to hear about.

You are most familiar with the other one. I am solely requesting the information you have about Kohl. It seems you are even more attuned to his situation than your innate abilities with the Nulls have led us to believe." There was curtness in Professor Nakshatra's voice.

"Not really. I don't really know the kid. He just showed up on the beach all grabby. That's what you saw too, right? I fell down and his grubby little hands were ready to be all over me. It was horrid. Then, yeah, you came in, and he turned into a shadow and got away through the sea. What a bummer! Am I right?"

"You know not of his abilities?"

"No. He kind of gives me the creeps, honestly."

"You ensure there were no discussions of power? Of fun?" Professor Nakshatra accused.

Delphine's face paled. This conversation wasn't going the way she planned.

Selene finally made eye contact with the siren. "Give it up, Delphine. We all know you're a mole."

"Excuse me? I am not a mole! I am a siren! I am a descendant of the Olympian gods! How dare you!" She was on her feet, shouting.

Lena sighed. Delphine was not intelligent. "Not a mole as in the creature. A mole as in a spy."

Delphine's tone was scornful. "Of course you would think that, Lena Basil. You know what? I'm tired of your bullying! Professor Nakshatra, she has been cruel to me since day one! I cannot tolerate being treated like this any longer!"

Tao spoke up next, "It's not Lena, Delphine. It's all of us."

"We think you've been steering us off course for months, so you can try to use Kohl's darker side to get your powers back," Solei added.

"You guys don't know anything! I can't believe this!" Delphine went over and grabbed Selene's hand tight. "Are you hearing what they're saying about me? You can't believe them. We've been together through every culture of every world, helping every Null, studying every clue we could possibly find. You know me. No one has worked harder at catching Kohl than the two of us have together!"

"You're right, at least partially so. I have stood by you through everything, Delphine. I've defended you countless times to others, and I've let you come to me at all hours for comfort. I've never not showed up for you, even at the expense of what I've wanted and at the cost of my own happiness." He pulled away until she finally let go of him. "I kept telling myself it was my responsibility to take care of you, and you enforced that mentality every chance you got by telling me you didn't have anyone else. Everyone is saying you're doing this to get your powers back, but you don't even know how you lost your powers in the first place. No one here does except me."

"They got to you too?" Delphine was eager to be the wounded victim. No one else seemed to care. Furious, she stomped, "I'm tired of everyone telling me about my first day when I was the one that lived through it! I think I know my own life better than the rest of you!"

Lena wanted to comment and tell the mermaid she wasn't even conscious by the time she got to the fountain but knew this was Selene's moment for closure.

"Kohl did turn into The Bad One, and he did attack your city. He destroyed everyone in the castle. I was too late, too far behind. I knew he did things like that, but I thought I had a better handle on him than I did. I saw you, sitting on the street, watching it all happen. As soon as you noticed me, you came running to me, asking for me to save you, so I tried. The Bad One had already sensed my presence, though, and knew I was a threat. We fought often in those days. He was hunting us down, and I swore I wouldn't let him get you too. And I didn't."

"Even if he caused me to lose my powers, you'll always be the one who saved me. What we have is special." Delphine gave her best doe eyes to try to soften Selene's heart.

"You're not listening. He didn't get you. You were fine. I got us fairly deep into the water, and he gave up tracking us. I wasn't sure why, at first, until I realized the waters we were in were changing. They were turning from pure blue to having whispers of white and black. I wouldn't know until much later, but Hades was claiming the souls of the ones The Bad One took before the vampire could devour them himself. I made the choice to follow the strands in the water over going back to where we had come from. It was the wrong choice. I swam us from river to river until I made it back into my own reality. You had grown limp in my arms. I knew something was wrong, that I had done something wrong. Unintentionally, I had taken us through the rivers of Hades. I didn't know it at the time, though. I found it all out much later through Lena on what I had done. She had been told the water we all thought was your blood was actually from the Lethe river, the river of forgetting. You were fine before we went through the Underworld. Whether it was Lethe, Styx, or one I don't even know we touched, those rivers are what took your powers, and I'm the one who put you in them. I'm the reason you're powerless, Delphine. Not The Bad One. Not Kohl. Me. And I've held that guilt for months, causing me to do things I don't want to do, all in order to protect you and be there for you. I've traded large parts of my happiness to be present for you over and over again. I'm done now. I don't know what you have going on with him, especially after all the truly horrible things you've said about him to me, but you've created your own messes now. I'm not taking responsibility for these. These are all on you."

Delphine was enraged. "You? You did this to me? After all this time that I trusted you? How dare you!" She lunged at him, her hands stretched out like claws, ready to gouge his face.

Lena rose to defend him, but she was held off

by Professor Nakshatra.

"We will not be having that today." The professor waved her hand, and Delphine floated softly to the ground, fast asleep. I think our time here is done, and you all should refocus some of this energy. We need to return to the matter at hand, the reason you all sought me out in the first place."

Everyone was uneasy. Tensions were rising too high.

Professor Nakshatra carried on, "As you know, Baba Yaga has entered Astoria. Before you youths decided to get involved, this was a controlled situation. However, it seems not only has Miss Hikona gotten herself entangled in the witch's web, but Miss Basil has as well. I will work to remedy this."

"No way." Tao was crushed. "You knew the Old Hag was coming back this entire time?"

"Of course I knew. Principal Chromwell would never send something to Astoria like that without telling her confidants. Your father told me you knew as well, too. I had asked thrice to meet with you, but you never showed up."

Tao had blown off three messages from her. "Regardless, how could P.C. do this?"

"It's a part of their agreement, child. It's always been under control. At least it had been until today. With that, Lena Basil, please enlighten me. What are the exact terms of the pact that you made with Baba Yaga? It's incredibly important to be as specific as possible here."

All eyes were on Lena. She felt like this was a pop quiz she wasn't prepared for. "I was granted freedom to come here as long as I talk to whoever is in charge and gather kids for dinner. If I brought enough kids to end her hunger then Airess is freed too. And if I fail, she's going to eat both of us."

"I see. How many children were said to end her hunger?"

Lena hadn't thought to ask that. "I don't know."

"How many Baba Yaga were present when you made this pact?"

"One? Wouldn't there only be one?"

"No." The professor pressed on, "What size was Baba Yaga when you made this pact?"

"Normal, I guess. We were in her hut when this pact was made."

"That sounds like there was more than one pact, child."

Panic was setting in. She thought she handled everything so well. "I don't think so? We made a pact when she was a giant, but then she acted like she didn't know that pact, so we made this pact too. Oh! There was a thing too that if I did this right, she would tell me about my parents."

"What did she say about your parents, Lena?"

"That she smelled them before, and if she agreed to having them for dinner, she'd have me too. She was somewhat sympathetic about my mom, saying she was pure of heart or something like that. She didn't like my dad, though. She said he was deceitful."

"I see. That is not ideal, but we will manage."

"Why? What's going on?"

"Nothing to worry about at the moment. For now, we have to figure out how many Baba Yagas have come into Astoria and what deals have been struck with them. All the deals you made with them have the time frame of one hour?"

"Uhh . . . no. Only the first one."

"The first pact you made or the first one you told us about?"

"The one that granted me freedom."

"All right then. We will split up. I've held us stationary in time here, but once we leave, we will lose that benefit. Lena, you have fulfilled the task of talking to me. You will now need to gather other students."

"What?! There's no way I can bring actual kids to her hut! She. Will. Eat. Them!"

"I did not make that deal, child. You did. Selene can go with you. Tao, I need you to stick with me please; we have much to discuss. Solei, Chibi, and Mae, I need you to go through Airess' agricultural logs and see if there's anything that can help. You're allowed to persuade the Beboy twins to assist you as well if you'd like." The professor delivered that last statement very routinely. "Delphine will stay safe here in my space."

The teens' mouths were agape. *Did she just say what I think she just said? Can you use your powers on the Beboy twins?!* Lena asked Solei. *I want in on that!*

Ignoring Lena, Solei stood and emptied their bag on the table. "I grabbed these too. We have another shield, an electrical enhancer, a pouch of magic dust that seemed worthwhile, and a fireball bracelet."

"Why fire? Wouldn't that burn the forest down and trap us in it?" Tao was not hiding his judgment on Solei's pick of items.

"Aren't ogres scared of fire?" They defended.

Condescendingly, Tao replied, "That's trolls, Solei. Trolls are scared of fire."

"What weakness does an ogre or ogress have then?"

Tao gestured to Professor Nakshatra. "I think that's what she's trying to figure out for us."

"It'll be all right, children. We will ensure we follow the rules that have been agreed to, and we will prevail. Does everyone understand their role?"

"I have one more thing, I guess," Solei added. "Mae isn't with us. Only Chibi and I are here."

The professor was quick to reply. "Understood. Any other questions or concerns?"

"No . . .," Solei responded unsurely. *That was weird, right? She kind of blew me off?* Solei asked Lena.

100%, Lena agreed. *She's probably over-whelmed. She's changing colors again.*

I thought she was blue before?

She was, but when she came back, she was white.

What does that mean?

No idea.

"We're set to depart then. I will send us where we need to go. Good luck, my children. We shall meet at the hut when our hour is due. We all have three fourths time. Godspeed to us all."

Lena's vision was engulfed by puffy clouds. She was falling. As soon as she was about to panic, she heard Selene's voice and felt his hands on her waist.

"I got you," he soothed.

She landed with a thud in the courtyard of Legacy Academy. "Back where it all began, I see." She motioned towards the fountain.

"Hey, I'm sorry about that. I should've told you sooner."

"I thought we were done keeping secrets?"

"We were."

Lena let out a noise that sounded like a high-pitched "eh." She drew out the sound extensively.

"We are."

"Sure we are. At any rate, we need kids and a lot of them. I don't feel great about this. I don't even know where to start."

"You don't have any ideas?"

Lena squirmed. She had one, but he wasn't going to like it. "No good ones."

"Any bad ones?"

She was hesitant to respond.

"Out with it."

"There is one group of students that are numerous in quantity and centrally located . . ."

"You've got to be kidding me."

"Nothing will happen to them, I swear!"

"I cannot believe you're going to ask me to do this."

"I didn't even think of them until I had you with me. They wouldn't listen to me, but they'd listen to you!"

"You want me to take the dozens of kids I've saved and brought here for sanctuary into a magical forest where a witch wants to eat them?"

"Wants to, but won't!"

"This is unbelievable. If you're forcing me, I will ask the Nulls, but I'm not lying to them. If they're willing to risk their lives, they're better people than I am. I'm not tricking them."

Cringing, Lena affirmed, "Good, because that's one of the stipulations."

Selene stalked off ahead of her towards the dorms.

Trying to stay in a positive mood, Lena reached out to Solei. *This isn't going well, but it's going. Best of luck in the fields! Give the twins a special hello from me.* She hoped her friend would respond with good news soon.

~*~

Solei had no idea what they were going to do.

211

They asked Chibi to take them to Airess' logs, but the golem didn't move. They asked Chibi where Airess' botany books were, but the golem didn't move. When they asked what Airess had planted in the fields, the golem took them to what can only be described as an unlabeled seed library.

"This isn't helpful if it doesn't have words," Solei implored.

Chibi stayed stationary.

"Chibi, I need to know what is planted in the fields."

At the last word, Chibi started pounding their chest.

"The fields?" Solei asked.

Chibi nodded.

"Okay, then. Lead the way."

They walked out of Chibi's home. Chibi had to duck to get in and out of the entryway. He had gotten so big. A snake started to slither up the golem's body. At first, Solei was alarmed. They were ready to attack it, but they watched as Chibi tried to pet it with their clay brick arms.

Giving in, Solei greeted the snake, "Welcome to the team, little dude. I'd have stayed away if I were you."

The snake hissed in return.

Solei was looking at their phone as they trailed behind a determined Chibi. They were hoping to find some app that would give them what they needed about these plants. They knew the likelihood that

Airess' creations were anything a normal person would know was slim, but ideas were scarce at this point.

There was some shouting off in the distance and Chibi started to run.

"Chibi! What are you doing? Come back!" Sprinting, Solei tried to keep up.

The golem ran straight towards the Beboy twins who were covered in manure. Despite the twins being oversized, they barely made it up to Chibi's chest. He grabbed one with each arm, smushing the twins between his clay arms and torso. They kicked and flailed. They hit Chibi as hard as they could, but it didn't matter. Chibi carried them without strain. Solei watched as the cluster headed back to Airess' fields.

Unbeknownst to Solei, there was a creek behind Chibi's hut. That's where Chibi decided to sit with the boys firmly in tow.

"This monster is going to drown us! You're just going to watch?" one of the Beboy twins criticized.

Solei knew they wouldn't actually let the twins get hurt, but the boys didn't need to know that. "Meh. A life for a life, I guess."

"We're two lives! And what life did you lose, huh? I don't mess with the likes of you people."

Solei was unaffected by the insult. "I was being generous that the sum of you two equaled a full life. And as far as not messing with my people, that's not the story I heard from Airess."

"Airess isn't one of you. She's a true female.

Wanna know how I know?"

The snake slid down and bit the twin's arm. Solei couldn't be certain, but it looked like the serpent spit out the taste afterwards.

"Is that thing poisonous? You can't hold us hostage and do this! P.C. will have your head!"

"P.C. is gone. Plus, I have permission. You can go once you tell me how to free Airess."

The twins resisted at first, but Chibi and the snake made an extremely compelling argument without using any words.

"Babas always get what they want."

"Yeah. No one is smarter than grandmas! That's why P.C. always loses!"

Solei wanted clarification. "What do you mean P.C. always loses?"

"P.C. never knows how to handle her problems, so Babas always has to come to save her."

The second twin continued the first's thought. "Deal's a deal. P.C. gets what she needs, and Grandma gets to come visit. Grandma makes the best food."

"Why do you keep saying grandma? What do you fiends eat other than poor innocent children?"

"We only want kids."

"Adults are fine if we have to. Five bellies are a lot for small portions. Bigger portions aren't as soft though. They're not as good."

"Five bellies?"

"Us plus Grandma's three."

"There are three Baba Yagas?"

"One Baba Yaga. Three bellies."

"You don't make any sense! I can't believe you eat humans! How many lives have you taken here?"

"None yet, but P.C.'s gone now. We'll finally eat good!

The second twin fist-bumped the air. "Yeah! Eating is going to be real good! No more livestock!"

Annoyed, Solei kept going, "You've been going on forever about humans, but you've never actually eaten one?"

"P.C. always gets in the way. She's not in the way no more!"

Solei cut in before the other could talk. "You didn't even know P.C. was gone! If P.C. always gets in your way, why do you say she always loses? You make no sense!"

"P.C. never gets what she wants. Babas does though. Babas gets to come visit every time for longer and longer."

"Now Grandma will never leave us!"

Solei looked at Chibi. This new information was bad. They knew they had to tell the others. "Can you keep them here?"

Chibi nodded. The snake slithered out to sit in Solei's spot, keeping its focus on the twins.

Hello? I don't know if I can talk to both of you at once. I have bad news. The twins say Baba Yaga has three bellies and gets to stay here forever now with P.C. gone. Have you guys heard this?

Lena was the first to answer. *She did keep saying there were three bellies to feed.*

It was muffled, but Tao's voice attempted to connect as well, *So much here. We know about the three Baba Yagas. I know the original pact. I have to go. See you in half an hour.*

Solei hadn't been this terrified since Indra. They missed having Mae by their side. After this, Solei didn't want to feel this way ever again. They headed back over to the creek.

"I need to know what plants Airess might have to help free her from dinner."

"Babas doesn't like new things."

"Yeah, only old things, things from their country."

"What country is Baba Yaga from?"

"Slavic countries mostly but sometimes, others too."

"Slavic bones are the best bones. It's hard to find Slavic pigs."

"Aren't all pigs the same as long as you get the right breed?"

The Beboy twins thrashed at the thought. "You know nothing!"

"Grandma would know! Grandma would always know!"

"Fine. I think you've given me all your brains can handle. I'll ask Chibi and our new friend here, the snake, to let you go, but know that you better pray to whatever god you consider holy that nothing happens to Airess. If she's hurt, I'm coming directly for you, and I don't care if I get thrown out for the retribution I will bring down upon you." Thunder crackled in the background of Solei's threat. They nodded to Chibi.

Chibi fully submerged the brutish twins for less than a breath then let them go while they were underwater. They bolted out of sight.

"Chibi, how am I supposed to figure out what plants are Slavic? That's an entire region, and one I know nothing about. I don't want to bother Tao, but man, I don't know anything about this. Even if I came up with names, I don't know what any of those would look like."

"I could help," Mae's tender voice offered.

"MAE!" Tears of joy streamed down Solei's face. "Mae! Where are you?"

"I could do this in a less dramatic way but look down first."

Solei's eyes went to the ground. The snake was staring back at them.

"Are you freaked out?" Mae asked, their snake tongue flicking after every couple of words.

"Not yet. Will I be?" Solei tentatively asked.

"No one's ever seen me in this form before."

"Is it a new ability?"

"No. The drops of Pythia blood in my veins gave me this ability in addition to being an oracle. "

"Have you always been able to change into a snake?"

"It has to be a python, but yeah, I can change

into any python."

"I promise to be cool with all this if you can promise me one thing in return."

"Help you with this whole Airess situation? I've already been heavily involved in that."

"No. Don't tell Tao that you're a python."

"He wouldn't be the first to make the joke about oracles being snakes."

"It's not that, it's just that no one needs to hear him gloat, and I feel he'd be all in on this particular validation."

Mae let out a laugh. "I didn't know he cares so much."

"I thought you were a hat."

"A hat?"

"A nice hat! But he made me listen to a lecture about pythons instead."

"That sounds monotonous."

"It hurt my head."

"Where were you guys? I'm guessing you saw me with Chibi?"

"Yeah. I was in his head. He was in Ward B."

Mae cringed, "Oooh."

"Exactly. It was everything you'd expect it to be."

"There's a lot to unpack there."

"It was indeed a lot, and telepathy is not going to be his calling in life."

"I'm not surprised. Well, I'm ready to go look at the plants whenever you are. I have ideas of what we might need."

"Can I ask one more question?" Solei pressed.

"Sure."

"Why didn't you tell me you were going to come? I thought this was going to break us."

"I thought it might too. I knew you wanted to go charge into battle, and that's not my style. Plus, I knew a little more than you did. I had to hold back."

"Why? Why not just tell me?"

"Because Apollo said Baba Yaga wins, and I refuse to accept that. I needed to think things through."

"The Old Hag wins? What happens to the rest of us?"

Mae avoided eye contact.

"Then what do we do?"

"We prove him wrong. He's entitled and mildly obnoxious anyway."

"Can a god be wrong?"

"He will be today. I have an idea, and it begins with you holding some beets!"

"I've heard stranger things. Chibi, direct us to the beets!"

Chibi got up and started walking towards the proper row of plants, but Mae had already beaten them there. Back to her normal self, she stashed a bag full of freshly picked beets into Solei's backpack.

"When it's your turn to talk to Baba Yaga, you have to show these to her, okay? I want you to display them, squeeze them, and a hint of magic wouldn't hurt either. I want her to believe you're the descendant of a Sun God."

"My last name IS Morningstar."

"Precisely. We're going to lean really far into that lineage today. Plus, you've been a sun for Airess before, haven't you?"

Begrudgingly, Solei nodded.

"And that seems to have gone successfully?"

Solei gestured another halfhearted agreement.

"Then, let's repeat what we already know works. I have a few other things to grab. I want a few vials of water, a couple handfuls of seeds, and bark from a tree, but I can grab the bark on our way. Anything else you need?"

"I have no idea what I need right now."

Mae turned to Chibi. "How about you, you good?"

A proud chibi beat their chest.

"Fantastic. On we go then! Do you know the way?"

"More or less."

"Time to go, then. I'll follow you anywhere." Mae reached for Solei's hand.

Solei happily held their love's hand and kissed their head. "Maybe when this is all done, we can go back to Rome?"

"Planning vacations already, are you?"

"I don't mean for vacation. I mean for good."

"I'd like that." Mae bounced with happiness.

"I love you." Solei leaned in to kiss Mae's lips.

For a moment, Mae forgot they were headed into certain death. All she wanted, all she needed, was standing right there in front of her. Words she had never said escaped her mouth, "I love you too."

{ 11 }

Secrets and Scheming

"**Y**ou're sure you're okay with this?" Selene asked hesitantly as he donned Lena's bag.

"It can't be a worse fate than trading all these Nulls to Baba Yaga, right?" Lena shrugged.

In total, twenty-two Nulls had agreed to accompany Lena on her journey. She had expected it to be a hard sell. None of her friends would have willingly agreed to risk being eaten for a stranger, but the Nulls they spoke to had no qualms about it. They didn't care. They didn't care about anything. The Nulls' wing of the dorms was the most depressing place Lena had been to in quite some time.

"I'll be as quick as I can, and no matter what, I promise I'm coming back right away this time. I won't leave you alone. Not again. Not after everything."

"Listen, I love you, but you need to go do this. I'll be fine. I'm always fine. I'm used to working things out on my own at this point. You do you, we'll figure

222

everything else out after all this."

He knew her statement was true, but it still made him sad. He regretted a majority of the decisions he had made these past few months, and his next actions were not going to reflect the change he wanted to make in his life. "I'm coming back this time, I promise."

"I believe that you're going to try your hardest. Life just has its own plans sometimes. I hope I'm wrong."

"Me too." Selene kissed Lena's cheek and started back towards Legacy Academy.

It was a quiet trek. Lena wasn't exactly lonely, but it was awkward walking with a large group of people in utter silence. She had assumed the Nulls were friends, or at least friendly, with each other. She thought they would be exactly like her and her friends. Lena knew they were powerless, and ripped from the world they lived in, but Lena was new last year too, and that had turned out well, more or less. This wasn't the case for them. They were closer to zombies than students. Not that Lena had ever met a zombie, but she was confident nonetheless. She remembered Selene not liking the undead. That was going to complicate his day.

There was no path to the kicking chicken hut, but Lena could feel Baba Yaga's magic now that she knew it. It was strong and strange. Lena undoubtedly knew the Old Hag would eat the children if given the chance, but the witch's patience and willingness to make deals offered a sense of hope. Lena desperately wanted that feeling to be legitimate. Lately, she had not been as in control as she expected to be, and this was one situation she didn't want to mess up. She'd never let these kids get hurt, especially after seeing how much they were willing to be. They needed help. Maybe helping them could give her more time with Selene too. She desperately wanted to go back to being on the same team as him. That pipedream had to rest on the back burner for now, though. Child eating ogress' came first, everything else had to be second.

I see you. We're about fifteen feet ahead and slightly off to your right, Solei directed.

Lena walked over and told the group behind her to make themselves comfortable. Most didn't listen and kept standing around idly. Disheartened, she went to sit over by Solei, Mae, and Chibi Chan.

"Wow! Someone has surely grown!" Lena patted the core of an extra-large Chibi. They towered over her even in a sitting position.

"It seems like he sprouts a foot every couple of hours now," Mae added while picking at the flora around her. A hefty pile of four-leaf clovers already sat between her and Chibi. "It's pretty incredible. I've never seen anything like it."

"I think all of us can say the same. It looks like you got a whole crew there, Lena! How'd that go over?"

"Way too easily . . .," Lena said, uneasy.

"That seems like a story."

"They're doing the best they can, I think."

"If you want to talk about it, I'm happy to listen. Otherwise, want to see what we grabbed?"

Just then Tao arrived. "I want to see what you have! I have my own stash to share as well," he chimed in.

"Tao! How are you?" Lena greeted.

"I'm all right. I have some pieces of paper to share with the group. Shall we start a lightning round of show and tell?" He grinned at Solei, waiting for approval on his pun.

All the friends agreed, but Professor Nakshatra saw no need for it and interrupted.

"Lena, I see you have gathered all the students you could?"

Forcing herself to listen to the adult present instead of the conversation she actually wanted to be in, she replied, "Yes, ma'am."

"And where is your partner, Selene? Is he rounding up more children as a part of this task?"

"Yes, ma'am." It wasn't the full truth, but it wasn't a full lie either.

"That will be helpful. From what I've been told your tasks were to talk to me and gather students. Those points have been met. That means it's time to go face Baba Yaga." The way Professor Nakshatra's green robes billowed out behind her made her presence reminiscent of P.C.

"We're almost done here," Lena gestured to

the rest of the core group. "Can we go after we've had a chance to discuss our parts of the plan?"

"That will not be necessary, child. They will not be joining us."

"What?" Solei and Lena said simultaneously.

"It's time to go, Lena. Don't stray." Professor Nakshatra began to walk off.

Lena had no idea what to do, but the professor was not walking at a normal speed and the distance was building between the two quickly.

Tao snuck two pieces of paper into Lena's open hand and closed her fingers around it. "Go!"

"Okay!" Lena took off to try and catch up to her leader. It was hard finding the professor's green colors amidst the forest. She finally saw her teacher standing in a clearing and ran to their side.

"You fell behind. We have arrived. When we go in, I will do the talking. Understood?"

Lena knew there was no arguing that point.

The professor addressed the surrounding forest, "Baba Yaga, your presence is requested to uphold the oaths you have made. Please come forward and be visible to all parties we have brought here today." Professor Nakshatra held up a blue lotus. Eight tiny wisps floated up from the lotus' center and started to circle above the flower. The professor blew over the pea-sized spheres, and one went off into the forest.

Lena waited. She got the distinct impression she was not supposed to speak whether Baba Yaga was physically present yet or not. She inhaled the scent of the lotus. If she was going to feel useless, at least she was going to enjoy what she could.

Heavy footsteps came from deep within the trees. The wisp wafted back to its creator. The chicken hut had come into view. A single eye-like window peered out between the trees. The shutters blinked as it scanned the area. Then, as it stepped forward on its sturdy chicken legs, the front door opened.

"That's our welcome," Professor Nakshatra whispered to Lena. She confidently strode towards the hovel.

Lena stayed close behind. They walked straight from the ground into the hut. Airess was sorting out plants on the counter. Too scared to speak, Lena rushed over and hugged her friend.

"Hey. I'm okay. Things are good here," Airess consoled.

"Baba Yaga, I am Tara Nakshatra, interim headmistress of Legacy Academy. I am here to discuss the pacts you have made both with Lena Basil and Theodora Chromwell."

"Yes, yes, my pretty. No need to be so formal. Come. Sit with Baba Yaga. I'll brew us some tea."

"No, thank you. I'm purely here to right the wrongs that have been made in accordance to your recent actions and dealings."

Baba's demeanor tensed. "No wrongs here. Only willing participants. Them's the rules."

"In the pact with Theodora, I believe there are

three rules to be followed, and all have been broken."

"Baba Yaga breaks no rules! A deal is a deal."

Professor Nakshatra waved her hand, summoning a piece of paper. Rule one: Baba Yaga is permitted to stay at the designated magical residence in Astoria during each interaction's agreed upon time." She paused, letting the weight of the rule linger. "This rule was broken when you went into the livestock fields."

"Babas was invited! Invitations are allowed in rule two! Rule number two says that no student shall interact with Babas without full knowledge and consent of what the dinner shall entail."

"That does not give you permission on school grounds."

"Babas says it does. The twins are very aware of what the dinner shall entail and are exceedingly happy to eat with Babas. They wanted us to come to their fields, so Babas did."

Professor Nakshatra did not hide their displeasure. "Rule three is the primary rule of Astoria. It is one set forth by the mayor that we all abide by. No magic shall cause alarm or harm to those who call Astoria home. I think we can all agree here that there are several instances from today alone that break that."

"Not one." Baba was unwavering in their position.

"You've kept Ms. Hikona as your captive."

"No alarm or harm. She chose to come with me

and not a hair of hers is hurt. Ask the girl. Her and Babas gathered plants together, nothing ill to be had."

"Airess, is that true?"

"Unfortunately, it is, ma'am. I didn't want anyone else to come here, so I volunteered myself, and while Lena was gone, things were peaceful, enjoyable even."

Lena did her best to not take that statement to mean her presence was the problem.

"I see. Thank you for your honest response. Even if that is the case, Lena was certainly alarmed, and she also calls Astoria home."

"Babas' magic had nothing to do with that girl's emotions. She is emotional by nature."

Rude. Lena was tired of staying quiet. "Your house kicked me! You went from like a fifty foot ogress to a five foot ogress! You were going to eat my friend! You threatened to eat me! There are almost two dozen other kids out there you asked me to gather for you to eat, too! None of this is okay, and you're withholding something about my parents!"

"You have so much of your father in you, my pretty. You really should consider being more like your mother. Babas' house is not part of Babas' magic. The dancing hut belongs to the forest and follows its own will. Also, whether my sisters and I are together as one or apart as three, that is how we move. Our travel is a true essence of our existence. One cannot limit Babas' way of being. Our stomachs three are the same. The charming girl in the corner asked to be eaten. Babas can't say no. Babas is grateful for her gift! You also agreed, never threatened, both to yourself and the others you gathered."

"You said if I didn't bring enough students for you, you would eat me too! That's a threat."

"No threat. Pact. That was the rule of the pact. You agreed. No magic."

"Lena, everything is under control. Please sit down."

Dismissed, Lena pouted in the corner next to Airess.

"Where are her parents, Baba Yaga? Theodora, Ina, Millie, and Kasim all traveled together to your portal, and they have not come home in their estimated allotment. They all sought out your audience, and the fact that you're here gives me reason to believe their endeavor was successful."

"Yes, Babas saw them. Babas helped them too because Babas is so kind." A wide iron-toothed smile spread across the ogress' face.

Covering her revulsion, Professor Nakshatra continued, "Where is the group?"

"Millie did not want to stay, so she left. Babas doesn't know where Millie is now."

"You're avoiding my question. Where are the other three of that group?"

"Waiting. They chose to wait until Millie comes back."

"Wait where?"

"Babas doesn't have to answer this. Babas has

a pact due with the loud girl in the corner."

"If you have hurt any of them, your pact with Theodora will have been broken. I believe there are some strict punishments that should happen if that is the case."

"Babas has had enough!" The Old Hag grabbed her broom and with one solid sweep, Professor Nakshatra vanished. The hag faced the two girls on the bed. "Time is well past! Time for Babas to eat!"

Lena moved in front of Airess. "I brought over twenty students. That should be enough. Can't you let us go? They're all in your forest. I don't even think they'll fight you."

"Lena!" Airess smacked her friend's back. "Absolutely not."

"You agreed Babas be free of hunger. You go when all three bellies are full. No more tricks." With the broom still in hand, Baba swept the girls away with the same vigor she did the professor.

All Lena could see was darkness. All she could smell was the earth. What had she done? She was angry with herself. She was angry at the others too. She swore and kicked the solid soil around her. They had all screwed everything up. Nothing had gone her way. She never had the control she wanted. She would never forgive herself if the Nulls got hurt because of her, and Selene probably wouldn't either. *Oh, Selene,* she thought. What disaster is he going to be walking into if he does actually come back? She wondered where he was now, wishing with all her might that he was safer than she was. Truly hoping for the first time that he would get too busy to keep his promise, she wondered how his plan was going. She'd give just about anything right now to have it fail.

~*~

Selene raced to Professor Nakshatra's door. He used Lena's skeleton key to get in. The study had been turned upside down. Books and other belongings were scattered across the floor.

"Delphine?" He called out slowly.

"Selene!" She popped out from behind a corner. "I should've known you'd come for me!" She went to throw her arms around his neck.

He stepped back, causing her to stumble. "No."

She scrunched her face in anger.

Before another attack tried to come his way, he wanted to make his intentions clear. "I'm here for Kohl. I want to know how to find him. No games this time."

Delphine laughed in his face. "He wants nothing to do with you all. Now if you take me with you, he usually can't get enough of me, no matter what form he is in."

"That is not an option. I'm done dealing with you. Tell me where Kohl hangs out."

"One: you'll never be done with me. The Nulls need me. This only ends if I decide I'm done with you, and I have to warn you, Selene, you're getting awfully close. Don't make a decision you regret later." She jabbed him with her finger. "Two: Why would I help you? What's in it for me?"

"Knowing you did the right thing." He stood his ground.

"Pass. Next offer." Delphine looked disgusted at the thought.

"I'm not making a deal with you."

"Then, I'm not giving up Kohl. Everyone has wanted him for months, and I made sure he only wanted me. No way I give that up without a payout."

"You're so selfish it's despicable."

"It's a god eat god world out there, Selene. Get with the times. You'll never be on top without leveraging your way up."

"Did you even love him? Even the smallest amount?"

"Kohl? Ew, no. He's gross and smells like the dead. You on the other hand . . . I'd have let you get more of me than he ever did, but you're blowing that all now! And for what? Nothing!"

"I never wanted you. I'm here to save a friend."

"I bet he's barely recognizable now. He's been without his precious necklace for a while."

"Help me save him!"

"Not a chance. When The Bad One takes over, he'll come here. He'll want to find me, and I'm aching to be found by him."

"What's your endgame, Delphine?"

"To win. The same as everyone else's."

"No. Most people care about others before themself."

"Like your stupid Lena Basil? Sounds like she's off to offer herself up as ogre chow. I couldn't have designed a more suiting fate myself."

"Enough!" Selene slammed his foot on the ground, and a line of fire shot straight out towards Delphine.

The siren had to jump onto a bookshelf to keep from being cooked.

"No. More. Games." Selene's eyes were ablaze. "Tell me where Kohl is, NOW!"

Delphine always enjoyed his powers when they went to save the Nulls. It made her job supremely easy, but Selene's Hephaestus vibes in close quarters weren't exactly her vibe. "You wouldn't be able to find him even if I told you!"

"I'm not worried about that. If he's in his other shape, and I get close enough, he'll come find me. I'm a threat he can't stand."

"You know what? Fine! You boys and your childish feelings. He'll destroy you! The Bad One has the power of an ancient god! You've said it yourself!"

Selene stood in silence and waited. He hadn't meant to intimidate Delphine, but the fire shot out of him. She had pushed one too many buttons. He needed to scale back, so he didn't accidentally hurt anyone, but he wasn't budging on finding Kohl. "I'm not leaving until I know where he is."

Delphine's toe burned from the fire. She was

ready to be done with Selene and his immature emotions. She was a woman, and he had yet to evolve. "Prague."

"Where in Prague, Delphine?" His irritation was evident.

"I couldn't even tell you if I wanted to. No-where obvious though, that's for sure. He hangs out with a seedy crowd, that one."

"I finally get everything Lena's ever said about you. This is it, Delphine. I'll see to it personally that you're never back in Legacy after this."

"Don't you have a death wish to go fulfill? I gave you what you wanted," Delphine chastised.

"I can't believe I ever protected you. I regret everything."

"You'll regret more than that," Delphine sneered.

Selene grabbed a wobbly disc from the backpack. This was his ticket out of here. He did his best to manifest an image of Prague in his mind, threw down his mini portal, and jumped in. Once he landed on a cobblestone street, he snatched the item back instantly to prevent Delphine from having a chance to join in. He hoped he got his location right.

It was nighttime on this side of the world. The cobblestone was illuminated by a nearby building. The buildings were large and ornate in what looked like a town square. They were beautifully chiseled and astonishingly old. Before him was an astro-nomical clock with the most intricate design he had ever seen. The attention to detail was miraculous. The face had so many dials they were hard to differentiate, but one, without a smidge of doubt, followed the moon. He could stare at this structure for hours and still want to see more. Selene wanted to get a closer glimpse, but any light here lent itself more to the shadows than to clarity. Any one of these patches of darkness could be Kohl. A mass of people were coming towards Selene. He pushed himself up against a wall.

A gentleman in a wide brimmed black hat and long black cloak stood within his arm's reach. He held a lantern to his face as he talked to the crowd behind him, "And that is why they call it Old Town Hall. Now, if you gaze upon this wonder next to us, we will wait for the apostles' blessing before we move to the next part of the tour." The ornamented clock chimed as statues and figures moved about. One skeleton in particular caught Selene's eye. "Blessings have been granted folks! If you'll follow me, we'll go down a flight of steps in here and venture into Prague's mysterious and deadly underground city. Try not to be fooled by its appearance, this household turned prison may look abandoned, but I have yet to go a night without being properly greeted by its eternal residents." With his free hand, the man held up a device with a singular green light. The crowd facing him grew giddy with excitement.

Selene sifted through the crowd in his shadow-like state, listening to the chatter between the paying customers.

"If we don't see a ghost tonight, I'm asking for my money back."

"I saw that on TV before! I hope it lights up red for us!"

"I heard there's a pit inside that they used to drown their prisoners in. It'd be a shame if someone got pushed in." On the word pushed, one of the men in the crowd mimicked that action to their smaller counterpart causing them to scream. The brute laughed at his companion. Upon witnessing this interaction, Selene's feet accidentally intertwined with the bully's and as the man moved forward, he fell face first into a puddle of mud. The crowd moved on without him.

Selene had never seen a tour like this before. He was skeptical about its ability to find actual ghosts, but he admitted if it did the work for him, it'd be a nice change of pace. A creepy underground dungeon didn't not seem like a place Kohl would be, but Selene kept his hopes up. He turned himself into a mist and blended into the herd to find the way to descend below ground. Once underground, he went off on his own.

He passed rooms with pottery and medieval clothing. Some areas had beds, others had cooking instruments, and one did, in fact, have a peculiar looking well. However, none of these screamed Kohl. Further into the web of tunnels, metal cells built into the walls decorated the space. A sour odor accompanied them as well. The next area had wooden pillories set up on the floor and crosses lined up against the walls. Coffins lay just beyond the archway. In the final chamber, a wax figure with a hood over his head held a large axe. He stood next to a wooden structure. The top had a divet for one's head and a basket lay a few feet below it.

"What is this place?" Selene asked himself.

"A personal favorite, honestly."

Spooked, Selene demanded, "Who's there?"

"Not me, and it looks like not you, either."

"Who are you? Where are you?"

"Who am I? Who are you? And as for where, I am everywhere. Also, nowhere. It depends on who you are."

"I don't have time for these games. I've come to meet someone who calls themselves The Bad One. Do you know him?"

"I've met too many bad ones to tell them apart."

"That is his name, not his description. We believe him to be a Slavic Vampire. Have you seen him?"

"We? Who is 'we'? You certainly ask a multitude of questions. Shadow to shadow, what do you truly expect to get out of me? I don't know you. I'm not inclined to help you. You are in my house though, and I'd like you to leave."

"You live here?"

"No."

"You lived here?"

"Also, no. How many questions must you ask? I'd much prefer it if you could dissipate out the same way you came in."

"I'll leave when I know where to go."

"I'm happy to light an exit for you." An upside down torch cast light through a doorway.

"I need to know where to find my friend."

"Your friend, you say? Funny to call your friend such a foul name."

"My friend is Kohl. The Bad One is consuming him. I'm here to save him."

"Hmm, and you say he's a vampire?"

"We believe so. He steals the spirit of others and leaves shells of who they once were behind him."

"He doesn't let them cross over?"

"They aren't that lucky."

"Blasphemous. He's a coward to deny the dead proper transport."

"Then help me stop him."

"I could help if I chose to. I want something in return."

Why does everyone always want something? "What is it?"

"I want to meet the soulless ones you speak of."

"The ones I save aren't here."

"Those are my stipulations."

"I can't leave until I get Kohl to come with me."

"Sounds like you ought to be extremely

convincing then."

Selene's patience was growing thin. "If we don't go now, we'll miss our chance. I have people that need me to get home to them. They're in danger."

"Stop wasting time then."

"WHERE DO I GO?!"

"Do I get to meet the soulless ones?"

"They're called the Nulls."

"Oh, yes, that's obviously significantly more respectful. Tick tock, shadow boy."

"Yes! Just help!"

"Indeed, help I shall." A shade, darker than the night, began to traverse before Selene.

Selene held out his hand, creating a handful of marble-sized fireballs to light his way.

"Stay close. Beings darker than us roam these streets at night."

"I'm not scared."

"Good. You can meet the golem then. I know enough to avoid it entirely."

Selene thought of Chibi Chan. They weren't that intimidating. Ugly, maybe, but not intimidating. "Lead the way."

"Suit yourself." The dark figure led Selene back up to the streets of Prague. There was a slight chill in the air. The stones were damp; the air was misty. The duo had only been traveling a few minutes when the ground started to shake. "Hope you're ready to be brave."

A giant glob of monster lurched in the distance. It was easily as tall as the wondrous clock from earlier. "What is that abomination! It's huge!"

"That's the golem you're not scared of. Want to go say hi? It looks like it's scouting for something. You could be just the ticket!"

"That thing is wretched."

"It actually protects the city if you're not already aware. A rabbi created that for his people hundreds of years ago, but it's still needed today. A shame really."

"What does it do?"

"Anything it needs to, I imagine."

"Brutal. I wouldn't want to get involved with that at all."

"Best we make it to the river then. Top speed!"

With the help of his guide, Selene covered a lot of ground at a rapid pace. He hadn't traveled with someone as a shadow since Kohl. It was nice to feel akin to another again. "I still don't know your name."

"Right you are, and here is our destination, the formidable Prague castle," the guide said ominously.

"This place is stunning." The castle was breathtaking, vast, and expansive. Even Ward A rarely had sights as stunning as this in it.

"A palace fit for a king, am I right?"

"I can see why The Bad One would want to stay here."

"The glamor of royalty attracts all kinds. Time to go in."

The statement was said as a fact, but Selene

nodded anyway. The embellishments around the castle were jaw dropping. The attention to detail rivaled the clock's. The entire building was astounding, all except the vicinity of the dungeon. Selene could feel the walkways narrowing. Sounds of the outside world drowned out as the walls thickened beside him. Selene felt isolated and constricted in this tiny tower. He seriously doubted there would be enough space if both he and his counterpart materialized in this room.

"There, below us. I believe the one you seek enjoys the oubliette."

Selene turned to his regular form to pull the cover off the circular structure. Inside a deep dark pit sat Kohl. "Kohl!"

Scared, the boy stared back up at his rescuer. "Selene! What are you doing here? You don't belong here! Close that now!"

"I'm here to take you back! I can help you!"

"No! Quick! You need to leave!"

"Look!" Selene fumbled around the pockets of Lena's bag before pulling out Kohl's necklace. "Let me put this on you!" Selene reached down as far as he could into the cell.

A hand gripped onto Selene's, but it wasn't Kohl's, and it was anxious to climb out.

Selene jumped back in horror, accidentally pulling The Bad One up with him.

"So we meet once more, moon god. I see you brought a friend this time too. Moxxi, to what do I owe the honor?"

"I had hoped never to see you again, vampire, but it seems you're upsetting the way things should be. Leaving beings behind soulless? You know I can't accept those terms."

"I left your underground haven. I don't bother the people of your town. You're already getting more than you deserve."

"Prague or not, life is meant to live or die. What you're doing is unnatural. It's not right."

"When did you become so noble? It's not a good look for you, Mox."

"I am unashamed of who I am. You should take note."

"No thanks. It seems I have an old friend seeking my company tonight, and I'm dying to see him." The Bad One reached out a hand behind him, clutching Selene by his neck.

Selene struggled to break free. "Let me go, you creep!"

"And end our fun so soon? I know you've been trailing me unsuccessfully for some time. I bet you're desperate to see what I can do. I'd hate for you to have come all this way for nought. Let me show you, old friend, just how far I've come." He threw Selene down in a heap by his feet. With one hand, The Bad One touched a nearby torture device. With the other, he created a portal. "That's our cue." The Bad One picked up Selene once more and jumped through the freshly created portal.

The power from this new world was debilitating. The ground was made of sharp, dirty rocks. Everything was black except the vibrant flames that lashed out to greet its inhabitants. It was hard to breathe; it was hard to stand. Selene lay crumpled into a ball on the rocky floor.

"Down so soon? I remember you being harder to beat than that. You've grown weak, Diablo. You're pathetic."

With no other choice, Selene decided to coat his body in his own flames to protect from these godly ones. The licks of the realm's flames continued to sting, but changing his oxygen intake at least allowed him to stand. "It's time to go home. Bring me Kohl."

"If I did that, I'd spoil all our fun we're about to have. I can't take that away from you after you've traveled so far." A wicked grin spread across The Bad One's face. "Have you ever been to Hell, Diablo? It seems so fitting after all. Why don't I help you get a closer look?" An invisible force started to push Selene towards the edge of a steep ledge.

"Vampire! The dead shall not be manipulated to serve your bidding, especially not the dead that belong to another. This world's ruler will not be pleased if he notices."

"Didn't we already discuss that being so noble wasn't your best look, Moxxi? I recommend you stay out of battles that don't pertain to you. I'm not above casualties of war."

"The dead pertain to me far more than they do to you."

Selene tried to find any cracks in the unwavering force. He hoped to slip through their gaps. His fire made the outline of fully armored ghosts, using their shields to press onward. He couldn't find a way through it or below it, but his fire was able to rise and crawl above the crowd. It was painful and clumsy, but it was effective.

"Now, see what you did, Moxxi? You prevented our little friend from meeting his namesake. I'm disappointed in all of you." The Bad One reached out, and smoky black tendrils extended towards Selene, leeches spreading in each tentacles' wake. "Why don't you come a little closer, old friend? I'd hate to lose you."

Moxxi flew towards Selene. They had no wings, but their speed of flight was remarkable. The upside-down torch from earlier scooped up Selene's entire flame. He was captured but grateful. Moxxi held their other hand out as they went. They were flying straight toward a spiky pillar. Moxxi yelled words from another language Selene only partially understood. A portal opened right before them as they soared through it.

They came up through a deep well into a stone room. Selene returned to his normal form. He was feeling depleted from using so much of his essence without pause. This space appeared very similar to the underground tunnels of Prague. He gazed into the well to see if they were being followed.

"I wouldn't do that."

"Is he going to follow us?"

"If he did, that would be the least of your worries. The local residents here don't like to be disturbed. Less talking now, I'll take us out."

Selene did as instructed. The corridors were dark, matching the rest of his experience in Prague. Moxxi led him to a square courtyard.

"We should be safe here for now, but we need to prioritize leaving sooner rather than later. Bad things happen here."

"Where are we?"

"Right now? The proper part of Houska's Castle."

"How'd you get us here?"

"Through one of the gates of hell."

Selene didn't know how to respond to that. "Can you do that anywhere?"

"Like your friend the vampire? No. If a spirit or soul is in need of transport, I can take them down, and I can come back up at any point. That's the extent of it."

"I need to go back soon, but I need Kohl to go back with me."

"I haven't seen Kohl much before, however his other side is overly apparent as of late. He's full of gusto and bravado. I am surprised to see he hasn't gotten himself trapped yet. Gods don't take kindly to uninvited guests. And using Slavic powers over

Christian souls! I don't even think you're that dense."
Moxxi dusted off their white robes and blood red sash
as they ridiculed Selene. They readjusted their golden
rope belt and smoothed out their blonde hair.

Selene sulked. "It's probably hopeless anyway.
I lost the necklace when I reached in the oubliette."

"Oh, right! I grabbed that. It seemed important." Moxxi threw the amulet over. "What does it do
anyway?"

"It takes out the poison," Selene lamented.

Odd sounds started emitting from the castle.
There was a rumbling intensifying from inside the
walls, ready to explode. "Ick!! I hate this part!! Hide!!"
Moxxi vanished into the shadows.

Selene tried, but his body was too weak. The
moonlight shined upon him in the open courtyard. He
was defenseless and impossible to miss.

Creatures started pouring out of the
entryways. Large black-winged creatures escaped
viciously, clawing their way out of the building,
screeching as they took off into the night. Selene sat
petrified as he watched dozens take off into the sky.
They were morbid abominations. When all of them
seemed to have escaped, Selene attempted to stand.
He wanted to find Moxxi and leave.

"Don't. Stay hidden," Moxxi whispered.

That didn't make sense to Selene as the
spotlight of the moon was cast solely upon him.

A loud croak interrupted his thoughts. In the
doorway in front of him, a half-human half-toad

hybrid emerged. The initial sight churned his stomach. It hopped closer to Selene. Other half-animal humanoids entered the scene behind it; surrounding Selene were bloodthirsty bat-like, lizard-like, ant-like, and crab-like demons.

"I'm so glad you got to meet some of my new friends. You see, I'm running with a new crowd these days. They understand my hunger, my need to survive, and the frustration of being trapped for years on end. They get how good it feels to finally break free." The Bad One towered over Selene just outside of the moonlight.

"You're full of lies! Kohl's the one who's been trapped. You've taken everything from him."

"I've shown him the world and even kept that annoying girl around for him. He owes me!"

"Bring. Him. Home!" Selene demanded.

"Bossy. You want to make deals? I can make deals. Come out of your little fortress there, and let's have a chat. All of us are starving for your attention." The demons encroached closer.

Selene realized none of them would enter the moonlight. He was frantic to figure out how to use this to his advantage. "I'll come out for Kohl," Selene stalled. A red and white butterfly with golden accents descended from above and landed on his wrist. He watched the insect crawl onto the necklace in his hand. It tugged ever so lightly on the chain. His intuition instructed him to let go. He fussed for a moment then gave in.

The Bad One had been rambling on, but Selene missed it, having been distracted by the insect who now flew so high he could barely see them.

"I'm out of time. Kohl or nothing," Selene asserted.

"And where are you going to go, Diablo? Have Moxxi take you back to Hell? To Oculus? Skip the middleman. I'll take you myself. I've been longing to show you all the best spots."

Selene repeated himself, "Kohl or nothing. Last chance."

"Shake on it, then." The Bad One extended his hand.

Selene stepped closer to the edge of the moonlight. "If you want me, you have to come get me." And with both hands he pulled his rival into the stream of light. Selene pushed him to the ground and climbed on the vampire's back. The Bad One was less solid than expected. Selene fumbled trying to find the best way to secure his foe. The Bad One's tendrils snaked up Selene's body, keeping them tied as one. Selene did his best to contain the undead beast, but he was faltering.

The butterfly swooped down and draped the chain over the vampire's fluid shape. Selene reached for the crystal and pressed it into The Bad One's chest. The crystal glowed in the moonlight. Selene shifted to keep it within the moon's powerful beam. He watched the darkness slowly being dismantled. It was happening! Selene's arms stung with pain as The

Bad One resisted his fate. A few of the vampire's leeches had pierced Selene's skin, and as they were called back to the supercharged crystal, they burrowed down deeper into his body. He screamed in agony.

"Moxxi, we need to go. Grab the disc in my backpack and drape it over all of us," Selene ordered.

The butterfly struggled, but managed to achieve the request. As they dropped the transporter in place, all Selene could think about was that he hoped this was enough to save Lena.

{ 12 }

Witches and Worries

Lena wished she had Airess' powers. Being able to grow plants would be seriously helpful when you're stuck, who knows how many feet, underground. Lena had been kicking and clawing the soil for a while now. She was excited at one point to have a root to use for heightened stability, but that proved pointless. The only thing it was successful at was ripping her pants.

Lena readjusted in the tight, earthen space. Paper crunched beneath her feet. *What's that?* she asked herself as she bent down to look. The pages were torn and crumpled. They were the letters Tao had given her earlier. Their writing was illegible now. As she fiddled with them in her fingers, the remaining ink started to glimmer.

They were the same hue she had on her skin from the beach. Tao had given her talismans. She studied them again to see if she could make out their purpose. All she could tell was that they were most likely the same. Not wanting to waste the gift, Lena put one in her unripped pocket and the other up to her chest until her skin absorbed the note.

Lena placed her hands on the dirt walls. Roots jutted out of the soil like rungs of a ladder. She started to climb her way up. When she reached the ceiling, she pushed hard against the solid construct. Dirt crumbled around her hand, falling onto her face. She tried to be more tactful on her second attempt and created an avenue upwards. The ground was amenable. She was altering the earth to her will.

Up and up she climbed until her fingers touched air. She pulled herself out of the forest floor. Immediately, she scanned for other holes around her. The topsoil in this area was undisturbed.

"Airess?" she called out. "Professor Nakshatra?" Lena paused, hoping to hear a familiar voice call back. No one answered.

Solei? There was still no response.

Lena scanned the area around her. This was the witch's home for sure. It was eerily mute. No voices, no birds, no bugs. She crouched closer to the ground investigating for tracks. As she moved tall grass to the side, the blades fell like dominoes. The grass was creating a path for her. With no better option, Lena decided to follow the walkway before her.

As she trekked through the long grass, a morbid smell was intensifying. Lena knew she was close to the fence. Nothing else smelled that way. Her stomach retched. This was her way out, but that wasn't what she wanted. She wanted to be with her friends.

Lena got to the edge of the forest. She was at the part of Ina's property that faced towards her own home. A brief wave of emotion hit her. She missed her parents. Stepping out past the boundaries of the witch's forest instantly returned sound to her ears. A weight was lifted off her body. The air beside her started to shimmer. Unsure of who, or what, that magic belonged to, Lena ducked back behind the tree line. Two shapes emerged. Lena recognized one of them instantly.

"Selene!" She hurried towards him.

He caught her eye and got up to greet her. "Hey. Are you ok? Am I too late?"

Lena swiftly gave a recap of getting to see Airess again, the argument with Baba Yaga, and getting trapped. She was talking at mach speed, and her emotions were swinging wildly from fear to anger and back again. She was so caught up in her story that she completely missed Kohl righting himself next to her.

"I see you haven't changed much, Basil."

Lena jumped. It had been months since she had seen Kohl's smoky eyes. "Uh. Hey." She offered a small wave.

"I overheard what you said. Baba Yaga is super powerful, and P.C. paves the way for her to do as she pleases around Astoria. If you made a pact with her too, fulfilling it is the only way out. That crone is brutal."

"You're as helpful as ever, Kohl." She faced Selene. "We need to save the Nulls."

"No time like the present then." He picked up the wobbly disk. "Can you get us there?"

Lena nodded and grabbed the transporter. She thought of the chicken hut, its bumpy chicken skin, its widow-like eyes, and the giant cauldron waiting to be filled inside it. The images flooded her mind. Their location was prepped. They all leaped in.

Sounds of battle filled Lena's ears. The scene looked bleak. Chibi was trying to smash the chicken legged hut, but their assault wasn't notably successful. For a cabin on legs, it was surprisingly nimble. Professor Nakshatra was fighting with Baba Yaga. Solei, Mae, and Tao stood defensively around the Nulls who were engaged with . . . another Baba Yaga? A cackling creature flew overhead. Lena ducked and noticed they seemed to be flying in a large stone cup. The figure blasted a shot at the newcomers, knocking Lena off her feet. A pair of muscular arms steadied her.

"Easy there. Can't have you getting hurt already. Save it for the end. It's more dramatic that way." Moxxi winked at Lena.

Selene inserted himself into the conversation, "I see the Nulls!" The group of four ran as one.

Kohl shouted, "Where's Airess?"

Lena pointed to the house, and by proxy, Chibi.

"Is that a golem?" Moxxi asked, concerned.

"He protects our friend, Airess. He's on our side!" Lena reassured. The troop had reached Solei. They looked the worse for wear. A sticky reddish-purple liquid covered the top half of their body. "Solei! What's going on? Is that blood?"

Distressed, Solei looked to Lena and those behind her. "Thankfully not. It's beet juice. Things are bad here though, Lena. The Baba Yagas are everywhere, and they're sinister to the core." They glanced at the others behind their friend. "Is that Kohl?" Their disapproval was evident.

Selene stepped forward defensively. "I brought him to help us."

"And is that what you're actually going to do?" Solei posed aggressively.

"I . . . I don't know," Kohl stammered.

"I figured. Get with the rest of the pack then. The rest of us have some ogres to fight."

Deflated, Lena dragged Selene and Kohl under Solei's electrical net to be with the Nulls. Moxxi seemed to have already made their way there.

One Baba Yaga swooped low for a strike. Solei blocked it with a loud zap. Baba Yaga kept circling and avoiding bolts from Solei. Mae and Tao used their bodies as barriers over the Nulls any time the Old Hag cast a spell. Lena did her best to protect all of them under her shield.

"Babas! See what we have here!" The other

two witches gathered close to their sister.

"Oh. Babas sees."

"Babas undoubtedly sees."

The three Babas stood so close they started to merge into one. They grew taller and wider into the ogress Lena first saw in the fields. Her warty hand reached into the middle of the group, breaking Solei's net and piercing Lena's cover, to pull out Kohl. Professor Nakshatra tried to stop her, but it didn't work. The Old Hag held Kohl up to her nose. "Your bones have almost the perfect smell. You may be a death bringer, but you are from Baba's land." The ogress danced in happiness.

"I know of you. You eat children and steal them during the night."

"Only the willing and the naughty! Tell me, my pretty. Which one are you?"

Kohl turned into a mist and reappeared over the ogress' nose. "That depends. I could be either if the right terms are met."

"You try to trick Babas! Babas hates tricks!" She hastily grabbed at Kohl.

As a black shadow, he bounded all over the giant's body, exhausting the witch.

Kohl's voice echoed as he trailed from one spot to the next. "One of me is worth more than all those willing below. Their life source is already gone, and I'm the one who consumed it all. I can even be more than I am now. But that many souls is costly. One must be prepared to pay the price for such a feast."

"You! You don't look like a feast," the witch sneered. "You are too much trouble! Babas will go back to the other offerings." The Old Hag reached down to the group. She watched as Lena threw up her shield again. Not wanting to put forth more effort than was needed, Baba Yaga dug her hands underground to lift up the mass of children.

Sensing an opportunity, Professor Nakshatra slashed at the ogress' wrists with a curved blade. Baba Yaga shrieked in torment and reflexively yanked back her hands. The pain was immense and jarring. The witch stumbled and crashed into the forest, knocking a plethora of trees over in the process. Professor Nakshatra's blue hue switched to green as she used the recently fallen trees to bind the large witch. Vines started to wrap Baba Yaga. Chibi sprung forward to aid as well. The golem stood on the Old Hag immobilizing her as she yowled. The chicken hut kicked him from behind.

Kohl hovered near the golem and watched. Four-leaf clovers were stuck to their clay body. "That can't be ..." Kohl inched closer. "It is. That's raskovnik." Kohl appeared back in his human form to gather a handful of the clover-like plants and caught Chibi's attention. "Bring this to the witch's hut! It will unlock the door!" He pressed the bundle into the stump of Chibi's arm.

Chibi listened and leapt to tackle the chicken hut, pressing the raskovnik onto the door. It worked. The door flung open, and a disoriented Airess climbed onto her dear companion.

Kohl observed his desired outcome then went over to the unattended ogress. He knelt by her ear and whispered, "I can help you. I can take you to the healing waters you guard and even offer myself up as nourishment. But you have to leave here, Baba. This is their world, not ours."

Baba Yaga was livid. She thrashed about, but each branch she broke grew three thicker limbs to restrain her. The strength of her bindings were stifling. The Old Hag stared at Kohl as she fought for her breath.

No longer waiting for the ogress' acceptance, Kohl touched the witch and waved his hand. A portal started forming. "We have to go back to where we belong. "

The witch's anger turned to fear as she screamed, "Nooooo!! " One of her hands broke free. Baba Yaga scratched through the portal. Professor Nakshatra and Airess were quick to fix the restraints, keeping the Old Hag at bay.

All other eyes were on the circular doorway that had become fully formed. Through the gateway was a small cabin. It was an exact replica of the chicken hut they'd encountered in Astoria. Only in this one, the viewers could see inside. Three familiar faces that were bound and gagged filled the central cauldron.

"Dad!" Lena dropped her shield and rushed full force towards Kasim. A few of her friends tried to stop her, but she was too fast. She took out the gag in her father's mouth. Once she assessed his face, she held him close, the top of the cauldron pressing into her ribs. They sobbed on each other's shoulders.

Baba's scratch had loosened the ropes over Principal Chromwell. The gash gave her enough space to wriggle free. Her eyes were locked on Baba Yaga. Rage consumed her as she took in the view of Astoria. Ever so gracefully, she exited the cauldron and headed straight for her staff. As she passed by Kasim and Ina, she snapped her fingers, relinquishing her friends from their imprisonment. Lena clung onto her father's arm. Once all were free, the four of them walked out of Baba's homestead and into their own realm.

Theodora Chromwell strode forward with the confidence of a god. "This was not our agreement," she spoke sternly and directly to Baba Yaga. "I was willing to bend the rules a smidgen in order to help Millie. We sat in your foul cauldron. We let you tie us with rope and stuff apples in our mouths. We played your game to save our friend. But this . . .," the Headmistress addressed each of her students. "This breaks our treaty. We shall release you. You will go home and never be heard from again. Your land in Astoria will be wiped from existence. Never again will you bother this town's inhabitants. Do you understand?"

"Babas understands, and Babas will remember this next time you come ask for favors."

"I have undeniably relied on you too much for too many things. That is a failing of mine, and mine alone, usually, with little to show for it afterwards. I should have learned, but I was naive. That is over now. Helping Millie was my last favor."

"Yes. Help for Millie, help for Ina, help for your town and your school. You're always asking for help from Babas!"

"And now, it is done. The burden has ended." Theodora waved her staff and freed Baba of the roots, trees, and Chibi. "You are no longer welcome here."

"Silly human freeing Babas. If Babas is free, then Babas can eat!" With an open mouth of honed iron teeth and gnarled nails, Baba Yaga pounced onto Principal Chromwell and scooped the rest of the team towards their mouth.

"Eat you shall!" Chromwell twirled her staff above her head. Ravens inundated Baba Yaga's jaw, forcing the Old Hag back as they pushed into her mouth.

Ina, Kasim, and Lena rushed to Professor Nakshatra's side. Her robes had turned into a dark navy, and her skin was crimson red. In one hand, she held a long studded club. In the other, she held a skull cup that had been filled to the brim. Lena was shocked to see the calm and nurturing professor appear so deadly. The other adults stood in solidarity with the professor. Lena hid behind the three of them.

Lena scanned the forest for her friends. Selene, Solei, Mae, Tao, and Airess were on their way to join the huddle with Lena. Chibi stayed in the thick of battle, determined to knock the Old Hag over again. Almost everyone was accounted for except Moxxie, the Nulls, and Kohl. They were nowhere to be found.

"Where are the others?" Lena asked her approaching friends.

Mae and Solei shrugged.

"Kohl never left Baba's portal. He's inside there." Airess pointed to the cauldron. She was right. Lena could still see Kohl's faint shadow inside the metal pot.

"What is he doing in there?" Lena pressed.

Solemnly, Selene responded, "I don't think there's an answer to that that any of us will like."

"I'm going to talk to him. I've had enough of him being like this!" Airess got up in a huff and beelined towards the portal.

"Airess!" Lena called out, but the healer didn't turn.

"Lena, do you still have that other piece of paper I gave you?" Tao inquired.

"Yeah. Here." She handed it back to him. "Why?"

"If Airess is going into that portal, she's going to need to be able to find her way home. I'll be right back." Tao chased after the healer.

"Are we really just going to let them do this?" Lena rebuked.

"Little cub, I think some battles aren't ours to fight." Solei pulled Mae close.

Frustrated and uncertain, Lena turned back to Selene. "Where do you think Moxxi and the Nulls went?"

"I don't know, but I'm sure Moxxi is figuring it out. They only came so they could meet them. I'm sure they have a plan. They were really upset about The Bad One taking away souls and leaving behind whatever it is that the Nulls are."

"Oh." Lena felt uncomfortable. Everyone had their own agenda, and none of them felt cohesive to another.

"Incoming!" Kasim yelled as a normal sized Baba Yaga flew towards the group. He threw a large cloak over the kids.

"Tricksy, tricksy man. No one is safe from Baba Yaga!" Baba dove towards the huddled teens.

The ogress must have broken up into three again, Lena thought to Solei. She wanted to provoke a response, but it didn't work.

Professor Nakshatra raised her staff and swiped it through the air. A large axe sliced at the Old Hag as she flew by, knocking the witch out of her saucer and onto the ground before Ina. Ina wasted no time in drawing her flaming sword and pinning Baba Yaga down with it. The witch dug her claws into the soil, cackling at her actions. Not only did she start to lower into the ground, but so did Lena and her friends.

"She'll trap us underground if she can!" Lena yelled to anyone who would listen.

Kasim dropped down to the witches' side and

shackled her wrists in cuffs. The earth stopped sinking. "I may not have been able to stop you from sending off Millie, but there's no way I'm allowing you to take my daughter away from me too." He pulled a crackling strand out of a small bag and started to wrap Baba Yaga in it.

"Focus all your attention here, fool. Leave my other sisters free, and let's see who prevails," the smaller ogress spat.

"Once she's secured, Kasim, take her to her portal. We'll start seizing the others," Professor Nakshatra directed.

Lena stood up next to her dad and put her shield over them as he lifted the heavy hag. She could tell he wanted her to stay under the protective cloak, but before he could protest, Selene covered the Basils in a thick mist as well. Lena and Selene refused to let Kasim go alone. Giving in, Kasim trudged to the portal. Tao, Airess, and a visible Kohl manned the entrance. Airess' chest glimmered a familiar red. She had taken Tao's talisman.

"You kids shouldn't be here. You need to get back behind Tara and Ina for protection." Kasim flopped the Old Hag into her own cauldron.

"We'll keep her here and make sure she doesn't escape," Kohl announced.

Airess nodded and started to weave vines over the top.

"Promise me, you all will get out before the third one goes in. I don't want to fight with you all in addition to what we already have going on here."

"I promise, sir. We'll get out in time," Tao affirmed.

Disgruntled, Kasim accepted the situation. "I'm trusting you three. Don't make me regret it." He walked back to his colleagues and ushered Lena back out into safety. With Kasim having returned, Professor Nakshatra went further into the battle.

Only Selene was left under the cloak.

"Where'd Solei and Mae go?" Lena inquired.

He pointed towards Chibi who was slowly being disassembled. "Chibi needed reinforcements. Ina went to help, but P.C. got confined by under-growth, and Professor Nakshatra wouldn't leave me by myself despite me begging her to do so."

Lena watched as a large python slithered around Chibi, gathering all of the golem's parts closer and closer together. Solei attacked the hag with lightning, but Baba Yaga was not deterred. Professor Nakshatra was on the scene now. She drank from her skull cup, and a large astral cleaver formed in the hand of a third arm on her right side. The arm swung back and cleaved right under the second Baba's head. The Old Hag's spell stopped as she collapsed to the ground. The professor's third arm disappeared, and holding her studded club, she performed a chant that levitated Baba Yaga's body.

Kasim turned to his daughter and Selene. "We should haul that one away for Tara. She's better situated to help Ina and Theodora." Eager to be part of the team, the two teens went into action. Kasim wrapped Baba Yaga up in the crackling ropes, Lena popped her shield, and Selene draped them in his obscuring mist. They dropped the second body off at the cauldron where the others were still standing guard.

"One more," Lena emphasized to Airess and Tao.

The last Baba Yaga was slightly bigger than the rest. Her features were darker. Her teeth and pointed nails were stained deeper than the previous versions. She was unmistakably ready to kill. With one hand, she shot a spell towards Ina. The angel swung her mighty blade, but missed. The spell caught Ina in the stomach and she started to shrivel. The witch cackled and grew as the tether drained her opponent and she absorbed Ina's life source. "I haven't eaten an angel before," Baba mocked, "Would taste good with butter and bread, Babas thinks."

"Ina!" Professor Nakshatra charged in, swinging her mighty axe through the spell's con-nection. The axe redirected the incantation, up through the professor, but she was able to stand her ground. Ina, on the other hand, fell lifeless. Kasim was swift to start his healing practices on the fallen angel.

"Tara! Drop your axe!" Principal Chromwell commanded while struggling with her own predi-cament. Vines were constantly twisting around her body, constricting her movement and abilities. The headmistress had to alternate between making attacks against her foe and trying to protect herself.

Selene was the first to P.C.'s side. "Focus on Baba Yaga. I've got this." With his hands in the dirt, he found the plant's roots. Orange flames snuck up through the soil's cracks as he burned the plant from the bottom up, forcing the plant to die.

Principal Chromwell narrowed her focus and held her staff up high with both arms. All the light within the forest began to funnel into the staff. The headmistress rose into the air, breaking free of her ties. She had an aura around her, an outline that was illuminating and other worldly. Her eyes changed from iris' and pupils to cavities filled with the cosmos. When she spoke, it was not her usual voice. "You have broken our pact. You have hurt those that call Astoria home. Therefore, you must suffer the punishment of your crimes. I have tried to spare you, yet you adhere to your foul ways. There will be no redemption for you, Baba Yaga. Your banishment from the lands of others shall be permanent. No exceptions are to be made. The memories your followers have of you in all other realms but your own shall be wiped. Your powers are stripped of growth and limited to only those who dwell in your forest. You shall exist in your culture and your culture alone. Here I see to it! Be gone, foul beast, and never return, or else the wrath of gods will descend upon you in arrant splendor!" Theodora aimed her weapon at the heart of the final Baba Yaga, and the Old Hag shattered into a million pieces, each controlled by the great staff. The headmistress swirled the pieces together, causing a tumultuous whirlwind, and aimed them through the center of the portal, not realizing three of her students had been standing guard there. The fragments of Baba Yaga were headed straight towards the bubblegum healer. At the last second, Kohl ripped off his necklace and compelled The Bad One to take over. He grew three times his normal size and pushed Airess and Tao outside of the entryway's space as his wicked side roared into power. P.C.'s magic struck him dead on, knocking him into the back of the hut and sealing the portal door as it passed through his body. The gateway faded out of view.

"Kohl!" Airess threw herself into the air that previously held her former love. Tao caught her before she hurt herself further. She wept in his arms.

"No!" Principal Chromwell's voice was back to her own. "What have I done!"

"You have saved our city, dear friend. You have protected us all." Professor Nakshatra assured her leader as she placed their hand on the headmistress' shoulder.

"But the boy . . ." Theodora's voice choked at the thought.

"There is unfortunately not much that can be said to ease that pain, but you did well, Theodora. You did what needed to be done."

"I hurt a child, Tara. A student! That's reprehensible!"

"What Tara says is true," Kasim added. "There

is nothing to be changed about what happened, but you did right by us all." He put his arm around Lena as he spoke.

"It's how . . .," Ina coughed, ". . . the fates intended."

Unsure of her actions, Principal Chromwell distracted herself and examined Ina. "We need to get her settled for the night. She's unfit to be on her own."

"I can watch her at my house. Lena can assist, if needed, as well," Kasim volunteered.

"Of course. Anything for Ina," Lena sympathized.

"With your permission, sir, I can stay, too. I can watch over Ina while everyone sleeps," Selene offered.

Kasim glanced between the boy and his daughter. "I'll permit it, but you sleep on the couch, and I'll put an alarm on the stairs until morning."

Lena rolled her eyes, but Selene's acceptance was genuine.

It might be nice for being in the same house tonight, yeah? Solei reached out.

There you are! I thought you were back to ignoring me, Lena chided.

Me? You're the one that ignored my messages. I sent over a dozen while dealing with that nasty crone.

Oh. I didn't hear anything from you. I'm sorry.

Me too. Chalk it up to evil witches being evil?

Sounds fair to me. Lena left her father's side

and walked over to Solei to put her head on their shoulder. Solei wrapped their arm around her and gave her a squeeze.

Principal Chromwell addressed the group, "Tonight, we rest. We must mourn our losses. After the sun rises, we shall meet again. And again, to my students, I am so deeply, deeply sorry for what my actions have cost you today. I never would have chosen this path."

"Principal Chromwell?" Airess' voice was barely above a murmur.

P.C. wasn't holding together well, but she was trying so hard to be strong for her remaining students. "Yes, my dear?"

"I think you should have this." Airess placed Kohl's necklace in the principal's hands. "Try not to blame yourself. Kohl made up his mind about his future a long time ago."

The headmistress mouthed the words "thank you," but no sound was able to come out. It was time for the headmistress to go. She wasn't able to offer any more to her pupils. Seeing this, Professor Nakshatra nodded to the students and escorted Theodora out of the forest.

"That was really kind of you, Airess," Tao complimented. "I'm sorry about . . . well, everything."

"It's okay, I think. I just need some time." Airess was downplaying her heartache. "Chibi and I should head home."

"Here, take this. It might help." Lena dug into

her bag and handed Airess Ward A's skeleton key.

"I'll text you tomorrow?" Solei checked.

"I look forward to it. Thank you both." Airess fidgeted with her clothing. "I'm a little unsteady on my feet, I guess. Tao, do you think you could walk me home?"

Tao jumped up at the request.

Lena had to suppress a giggle. *Good for him.*

"We should head out too," Solei said, picking up a very oversized python.

"Do you guys need anything?" Lena directed her question towards the large snake. It shook its head. Lena looked up to Solei. "I'm just a thought away, all right? Let me know."

"If you walk down the stairs at night to help us, your dad is going to have a heart attack," Solei playfully teased.

"Out the window it is then," Lena said with a smile.

"I'm going to pretend I didn't hear that." Kasim nudged his kiddo. "We should start heading back too, Magpie."

The friends bid their adieus and headed for their respective homes. It had been quite the day, and they all required some much needed rest.

~*~

Selene drifted into the dream world with ease. It felt good to be surrounded in his element.

"You guys aren't much for skipping the theatrics, huh? I haven't seen so much showboating since the medieval ages rode prisoners around for public ridicule."

"Moxxi? What are you doing here? I'm busy. You'll have to come again another time," Selene scolded.

"Wow. Your concern for the soulless ones is astounding. I almost feel bad for taking them all away from you."

"Wait! You did what? Moxxi! What did you do to the Nulls?"

"I'm sending them home, shadow boy. It's the right thing to do."

"They belong here at Legacy!"

"They belonged in their own realms. After what your friend the vampire did though, they won't survive there on their own. They need to be transported to their proper resting places. You saw it yourself—almost two dozen of them were willing to walk into a trap where they'd be eaten and killed. That's not normal. No one should want to live like that."

"Then we help them! That's what we do here!"

"I talked to them, some have been here for months and the only help they had was getting set up in a fancy dungeon you all called a dormitory."

"I can do better. I'll do more."

"Listen, I'll at least let them make the choice. If they choose to go back to their roots and find asylum in Valhalla, or Aaru, or Heaven, or whatever, then they should be allowed that. Right?"

"I see your point, but I don't like it. I feel like I failed them."

"I think your town has plenty of that going around lately."

"Whatever. Do I at least get to say goodbye?"

"I can give you one day before I start my transport. I have already begun feeling out who wants to go where. I can't stop a ball already in motion."

"What about Delphine?"

"Which one is Delphine? I have to be honest, names aren't super popular among the half dead."

"Kohl's girlfriend. The siren."

"The annoying girl. What about her?"

"Are you going to transport her too? I doubt she'll go without a fight."

"I've already said if they want to stay they can, but she's not one of the soulless."

"What are you talking about? She was the first Null."

"She has powers and an absolute will to live. She's not on my roster."

"Delphine has powers? Since when?"

"That has nothing to do with me. I've made my stance perfectly clear. I transport. That's it."

"How do you know, though? I just saw her before Prague, and she was powerless."

"She gave me some guff trying to get into the soulless ones' dorms, but nothing I couldn't handle."

"Guff?"

"Yeah, she threw a few fireballs my way. They

were weak though. Her bark is way worse than her bite. I'd much rather get hit with her tiny embers than listen to her speak."

Selene laughed. "My girlfriend would feel the same way. She has been saying that to me for months. I'm just now starting to listen."

"She seems nice, that one. Don't screw it up with her. She's got a special thread tied to her lifeline, I can tell."

"That's probably solid advice, Moxxi."

"I got to go off into some other dreams before night end. Don't forget what I said. One day, then I'm gone with whoever wants to come with me."

"Can I ask one question before you go?"

"You and your questions, shadow boy. Do they ever end? Go. Quick."

"What should I do for the Nulls that want to stay?"

"That sounds like a question for the living, which I tend not to associate with."

"Fine. Good night, Moxxi."

"G'night, shadow boy. See you within twenty-four hours."

{ 13 }

Goodwill and Goodbyes

Lena's night went off without a hitch. There were no causes for alarm and no big scares. She tossed and turned while she slept, struggling to let her guard down. The night passed quietly, and Lena woke up to the smell of food. The aroma of fava beans was making its way through the house. That meant her dad was cooking, and it was going to be good. Selene was mildly talented in the kitchen, but this smelled more than mediocre.

Lena didn't bother putting on real clothes or brushing her hair. She went downstairs with full bed head. "Morning," she called out to her dad and Selene.

"Morning, Magpie! These ta'ameyas are just about done. Take a seat."

She sat down at the table next to her boyfriend, kissing his cheek as she passed.

He poured her a glass of orange juice. "Morning. Love the look," he teased.

She noticed he hadn't gotten ready either. "I see you're copying my style already. How did you sleep?"

"Okay, I guess. It was smooth sailing in regards to Ina. She was restful without being too out of it. She's still down in her peaceful, happy state on the couch. The only disruption was Moxxi."

"They came by the house?" Lena asked, surprised.

"Through my dreams."

"Weird. What did they have to say?"

"Info about the Nulls. I guess some of them want to go to their line's afterlife. Moxxi plans on fulfilling those wishes."

"Whoa!"

"Yeah, it seems like a large number of them will be leaving within the next day or so."

"That's so fast . . ."

"Yup," Selene responded. It was clear he wasn't thrilled about this new development.

Kasim came to the table. "Here we go, kids. Breakfast is served!" His high spirits were unexpected.

"You seem chipper this morning. Hiding some good news?" Lena couldn't imagine anything with P.C. or Ina perking up her dad's mood from the night before. He had been so exhausted and had barely said a word. She hoped her dad's change of mood was in relation to her mom.

"I have you, Magpie, and that brings me great joy. I wasn't sure the next time I was going to see you, for a minute there. I'm very glad to be home with you in this moment." Kasim reached out to hold his daughter's hand.

"You and mom both felt that way, I guess."

Lena had piqued her father's attention more so than what she already had. "You heard from your mom?"

She filled him and Selene in on the prayer Jibril delivered and how none of it made much sense.

"Poor Kamilah." Selene was moving around the food on his plate, but not actually eating. He couldn't help but think of how much more exciting the meal would be if Mrs. Basil had cooked it. Every meal of hers created a memory because no two of her meals were ever the same. Kamilah thrived on being unique, and that created such a safe space for Selene to be himself too. There were no social pressures with Mrs. Basil, no expectations of perfection. He could just be him, and that was always enough to be welcomed into the family.

"I actually think this is a good thing," Kasim stated matter-of-factly.

"How? It doesn't make much sense." Lena was skeptical at best.

"It may not have gone as planned. However, it wasn't a failure. Theodora's plan half worked."

"What does that mean?" Lena stuffed ta'ameya in her mouth as she spoke.

"It means that Baba gave Millie a way to confront the deity that stole her mind. Not only does your mom have a solid plan to get where she wants to go, but Baba Yaga helped build her confidence too. The witch wanted Millie to win and succeed. I have a lot of horrible things to say about Baba Yaga, especially after coming back to Astoria, but how she interacted and protected your mother on this new journey isn't a part of that."

"I'm no fan of the Old Hag either, but she did speak positively about mom, and often. She didn't like you though."

Kasim's expression turned sour. "I may be the reason things turned belly up in the portal."

Doubtfully, Selene asked, "How so, sir? You're always so calculated."

"That, son, was my failure. I was so certain that Baba Yaga was going to trick us, I never gave her a chance. I don't regret not trusting Baba Yaga, but I do regret getting caught by her. Theodora, Ina, and Millie went into the chicken hut, but I stayed outside. I wanted a backup plan, a way to protect Millie if things went south. I needed her safe, and I needed to get home in the timeframe I promised. Nothing was more important than those two things. I guess while Baba was wheeling and dealing with Theodora, my plotting was used against them. Baba said she couldn't trust us being free so in order for the witch to help Millie, we all had to be restrained to make sure we didn't hurt Baba. I still think the whole thing was a ruse, but it's how it happened. One of the Babas grabbed me from outside, threw me into their mortar and pestle, and flew me into the hut. I was the last one to be tied up and put into the cauldron. They stuffed apples into our mouths and from thereon, we could only answer yes or no questions and were at the mercy of the Old Hag herself. I had no idea she could come to Astoria, or had been coming here. I imagine if I did, I'd have likely been even rasher in my decisions, which probably would have made things worse. I can't describe the level of fear I felt, and the time seemed endless." Turning to Lena, he continued, "Losing your mother, not coming home like I promised, and knowing that awful crone was right by our house, it almost broke me. The whole situation really got to me." Kasim's tone was getting more emotional by the sentence.

"It was less than a day here, if that helps." Lena squeezed her dad's hand.

"Thanks, Magpie. I'm not sure if it does, but it's the thought that counts." He faked a smile.

There was rustling on the couch. Ina popped up her head. "What's that smell?"

Selene felt a sense of relief. "I haven't fully learned the name, but it's delicious. Want me to bring over a plate?"

"No need for special treatment. I can make it over to you all." Ina was wobbly as she attempted to stand.

Selene wasted no time and was by her side within seconds. He walked the angel to the table.

"Is this seat taken?" Ina joked, unknowingly

gesturing to Kamilah's seat.

"Not today, it's not. Please sit, old friend. We'd love for you to join us." Kasim's response sounded earnest.

Lena felt a great deal of pity and admiration for her dad. He was going through so much and having to face it in the most unpleasant ways, but he was still able to avoid sinking too far into his sorrows. She didn't think she could pull off a stunt like that. She figured she'd most likely let herself drown in that type of pain.

"I haven't heard from Theodora yet today; however, once we're done eating, I was planning on taking you to Ward A to finish your healing process, Ina? I expect Airess will want to have input about how your care is handled. I have a few incantations on an old papyrus I can use, but I was going to defer to our resident healer, if that's okay with you?" Kasim posed to his friend.

"I had similar thoughts. Airess tended to me tremendously for many years. Going back under her care until I'm fully myself again is the plan I'm most comfortable with."

"By the way Ina, that was a brave thing you did—taking on that spell for P.C. I don't think most people would have done that for another person," Selene complimented. Lena wondered if Kohl was actually who was on his mind.

"She is my sister, not by blood or by religion, but by choice. I couldn't let her suffer alone." Ina came off so certain. Then, under her breath, she added, "I tried that once before. I won't do that ever again."

Lena felt awkward. She had finished eating and did not love being in the middle of her parents and mentor's past. "I can go to Ward A. I just need to get ready."

Kasim was not surprised by her desire to leave. "I can make sure Ina arrives safely. Would you like to find your own transportation?"

Yes, thank the heavens. "I can make that work." She tried to hide her smile.

"Take care of her. You can help her pack." Kasim dismissed Selene as well.

Excited to be free, Lena ran up the stairs. She texted her friends immediately. "Heading to Ward A with Selene. Anyone else there or want to meet up?"

Tao was the first to reply. "I'm at Legacy with my mom. P.C. wanted to meet with my dad, but you know how he can be, so we came instead. I should be done in an hour or so."

Airess responded next. "I brought Chibi in last night and have been here since. Let me know where you're at, and I'll come out."

Lena waited for Solei to send something, but after a few minutes, they still hadn't read the messages yet.

Selene interrupted Lena's focus. "Hey, there's another thing Moxxi told me last night that you should probably know."

That doesn't sound good. "Oh? What's that?"

"Moxxi said Delphine has powers now."

"The mermaid got her powers back?!" Lena was floored. Delphine had been desperate for that for months.

"No. Not her powers."

"What do you mean?"

"Moxxi said Delphine has fire powers now, albeit weak ones."

"Fire powers? How does a mermaid get fire powers?"

"I have a hunch, but I want to run it by Tao first."

"Wow. She's going to be even more of a pain now, isn't she?"

"Probably."

"Hopefully she's still locked up in Professor Nakshatra's study. That'll at least keep her contained and minimize the spread of her chaos."

Selene sighed. "Moxxi saw her at the Nulls dormitory. I don't think Delphine stayed cooped up in the study for long."

"That is less than ideal."

"I know, but I wanted you to hear it from me before someone else."

"Thanks. I wish I knew what to do."

"That's what friends are for, right?"

Lena agreed completely. "Right!"

The two decided to walk to Ward A. Ina's house was back to normal. The smells of Astoria were pleasant once again. The only views to see were that of suburbia, and Lena preferred it that way. The walk took them under an hour, and Lena was pleased to see Ippy manning the front desk.

"Welcome back!" Lena greeted her friend.

"Glad to be here! The world wasn't right there for a minute. I was at my wits' end!" Ippy chattered.

"I hear you! Have you seen Airess? She said she took Chibi here last night."

"I saw her dropping off the skeleton key this morning, but that's it. I also noticed that the key was never properly checked out." Ippy gave a meaningful glare.

"I wonder who did that? Completely unprofessional if you ask me!" Lena dramatically embellished. "I'm off to find Airess! See you soon!"

"See you soon. Tell her I say hi."

"Will do!" Out of habit, Lena started walking in the direction of Selene's room. "Think I should text everyone again?"

"You can. Mind if I freshen up at my place though? I'm more comfortable getting ready there than around your dad."

Lena understood completely. "Of course. I'll text them while I wait on the beach."

"Great! Thanks." Selene put his arm around Lena as they walked. Things were getting back to normal. They turned down the hall where he lived.

"Uhh . . . Selene . . ." Lena was the first to notice the burnt image. On his door was a scorch mark in the shape of a skull and crossbones. "Presents from your former partner, I take it?"

"Hell hath no fury like a scorned siren, I guess." Selene tried to wipe off the marks but couldn't. "That's messed up."

"Just like her head." Lena snapped a picture of the door. "Go, shower, and I'll get the message out that Delphine is even more off her rocker than usual."

"All right. Give me five minutes."

"Take your time. I'm in no short supply of words to say." Lena made her way to the sandy beach and started texting the group in rapid succession.

~*~

"So, what do you think? Is it possible?" Selene was eager for Tao's opinion.

"I don't know. I guess it's possible? There isn't a lot of research on the Nulls, so I can't be certain of anything. But, yeah, unsettling as it is, I can see a way Delphine's fire powers came from absorbing yours," Tao attempted to ascertain.

"She's the worst," Lena repeatedly declared.

Airess wasn't sure how to react. Delphine had been a good friend to her many times, but she couldn't deny that not all actions by the siren were favorable. "I wonder if it's like a plant. If you put a cut flower in colored water, it absorbs the color along with the nutrients it needs to live. Perhaps, she absorbed Selene's flame because her body is des-perate to find what it needs to, to survive."

"Does that mean that any time someone directly uses a power on her, she'll absorb it? Or is it only in extreme situations? Or could it be a more selective process?" Selene was fighting to understand.

"I don't think any of us can answer that question. It wouldn't surprise me if Delphine wouldn't even know," Tao postulated.

Chibi pounded on his makeshift bed, and Airess went to tend to him. She had mostly gotten him put back together, but it was obvious his life source was much fainter than usual.

I'm sure you have the best reason for keeping to yourself today, and I don't want to intrude, but Mae is close to Chibi, and the golem isn't looking their best. I thought she might want to know, Lena thought to Solei. Her friend had been missing in action so far today.

"When you met with P.C., did she mention anything about Delphine?" Lena questioned Tao.

"No. She's not in a functional place right now. She's incredibly distraught over Kohl. She reached out to my dad, basically to try to pay penance for her actions. He, of course, was not having it. My mom offered to come onto campus to 'cleanse her spirit', but really, we were just there to activate talismans that could help P.C. heal from the wounds her mind is inflicting. We stayed with her to make sure she handled the process all right and left soon after. P.C. kept mumbling about regret and had a ton of negative self-talk but nothing relevant to this conversation. She has her own struggles currently."

"That's sad to think of her like that," Selene sympathized. "She should've never made the deal she did with Baba Yaga, but I don't think she meant to hurt anyone."

Airess chimed in, "We all make mistakes, and Kohl will always be a wild card."

"Even when he was here, P.C. struggled with him. He told me all about the meetings they would have, where she pushed him to try to find what he wanted for himself. He hated them. Most of the time, he just wanted to be left to his own devices and keep others out of his own business," Selene divulged.

"I know it wasn't his preference, but I think it was probably a good thing that so many people cared about him, even if he didn't like it. No one should be left in absolute isolation." Lena attempted to console Airess.

The healer's voice was soft in response, "Even Delphine?"

Lena cringed. Airess was justifiably using Lena's words against her, but she really didn't want to do anything nice for that awful mermaid. "Ugh. Probably, but please, no."

"We shouldn't leave her alone," Airess spoke slightly louder.

"Airess isn't wrong. Between Delphine's un-controllable and unpredictable nature, there are a number of reasons why we should try to find her and figure out what's going on," Tao affirmed.

Lena squirmed. She did not want to do this.

Selene whispered into her ear, "I'll do whatever you want. If you want to sit this one out, we can do that together."

Lena had to admit it felt nice to have him pick her over the mermaid. His words were helping mend some lasting wounds. She hated knowing her friends were correct though. "Ugh . . ."

Airess bounced with glee. "I think that means we won!" She wrapped her arms around Tao.

He sat, blushing and paralyzed. "Thanks, Lena."

Lena wasn't sure if she was being thanked for the hug or the fact Lena gave in. Either way, her thoughts were the same. "Why don't you two get a head start? We'll check in with Moxxi and the Nulls first, and then try to track Delphine down through them. Text if you get a good lead."

"You want us to go alone?" Airess clarified, back to her mousy volume.

"Absolutely." Lena's mood was lifting. If she had to confront her own issues helping Delphine, she was happy to push Airess to confront hers as well.

"I'm almost certain Moxxi is at the Nulls dorms. Ready to go?" Selene reached out to help Lena up.

Lena grabbed all her belongings and made sure to give Chibi one last hug. "Ready." Before leaving, she observed her friends uncomfortably fidgeting side by side. "Text me if you need me, but you've got this. I'm sure of it."

Neither Airess nor Tao believed Lena, but they

were sure about to find out real soon.

Finding Moxxi proved to be one of the easiest things Lena had been tasked with in some time. She was able to spot them as soon as she entered the dorms. They were in the middle of the common space with Nulls all around them. Some were even smiling. She hadn't seen that happen once the day before.

"If that's what you want, then I say go for it!" Moxxi encouraged one of the Nulls. "Hey! Shadow boy! If someone came here from a shark realm, but they felt more at home on land, is that a problem?"

Selene was taken off guard. "No, I don't think so. Why?"

"And who would someone talk to, to get out of aquatics classes and be more into agriculture?" Moxxi ignored Selene's disorientation.

"Umm ..." Selene thought of Tao's recent description of P.C. "Probably Professor Nakshatra?"

Lena wanted to help bail him out. "Whoever is the designated headmistress can absolutely help, but I've found talking to your professors can go a long way too."

"See? There ya go! She knows stuff. I'd trust her." Moxxi patted the Null on the back and walked to a less crowded hallway, gesturing for the duo to come along too. "They've been on me all night asking for help. They said no one's ever spent this much time with them here at the school." They glared at Selene.

Ashamed, Selene accepted the jab. "They're right. I'll do better."

"I can help too. If they want, I could even pair them up with some of the gods in Ward A that share similar interests," Lena offered.

"I don't like to get involved in the business of the living, but shadow boy is the one who asked what he could do to help them. It's not rocket science. Go talk to them. Figure out what they want and what they don't want. Push their requests up the chain of command. Be present. You're not a hero if you pull them out of their home and abandon them. Don't be worse than the vampire, man. Be empathetic. So many of them are lost and have no idea what they're supposed to do with their lives. Help them find their way. The ones staying want to live, so figure out how they can do that."

"I understand. I'll do better."

"Good! If not, that annoying girl will get to them first. I heard her this morning trying to recruit people to her cause, and no one wants that."

Curious, Lena pressed, "Delphine was here? What did she have to say?"

"Mostly complaints about you all and asking people to feel sorry for her."

"Sounds about right," Lena retorted.

"It didn't go anywhere today, but if the annoying girl ever figures out how to give them hope, you're going to have a mess on your hands. Now is your chance to get ahead of it."

"We will. I promise." Lena was certain in this. "But, hey, we're actually supposed to be looking for

Delphine after we meet with you. Any leads?"

"Nothing specific, no. My guess? You'll find her wherever she thinks she'll get the most attention."

It was hard for Lena to deny that.

"Moving past that drama though," Moxxi was clearly ready to move on, "let's talk transport. I surveyed two hundred and eighteen Nulls, and a majority want to come with me. Only seventy one want to stay."

"Wow." Selene hadn't realized there were that many Nulls, and the percentage staying was far less than he had hoped.

"We leave tonight. They're going to take the few belongings they have. I'll handle everything else."

"We should probably tell Principal Chromwell," Selene said hesitantly.

"I can make a list of the different realms I'm visiting and how many Nulls I'm taking to each location. That's about the extent of paperwork I'm willing to do."

"We can make that work. Can I ask if they're all going to happier places at least?"

"I wouldn't, but most are. Not all."

It never occurred to Lena that some of the Nulls Selene had saved were potentially bad. She assumed they were just more manageable versions of Delphine. She really had to stop assuming.

Moxxi could see Lena's revelation. "Don't worry, bright eyes, I'm not leaving anyone behind whose intentions are to stir trouble. I'm taking all the rotten apples with me."

"Thank you . . ." Lena's voice trailed off. There was so much she never thought of. Selene didn't look too far off from her. She wondered if it was just them or if others were in the same boat as well.

Lena's ID started to blink and Selene's did too. "I think we're being summoned," Lena commented.

"I have to go, Moxxi, but thanks for coming back to Astoria with me. You've helped a lot."

"It's my job, shadow boy. It wasn't right leaving them here without offering transport."

"Where will you go after this?" Lena asked. "Back to Prague?"

"Probably. There's plenty of work there. Maybe I'll find a new haunt in my travels though. You never know." They gave her a wink.

"Wherever you go, I hope you enjoy it. You deserve a nice place to call home."

"Thanks, bright eyes. Keep shadow boy in line. He needs it." Moxxi pretended to tip their hat.

Lena nudged Selene playfully with a smile. He rolled his eyes at her. "Until next time, Moxxi."

"Until next time." Selene let Lena guide their way out. "Did you mean what you said back there?"

"Hmm?" Lena cocked her head.

"That you'd help with the Nulls?"

"Well, we can't let Delphine win, can we?" Lena's joke fell flat. Selene was being serious. She stopped walking to make sure he could see the dedication in her eyes. "I'm kidding. I know how much they mean to you. I want to be a part of that."

"I feel like I failed all of them." Selene's words were full of regret.

"We can't go back. We can only go forward. My mom was always good for reminding me of that. We'll figure things out with the Nulls, whatever that means. We make a pretty good team."

"We do. I believe in us even if I don't believe in myself sometimes."

"I feel that to my core." Lena embraced Selene in a tight hug.

"Whatever we do though, is going to need P.C. So, it kind of works out that we're headed to her chambers."

"Uhh Lena, that's not where we were summoned to go."

"What?" She couldn't think of anyone else who had the power to reach them.

"I checked my phone after our badges went off. We're supposed to go to Professor Nakshatra's study. She didn't say she was still acting as headmistress, but between this and what Tao said, I don't think P.C. has taken back her role yet."

"You don't think she quit, do you? She wouldn't leave us after all that?"

"I don't know. She's done a lot of things lately that I never thought she'd do."

Lena was reluctant to admit it, but she felt the same. "I get that."

The rest of their walk was filled with their own

thoughts. Their minds hopped from one potential outcome to the next; their hands held onto the others' for reassurance and stability. As they entered the familiar room, they were surprised to be the last one of their friends to arrive. Even Solei and Mae had made it before them. Solei had the biggest smile, and Mae was acting silly. A few pillows down were Airess and Tao. Lena was shocked at that development, too. Usually there was Airess, and there was Tao, but the way they were sitting strongly implied that they were close enough to be Airess and Tao. Lena raised her eyebrow to the bubblegum healer. Her reaction was seen but only met with a coy wink. Professor Nakshatra entered the room. Selene pulled the couple to the pillows in between their friends.

"Good morning, my children. Thank you all for meeting on such short notice. I understand most of you have other things that need tending to, so I'll be swift. My position as interim headmistress will continue. I plan to stay onboard at this capacity through the school year. This will be of no shock to the majority of your classmates as you all are the only ones who know that Principal Chromwell has come back to Astoria. The intention of this meeting is for me to ask you to keep that to yourselves, and let our Principal announce her arrival when she feels she is able to do so. Does anyone have any oppositions to share?" The group was silent in response. "Fantastic, any other comments before we disperse then?"

Lena raised her hand. "P.C. doesn't want a say

in anything? Selene and I have some issues with the Nulls and Delphine that we were hoping to address." Lena explained Delphine having the speculated ability to absorb powers to the professor, and Selene went into an emotional monologue about how neglected he had made the Nulls feel.

"You two have covered quite some ground in the little time you've been given. I had hoped you all would spend the evening sleeping and the morning resting. I agree that we should address the development within Delphine. Since we now know that her powers were stolen from the River of Lethes and not The Bad One, there will be some reassessment to be had as well. I will find her myself with the help of my own team. There is no need for you all to continue doing the adults' work for them." She wanted that to sink in but knew they were likely not to listen. "However, as far as the Nulls go, there is no one I trust more with them than Selene." The rest of her speech was directed towards him and him alone. "After you rest, as you should have done this morning, please go back in and talk with them. I am very interested in hearing their needs. I want every student here at Legacy to feel welcome and cared for. I also offer them my sincerest apologies in the oversight that is solely mine to bear." Her last few sentences aimed at Selene were spoken more as a mother than a professor.

"Yes, ma'am. Moxxi will give me their transcripts tonight. May I return to you tomorrow with them?"

"If you don't find yourself having other plans. . .," Professor Nakshatra snuck a glance towards Solei and Mae, ". . . then I am happy to receive Moxxi's paperwork."

Selene agreed but lacked clarity.

"I think we're up," Solei said to Mae, who gave an approving bob of her head. Solei took a deep breath and faced their friends. "We're going to leave again. Mae and I want to go back to Rome."

Airess jumped in with glee. "Is there another school there? I've thought about studying abroad with Chibi too once he's fully recovered!"

"No." They put their hand up to stop the healer. "This isn't for study, and this isn't particularly easy to say, but I want to do things right this time." Solei's eyes pleaded with Lena. *I'm sorry. Please don't be mad.* "Mae and I are going to move to Rome. That's going to be where we call home going forward."

Lena's heart hurt at the news. She knew she was going to miss her friend terribly, but the move made sense. Astoria was not working out for their relationship, and Solei always went all in for the people they loved. She stood to congratulate the couple. Tears were already welling up in Lena's eyes. "I can't say I won't cry. I'm already failing at that, but I love you, and I think this is the best thing for you. I'm glad we at least had a little more time together, and I'm so grateful I got to meet Mae." Lena moved closer to Mae and in the most sincere voice said, "You're their perfect fit."

Mae mouthed a "thank you" to Lena.

As soon as the oracle finished, Solei jumped into Lena's mind. *We'll still have this, and I'll answer this time, I promise. I'm not losing you again. I love you too, little cub.*

Lena smiled, knowing she had to make her way to her seat so others could share their final moments with the couple too.

Selene was the next in line. He gave Solei a half hug and patted their back. "Stay in touch this time?" He glanced at Lena and then back to Solei.

"Of course," Solei reassured them then transitioned their attention to Tao.

Tao gave a firm handshake. "It's been my pleasure. Make sure you take care of yourself over there and take care of Mae too. If you need anything, I'm only a text away." Tao was gripping Solei's hand hard.

The sincerity broke Solei, and they started to cry, but they blamed it on the pain of his grip. "You've been with me since day one. You never called me Simon, but you never yelled at me for letting everyone else do it either. You always let me be me even when I couldn't offer that to myself. I don't think I ever thanked you for that, and if I did, it wasn't as frequent as it should have been. You were such a constant in a life that was swept up in a maelstrom."

"Well, now you have Mae, and it doesn't have to storm so often anymore. You're in good hands. I'll miss you, friend."

Solei tried to laugh through their tears. "I'll be in contact enough that I won't give you the chance to. Only text though, okay? No more telepathy for us."

"That was the worst. I'd rather have it be you than anyone else though. I mean, could you have imagined if it was Lena?" Tao dramatized how horrifying that could be, obviously knowing that was Solei's preference.

They laughed past their tears at his horrible acting.

That was his goal. Feeling accomplished, he sat down, only slightly continuing his dramatics as he strode by Lena.

Airess was the last one to go. "I don't want to do this," she said, scared. Normally the healer was the first one to wrap someone up in their arms, but they were keeping a noticeable distance.

"It's for the best," Solei said with confidence.

"I know." Airess stared at her friend. "I'm not great with being held accountable for other people's emotions, or my own." She paused. "I know I haven't always done right by you, and there were probably some conversations I ignored when I shouldn't have . . ." This is the one instance where Airess hated being in the spotlight. "But I'm happy for you, and I think Mae is beyond amazing. It all worked out in the end."

"It did," Solei gently acknowledged.

"One last hug?" Airess asked sheepishly.

"Only if you agree to it not being the last one,"

Solei asserted.

"I can do that," Airess said with a smile and bounced up into a big embrace from Solei.

As everyone settled into their seats, Solei and Mae stayed standing.

Reading the room, Selene moved the conversation forward, "When do you guys plan to leave?"

Mae was ready to answer. "Our bags are all packed. We stored them here with Tara before she called everyone. We're ready to go now, actually."

"That's so soon," Airess squeaked.

Solei tried to soften the blow. "I know, but I'll text later today, okay? We have a few layovers on the way."

"Send pictures?" Lena hoped.

"You got it. Take care, everyone. I love you." Solei blew a kiss to the group and headed off to their new life.

No one knew what to say after that. Their moods and hearts were feeling down. Selene had tucked Lena into his chest before Solei had even announced they were leaving. He knew it wasn't Solei's style to linger. Bravely, Tao tried to mimic the same actions with Airess and much to his amazement, it worked.

Professor Nakshatra gave the kids a moment of silence then started playing her big Tibetan singing bowl. She hoped it would offer her students healing during this time of heartache. Losing one of your own was always hard, and she was grateful the departing couple agreed to announce their leave here. Tara knew she could keep everyone safe in her study. She could protect them and shelter them until they were ready to take on the world again, which seemed to be a common problem with this particular group of four. She had never seen such grit and determination in such tiny bodies. They had gotten themselves into more trouble during her time at Legacy Academy than the professor had gotten into in her whole previous life. She cared for them all so deeply. They were good children, and if her healing could ease the sting of what they were going through, she was honored to be able to provide it to them.

The meditation was soothing. Each note was more relaxing than the last. In almost no time, Tao had fallen asleep. He slipped into the world beyond reality, a world full of visions as he could no longer access his dreams. He saw Delphine trying to impress other students within the Academy; he saw her being laughed at and then attempting to provoke those students to see if they would cast their powers onto her. She sought out fights in the library, the lunchroom, and even interrupted a lacrosse game to gain a reaction. No one took her bait. Her anger, as always, was exceedingly apparent. She stomped around the school, kicking items on the ground as she went. She marched into Ward B, her memories presenting themselves to Tao. This was the place where her loss was presented to her. This is where her life began its downhill spiral. Coming back to the present, Tao watched the siren fill with rage and lift her fists into the air. She screamed as small fireballs caught the curtains between each bed.

Professor Nakshatra's ID started to chime. She was forced to stop playing, and as a result, most of the students opened their eyes, all except one. Simultaneously, Tao started echoing Delphine's screams.

Lena jumped into action. "This happened before. We have to get him back to Ward B."

"I've got this child, never fear." Professor Nakshatra held her white lotus while she chanted over Tao's head.

Lena hummed along to the rhythm. The chant was directing Tao to follow her voice, to come home. It gave Lena an idea.

Tao awoke in a panic. "Delphine! The curtains of Ward B are on fire!"

Professor Nakshatra sighed. "That is likely why I'm being called. My children, I will not keep you, but please let the adults attend to this matter. I am off to the healing unit, and I hope not to see any of you there for the rest of the day." She didn't wait for a response before leaving her students behind.

"Curtains?" Lena probed Tao.

"Yeah, she tried to impress people first, but it didn't go well, so then she started all these fights, but she still kept getting blown off time and time again. She got so mad she went into where she felt her life started to decline and set a bunch of curtains on fire."

Even to Tao, it all seemed rather ludicrous.

"Kudos to her, I guess," Airess offered. "I would've expected that area to be element proof."

Lena had thought the same. Before any more chaos snuck in, she wanted to share her idea. "Hey, Tao?"

"Yeah?" He had successfully snuggled Airess once again and was quite proud of himself.

"You know how you gave Airess and me talisman's to come home? Would that work for you if you're stuck in a vision?"

"I never thought of that. I don't know." He reflected more on what he knew. "It's worth asking my mom about. She'd know."

Airess looked up to Tao with her big doe eyes. "Would you do that? If they keep taking you over, it would be nice to know how to get you back."

He traced her face with his finger. "Yeah, I can do that."

Lena was proud. It wasn't her moment, but she helped, and that made her heart happy.

Selene noticed her grin. "I think we're sup-posed to be off duty today. What do you say we head to the beach then back to your place for dinner?"

"I could use a beach day with you," Lena admitted.

"See you two tomorrow?" Selene posed to the two new love birds on the other side of Lena.

"We'll be around in some time," Airess smirked.

Selene shook his head at Tao. "Good luck with that one, my friend!"

Epilogue

Cuddles and Companionship

"Can't we play hooky today and skip going to Ina's?" Selene was super comfy being curled up with Lena on the couch. Airess had healed Ina back to full health, and in turn, Ina was going to renew Chibi as a thank you. The ritual was set for when the bubblegum healer returned from her winter solstice rejuvenation. There was going to be an elaborate ceremony to celebrate the life they had all been given tonight. There was even a rumor that Principal Chromwell was going to be in attendance. Not even Tao had seen P.C. much since the incident with Baba Yaga though that might have been due to Airess too.

"I want to name off all the people that we would infuriate if we ditched, but I don't know if I should lump those who would walk over and kidnap us into one category or list them out separately?" Lena posed to her sweetheart.

"We could get away with it! Your dad's in Rome with Solei. No one would know."

"Oh yes, he would absolutely not find out that I missed my mentor's ceremonial debut and instead, stayed home alone with a boy."

Selene stuck out his tongue at Lena. "I'm not just any boy, you know. I'm Selene! He likes me."

"He likes you enough for you to tell him that we're home alone right now, even when we aren't missing an assigned party we have to go to? It can be the second half of your text when you're messaging him about the Nulls," Lena taunted.

Selene gave her a glare.

"Mhmm. That's what I thought." She kissed his lips. "I win."

He snuggled her closer. "Yes, yes. Of course you do. You always win."

"I like it. I'm a fan," Lena gloated.

"While you're enjoying your 'holier than thou' pedestal, have you responded to Solei?"

Lena scrunched her face. Things with Solei had been great since they left for Rome, but they were coming back for a visit over spring break and wanted Lena's help on an item for Delphine. "I can't wait to see Solei! Same with Mae! But why am I always the one that gets roped into Delphine things? I. Hate. Her!"

"Would you rather they ask me?"

Lena scoffed, "Obviously not! But why not Airess?"

"Her hands were already full with around-the-clock care of Ina, gaining her powers back after the winter solstice, and now Chibi is going to get added into the mix," Selene recited. This was not the first time they've had this talk.

"Fine. Then what about Tao?"

"If anyone asked Tao, he would say yes, so no one is asking Tao anything."

"That sounds like the perfect solution to me."

"You really want to be the one to take his time away from Airess after their separation? That kid is on cloud nine and is living his best life right now."

Lena knew it was true. Tao was head over heels for Airess, and she was putting her best self forward in their relationship. They were ridiculously cute all the time. It was gross in the best kind of way. "Ugh . . . fine! I'll do it. I just don't like it."

"You don't have to like it." He kissed her forehead. "You know Greek better than most people in Astoria. If you help them get the tania right, it might be enough to get Delphine back to her people. The whole thing could be a win-win."

"When you say it like that, perhaps writing on the headband could be worth it."

"We'll make it fun. We'll figure something out."

"All right. I'm in. But you need to do something to help a good cause, too. Will you finally ask my dad to help you with the Nulls when Solei is here? He'll have extra hands to help! It'll make it even easier than it probably is!"

"I don't know, Lena. He wants to find your

mom, and I want him to find your mom too. He shouldn't be spending his time on helping me."

"I don't think anything could stop him from searching for my mom," Lena said concretely.

"That's probably right. I just feel like this is my problem to handle."

"I think you mispronounced 'our problem to handle' again." Lena booped his nose.

"Okay. Our problem to handle. The Nulls just have so many needs. I want to fulfill them all, but it gets so overwhelming. I mix things up, and it's hard to keep all their wants straight."

"We're doing a great job. Almost a third of the Nulls that stayed are taking the courses they want AND have mentors from Ward A which, honestly, is helping bring some of those deities out of major slumps. It's a lot of work, but it's great and it's working. You should be proud of that."

"I am, but I feel I need to do more. They deserve the best I have, and I know they want extracurriculars too, which I don't blame them. I would want groups I fit into too, but seventy one schedules are overwhelming to juggle."

"Professor Nakshatra has offered to help with that exact problem more times than I can count."

"I know; they remind me of that too."

"Accept her help, Selene. This is not your sole weight to bear. You let me in, and things are going well. Think of how much better things would be if my dad and/or Professor Nakshatra weren't so blocked off from everything too."

"She has an entire school to run, Lena."

"Now that you mention it, you're right. She must have made countless offers to help while completely forgetting that key part of her daily life. No matter that we have been standing in said school the majority of times she has offered, and that she lives there, I am confident she completely forgot about that, and your reasoning is totally sound." Lena's sarcasm was coming off strong.

"You're the worst, sometimes," he teased and lightly rolled her from side to side in his arms.

"I'm also something else! Say it . . ."

"No."

"Say it . . ."

"I already said it today!"

"Tell me again . . . I . . . am . . ."

"Right."

"Yes!" Lena raised her fist in victory. Her watch lit up the time. "It's noon already. If we're not at Ina's by two, Airess is going to have our heads."

"Isn't that what Tao's for? Can't he set up?"

"You know, as well as I do, that he's working as hard as Airess is on all this, especially since he isn't blacking out with visions anymore. It wouldn't surprise me if he has talismans from his mom all over the place trying to make today perfect for Airess. "

"Yeah, that's true. All right, let's go be good friends."

"In matching outfits!"

"What?"

"Nothing, follow me!" Lena frolicked up the stairs.

Selene chased her. He had just tackle hugged her onto her bed when they felt her phone buzz. He groaned as she checked it.

Her mouth dropped. "Selene. You need to see this." She was shaking like a leaf.

He sat up to steady her and grabbed her phone.

There was a video playing of a jade door embellished with emeralds. The door was curved at the sides and pointed at the top. Deep carvings spread and shifted over the face of the entryway. There were people layered upon people in an overpopulated cityscape. They were living their everyday lives. Some were washing clothes, others were selling goods, or walking with their families. One second, the door displayed a crowded street, but the next second, some of the figures' faces changed into grotesque sneers. Squirrels, fish, people, and trees, all adopted heinous expressions aimed at the figures they were just so happy with. Then, it all went back to normal again. The video turned to face Kasim before he cut it.

"That's intense, Lena. Why did he send that?" Selene asked, perturbed.

"Look at the title." Lena pointed out.

The video was sent with the title "I found the portal to mom."

Acknowledgments

I can't believe we did it again! I am so insanely proud of us!

To Dj, B, and Bug: You all are amazing, and I cannot thank you all enough for the HOURS (days? months?) that you have put into this book with me.

Dj, you continue to amaze me. You are the first round of support when it comes to all of this. You help me keep my head together when it comes to outlining, help keep the story as close to the plot as possible (which may be the hardest job of all), and really think through and enhance the subject material. You help keep everything canon and are always willing to do another round of edits with me. Speaking of edits, you even stepped up your game in that regard, and I am so grateful. You're our all-in-one editor, designer (P.S. The cover is GORG!), and collaborator. I am proud of what we've accomplished together and proud of the story being told so far!

B, you are my first test reader without all the background info, and with the exception of your incessant shipping of Tao and Lena, your takeaways are worth their weight in gold. I always enjoy when I can insert quotes you've given me, and seeing this world I've made through your eyes is such a treat. In addition to all of that, the time and space you provide me to make this happen is invaluable. Writing a novel is no small task (for any of us), but you prioritize my dreams, and that means the world to me. Thanks for embarking on this challenge with me and being there through all the ups and downs this journey grants us.

Last, but never least, my sweet Z. You are my

favorite Bug. You helped create the title, championed Moxxi with full gusto, and your ideas are always enlightening. You inspire me at every turn. There are no words to truly capture how grateful I am for you, both as my kiddo and as a contributor to this story we're making. Your mind is brilliant, and I hope you never see it any other way. Thanks for engaging in my dreams with me. I promise to reciprocate that always.

About the Author

A. P. Goodman is a lifelong enthusiast of mythology and religion. From her first love of Disney's Hercules to her most recent love of Prague's legendary mythos, Ashley has spent much of her time engrossed in various accounts of past and present lore. She loves obscure stories best and feels strongly that no tale should be left untold. In her moments outside of cultural deep dives, she feels nothing compares to warm chai tea and creating core memories. Her loved ones and pets (especially her fluffy puppy) are always her favorite company. She also has two meddlesome cats and a bunny who reigns as king of the household. Astoria's Secret is book two of her debut trilogy.

WHICH LEGACY CHARACTER ARE YOU?

Scan the QR code below to find out!